WHITE LAKE

A NOVEL

SUSAN AMOND TODD

Copyright © 2016 by Susan Amond Todd

ISBN: 978-1-943258-28-4
Library of Congress Control Number: 2016917297

Edited by: Jessica Carelock

Published by Warren Publishing, Inc.
Charlotte, NC
www.warrenpublishing.net
Printed in the United States

*This book is dedicated
to the memory of
my parents,
Ralph and Joan Amond.*

PROLOGUE

*T*hey had such big plans.

If it weren't for the headlights of her car, she would have been in total darkness, the steady rain pounding on the windshield only contributing to her bleak view. Momentarily the wiper blades cleared a path, allowing her eyes to follow the steps up to the gloomy front door and dark windows. The view made her feel alone and unwelcome, as if she didn't belong.

Why didn't I leave a light on somewhere inside the house, she wondered, but when she'd rushed out earlier, flipping one on had been the last thing on her mind. Then the thought of sleeping here by herself came, with an anxious feeling she didn't want to face.

She turned the car off and sat for a good ten minutes, struggling to put what happened in perspective as the rain continued to pelt the metal roof above her head. Her vision trailed down to her hands. They were clenched into fists. She relaxed her grasp and extended her fingers on her left hand, slowly moving it into the light so she could see her wedding ring. She let out a long sigh and laid her head back, her eyes closed briefly in silence. *Might as well go in and get it over with*, she thought.

As she began to move, her body felt unfamiliar, not her own. She mechanically rose out of the car, into the rain, and put one heavy foot in front of the other, reluctantly making her way up the stairs to the door.

Her hands shook as she fumbled with the key. To her dismay, it wouldn't turn. A simple task causing her difficulty. Then she remembered earlier, he had jiggled the key slightly, coaxing it to budge, so she tried this with the same success.

The heavy door opened, and she walked into what was *their* house, but not yet *their* home. A home is where you know the creak of every stair and floor board, how to open every door that might stick a bit. A home is where you can get up in the middle of the night and walk to the kitchen for a glass of water without ever turning on a light to find your way. Memories of Christmases past, birthdays celebrated, summer picnics, friends for dinner, time with the kids, and sometimes companionable silence between the two of you.

There was a row of light switches to her left. She flipped on and off three of them before she found the right one.

The living area was full of boxes stacked and arranged around the room. To say she felt overwhelmed was an understatement. What was she going to do with them? He was supposed to help her unpack and start this new chapter of their life *together*. The one where the kids were grown and starting their own lives, getting married and having grandchildren for them. At least that's what he'd told her.

Maybe she should open a box and start the never ending process of putting things away. Would she really stay and live here? She wanted to turn and run back to their old house, but they'd sold it to a family she was sure already started making it theirs. She had to stay here, at least for now.

How could he have done this to her? How could he! She trusted and believed him when he told her they were going to build a life together here.

The anger came from deep down, like nothing she ever

felt before. She wanted to turn back the hands of time so she could ask him.

Maybe this was one of the dreams she'd periodically have. Soon she would wake up and her life would be back as it had been, and they'd both laugh at how silly she was to have dreamed something so impossible.

But her dreams were never like this. They were never this clear. They always took place in a blur, and most of the events were odd and unnatural, short and all in one place.

Then, with a shiver, she remembered how cold and unfeeling he'd looked only an hour ago, not the warm engaging man she slept with every night and cared for every day.

God, how can a woman prepare for something like this? Nobody believes it will happen, but yet it can, and it does.

There was a family picture on top of one of the open boxes, taken a year ago. Everyone with big smiles and no idea what was to come. She thought about how it was supposed to be and shook her head in disbelief.

They'd been fortunate to save enough money to put the kids through college and buy this beach house on St. Simons Island in southern Georgia. She was going to get a job as a nurse at the local hospital, and he would transfer his position with the bank where he'd been working for the past fifteen years. They had thought the beach house would be a great place for the kids to come visit and for them to use as home base when they traveled after they retired. That was the plan.

He told her he made good investments for them so it could be a reality. Then they found this beautiful house, everything falling into place, allowing them to make the big change and move to the island. She assumed they would live here, together, a long time. What a mistake she made believing this.

The kids. What should she do about them? She needed to call them but what would she say? How could she help them understand something she didn't understand herself? They'd be devastated. She couldn't deal with telling them right now though. She needed some time to regroup and be strong like they expected her to be.

A slow panic started in the pit of her stomach as it occurred to her she was all alone now. She hadn't been all alone since… well, ever. Again she shivered, chilled to the bone from the rain.

She needed something dry to change into, so she went upstairs to find the boxes of clothes. After opening two of them, she found a hooded sweatshirt and a pair of long pants. She felt slightly better after she changed into them.

She didn't know what to do next. After slowly descending the stairs, she stood at the bottom for several seconds, trying to hang on to the tiny amount of control she still possessed, eventually losing it and sliding to a sitting position on the last step, collapsing into sobs.

When at last she raised her head to look around the electricity went out, startling her and leaving her in the dark. What did it matter? The darkness allowed her to not look at the inside of this house, filled with what was to be their new life and dreams. The lack of light mimicked the ache in her heart, growing hopeless, empty, and dim as time moved on.

Her tears stopped, and as her eyes adjusted to the darkness, they were drawn to the panel of tall windows framing the view of the water where she noticed that the rain had finally stopped and the clouds were starting to clear in spots. She could see a silhouette of the winged-back chair and ottoman he placed in front of the huge glass windows earlier when he needed to rest. The sight of the chair and ottoman released a short sob from her chest as she pictured the last time she saw him sitting there. She pushed herself up from the bottom step, drawn to the windows by an increasing brightness.

The full moon was peeking out of the break in the clouds, producing an eerie grayish glow reflecting off the water.

The moonbeams accentuated the white line of foam along the incoming tide and seascape.

She dropped down into the chair and put her feet on the ottoman, thinking about how he'd sat there only hours ago. Was it strange that she felt comfort in sitting there?

She sat silently for over an hour, though it felt like only minutes. Outside the waves came in and out, in and out, over and over. She found them calming and hypnotic, as if she had discovered a tiny bit of control as her world unraveled. How could life change so quickly between morning and evening? She knew deep inside that she couldn't stop what had been put into motion, only deal with what happened the best she could.

Thank God there were no memories attached to this house — she could never live here if there were. It was still a blank canvas waiting to be painted. The only problem was she thought the painting was going to be of the two of them.

Her eyes and thoughts were back at the window when her stomach growled. She realized she hadn't eaten since this morning, and there was nothing in the house to fix. She started to cry uncontrollably again.

It occurred to her that if she put some distance between herself and this house, she might be able to start sorting through what happened.

She decided to get into her car and drive until she found a restaurant, order something to eat, and think about what she should do. She grabbed her purse and keys and headed for the car, having the same trouble locking the door as she had earlier when she tried to open it.

She sat in the car a few minutes before backing out of the driveway, in an attempt to build up the courage to strike out on her own. Finally, she started the car and began to back out when a deluge of rain started coming down. She cried again, but didn't allow it to stop her. She was determined.

After driving ten minutes in the torrential rain, a flashing neon OPEN sign caught her eye outside a barbeque restaurant. She parked her car in the gravel lot and forced herself outside, thankful for the steady raindrops on her face — they masked her tears.

The restaurant was not very busy. A middle-aged man in blue jeans and a red and blue plaid shirt stood behind a counter. He gave her a quizzical look but smiled. "Can I take your order, ma'am?"

"You're not getting ready to close are you?" she asked.

"No, ma'am. Just not a busy night," he said. "Probably 'cause it's rainin'."

She ordered a barbeque sandwich plate and a glass of sweet tea.

"Go ahead and sit at any table," he said, as he handed her the tea. "I'll bring you the sandwich when it's ready."

The dining room was nearly empty. She picked a table as far back as possible. She felt the need to be alone.

As she sipped her tea, she went over what had happened. In twenty-four hours her life had changed drastically for the worst. What should she do first? The kids. When she was back at the beach house, she'd call them and explain what had happened. The thought had her crying again.

She looked up to see the man behind the counter studying her, before taking his leave through a swinging door.

She pulled a pack of tissues out of her purse and wiped her eyes and nose, telling herself to stop crying and get in control. What would she do after she called the kids? She had no friends here so, whatever it was, she would have to do it alone.

She wasn't sure how much time had passed when she saw a figure dressed in white coming toward her. Through her tears, the figure looked like an angel slowly gliding closer.

It was a woman. She sat down opposite from her, silent for a few minutes, then said something she didn't hear. After that the woman rose from her chair and leaned over to wrap a shawl around her shoulders. The gesture not only made her feel warm but also loved, exactly what she needed at the moment.

She started crying again, and looked down. The woman took her hand, causing her to look up at her.

The man who had taken her order came over and set her sandwich down along with two steaming mugs.

"My name is Betty, and this here's my husband Jack," the woman said. "We own this restaurant. Honey, what's wrong?"

She looked up at the woman. She knew nothing about her, although she felt she could trust her. A calm peace came over as the tears dried up, and she finally found her voice.

"My name is Cynthia, and I've had a terrible thing happen to me."

"Well, why don't you start at the beginning and tell me everything?" Betty said.

So Cynthia did.

CHAPTER 1

One Year Earlier

The rhythm of her breath was steady and unlabored as Cynthia Lewis turned the corner onto Glade Valley Lane. She was at the end of her four-mile run, and she lifted her head to the sun, taking in the warm day and feeling grateful that she wasn't needed at the hospital where she worked. *Only in the South do you get the gift of fall days like this*, she thought. Cloudless, warm, and no humidity. It made the cool-down walk to her house at the end of the road pleasant.

She started running in high school and kept it up over the years, going once or twice a week when she had the time.

As she approached the house, she saw Christopher's car turn onto the road. It was too fast — she'd need to have a word with him about it.

Her son, Christopher, was a senior in high school this year. He'd always been a decent student, but last year had decided to "pick up his game," as he put it, so he could get into a good college. She was happy to hear him say this, but she still needed to encourage him frequently.

It was different when her daughter, Millie, had applied to schools. She was in the top ten of her class and had the whole college thing figured out. She applied to three schools, was accepted at all three, and decided on one. That was it. Christopher was still unsure and had only just started researching.

She thought about how fortunate she and her husband, Philip were to be able to live where they did. Millie and Christopher went to good schools, and the neighborhood was quiet and peaceful, filled with beautifully manicured yards and neatly trimmed bushes. You could tell it was a family neighborhood by the swing sets in the backyards and the occasional bike or toy in the driveway. Atlanta was filled with hundreds of neighborhoods just like this one.

When she reached her house, she headed into the garage and through the door to the kitchen. Christopher was sitting with his back to her at the table, a bottle of Gatorade in one hand and a leftover slice of pizza in the other.

"How was your day?" she asked. He jumped, taken by surprise.

"Oh, hi Mom." He turned around, pizza in his mouth. "It was okay. You know how it is."

She wasn't sure she did and opened her mouth to ask, but he cut her off.

"What else can I eat? When's dinner? Will Dad be late, or can we eat when we want?"

"There's a bowl of fruit in the refrigerator, I'm not sure when we'll have dinner, haven't heard from Dad."

"Okay." He went to refrigerator and opened the door to look.

He was a handsome young man, and reminded her so much of Philip when they'd first met in college. He was taller than his dad at 6'2," but he had the same dark hair, brown eyes, and build. They even walked the same.

"I don't see the fruit."

She walked over, pulled the bowl out, and handed it to him. He took a fork out of the drawer and returned to the table. She followed him.

"Listen, I saw Emily's mom, and she told me about a school dance coming up. I was wondering, are you going take someone to it?" she asked, joining him at the table.

"I didn't know you were friends with Emily's mom," he said.

"Well, I'm not friends with her, but I know her enough to say hi and visit."

"Where did you see her?" he asked.

"At the grocery store."

He smiled, changing the subject. "Speaking of the grocery store, I ate the last banana and finished off the deli meat."

"Put it on the list," she responded.

"Will do." He jumped up from the table. "I got to get going. Told a couple guys I would meet them to shoot some hoops."

"Wait a minute," she said. She would not be deterred. "The dance. Are you going to ask someone?"

He turned back and gave her a smile so similar to his father's. "Already did."

He was out the door before she could start to ask about the girl. *That's okay*, she thought. The dance was several weeks away. She'd have plenty of time to find out.

She went upstairs to take a shower, thinking about how much she was going to miss him next year when he went to college.

After her shower, Cynthia headed back to the kitchen to get supper together. She'd taken some chicken out of the freezer earlier in the day to thaw, thinking she'd grill it in a pan with butter, olive oil, onions, and mushrooms, and serve it over pasta with a salad.

Cynthia enjoyed cooking, and learned most of her skills at the side of her Granny and Mom where she grew up in Walden Falls, a small town in Wisconsin. They were both outstanding cooks and had given her much to live up to.

When she was a child, she and her brother Arthur spent summers at her granny's house on White Lake, about fifteen miles from their home. Cynthia became Granny's assistant in the kitchen. She even had an apron just her size to wear.

Granny was of German decent, so most of her meals were hearty, stick-to-your-ribs type food. Over the years, Cynthia had adjusted many of those recipes for her family swapping out things like bacon grease, lard, cream, and butter — she didn't think it was all bad, but just good in moderation. Granny would never approve of the adaptations, but she didn't have to know.

Cynthia always made an effort on the days she didn't work to have a family meal together. She remembered how her family shared dinner every evening, but today, it seemed like families were going all different directions and didn't use mealtime to touch base with each other.

She wondered how much cooking she would do next year after Christopher went away to college. The empty nest would certainly be different.

Christopher and college started her thinking about how she always wanted to get her master's in nursing but never did. Her career had advanced fine without one, but maybe this would be the time for her to pursue it. It seemed between Philip and life, there was always a reason not to. Babies came, Philip had his career as the major bread winner, the kids got involved in extra-curricular activities — the list went on, and soon her dream was forgotten by everyone, sometimes even herself. She remembered one of the times when she brought it up and Philip's response, "Don't you have enough to do without adding school to the mix?"

She bent over to get a pan out of the cupboard and her phone rang. Philip. When he called at this time of day, it only meant one thing. He would be late.

"Hello, sweetheart," she said. "How's your day?"

Philip sighed. "The usual. I've got a late appointment, so I won't be home till after seven. Just eat without me, okay?"

Philip was a financial advisor. Most clients could be met

during the day, but some had to be seen after hours. She hated how tired he was when he got home.

"Okay." She tried to sound pleasant. "What has you so busy?" she asked. He didn't respond. "Philip?"

"What... oh... what's the problem?" He sounded slightly annoyed.

"No problem, darling. I'll let you go. Love you," she said. No response. "Philip?"

"I'm sorry. Just preoccupied with work. Yeah, I love you, too, Cynthia. You know that." He didn't sound convincing. "Right now work is on my mind."

"Okay bye, see you later." She hung up. He hadn't even acknowledged her goodbye.

His job was high-pressure, but it had never seemed to bother him like it did lately. When she'd suggested that maybe he should take it easier, he would get angry, asking if she didn't think he could handle it. She was only trying to show she cared.

She heard the front door open — Christopher was back. He came into the kitchen taking a deep breath. "Smells good, Mom. When will we eat? Is Dad going to be home soon?" He was obviously hungry.

"Your dad has to meet a client, so he'll be home later."

Cynthia worried about her husband working such a high-stress job. Both his mom and dad had passed away, his mom five years ago and his dad when Philip was only ten. Philip told her the story of how his dad dropped dead before his eyes while they were raking leaves outside in their back yard. He told her that he never wanted his kids to go through the same.

"Why don't you set the table?" she asked Christopher. "It should be ready in 10 minutes."

As he set the table, Cynthia thought about her husband. He'd been so tired lately. A physical would be a good idea. She was sure he wouldn't agree, so she would suggest it to him when the time was right.

After pulling the key from the ignition of his car, Philip Lewis sat in the driveway for several minutes, attempting to get himself together before going inside.

Not only was he stressed out from the pressure of the day, but he was also hungry. He was sure Cynthia had left a plate for him. He started to feel slightly better and decided to go in.

The house was quiet. Christopher was probably upstairs doing homework or watching TV in his room, but he wasn't sure about Cynthia. She must have gone to bed.

He took a cold beer out of the refrigerator and removed the plastic off the plate of food, not bothering to warm it. He headed into the family room to find Cynthia sound asleep in a recliner. There was half a glass of wine on the end table and an open book in her lap.

She was just as beautiful as the day he met her, he thought, as his eyes went down to his protruding belly. He worked out when he could, but he hadn't much time lately. Between Millie in college and pursuing her master's after graduation, Christopher going to college next year, looming retirement, and the general cost of living, he felt as if he were on a treadmill. Too bad that didn't count as exercise.

Most of his stress wasn't because of work, but because of a situation he had gotten himself into that he wasn't sure how to get out of. A mistake he didn't know how fix.

Cynthia's voice broke his thoughts. "Hey. How long have you been home? What time is it?"

"About nine forty-five or ten," he said. "I haven't been home long. Do you work tomorrow?"

"Yeah, a twelve-hour shift," Cynthia responded through a yawn. "I was hoping you would've been home earlier so I could spend some time with you. Why are you so late? It seems we hardly see you lately."

He wasn't sure how to respond and didn't want to because

he would have to lie, so he changed the subject.

"Let me walk you upstairs and tuck you in," he said with a smile.

As he steered his sleepy wife to their room, he thought about how glad he was this day was over. He was ready for some alone time.

Cynthia sat on the bed and proceeded to undress. He grabbed her nightgown, and when he came back from the closet, she was naked. As she put her arms up, he slid the nightgown over them and thought how great she looked.

He was happy she was going to bed. He had one more phone call to make, a phone call that could put things right again.

"Sweet dreams. The morning will be here before you know it," he said.

He kissed her on the forehead and went downstairs to make his call.

CHAPTER 2

A few days later the house was quiet, and nobody expected home for hours. Cynthia went to the shelf her cookbooks were on and pulled out the folder containing her notes for the upcoming surprise birthday party she was having for Philip. It was hidden between *The Joy of Cooking* and *Betty Crocker's Cookbook*. No danger of him finding it there.

Philip was turning fifty-five, and if his current mood was any indication, a party could lift his spirits. She asked him what was bothering him several times, and he said nothing, so it had to be the birthday.

She paged through her papers until she found the number of Joe D's the sports bar, where he frequently met his buddies to watch football.

"Hello, Joe D's. Joe speaking," said the friendly voice of Joe.

"Hi, Joe, this is Cynthia Lewis. Are we set for the party?"

"Got it on the calendar," he said.

"We talked about using the patio, but do you think it will be warm enough?"

"I don't think it will be a problem. I've got outdoor heaters that make it warm as toast for fall. You'll never know you're outside when I'm done."

"Sounds great. Is it possible for me to come over with a cake and some decorations the day of the party? When would be good?"

"Absolutely! Let's say about three. Let me know a couple days before how you want the tables set up, how many people, and what food and alcohol you want. Can't wait to see the look on old Phil's face. Should be one of those priceless moments."

"I hope so. Say hi to your wife, Joe, and I'll be in touch." She hung up.

It was all coming together nicely. She'd sent out the invitations and was having everyone RSVP by email. Because they both grew up in Wisconsin, she and Philip were Packer fans through and through, so she was doing a Packer-themed party. It might be a little tacky, but Philip would love it.

Just then, her cell phone rang. It was her best friend from college, Purvell Whitlock.

The women couldn't have been more different. Purvell was a realtor in New York City. Tall, long blonde hair, blue eyes, single, and always going somewhere. Cynthia was petite, with shoulder-length light brown hair, hazel eyes, married, and involved in raising a family. Both women were happy where their lives had taken them.

They'd become friends their freshman year in college at the University of Wisconsin in Madison. The two had ended up living across the hall from each other both having regretted going potluck on dorm roommates. At the end of the semester, Purvell convinced the other two girls to room together so she and Cynthia could do the same. Even back then, Purvell could sell anything. The young women continued to be roommates all through their college years, developing a strong friendship.

"Purvell, it's so good to hear from you," Cynthia said. "What've you been up to?"

"You know, the usual. Working hard and going on a few

trips here and there. Dating a new guy. He's five years younger than me. Cute and smart. Does something with computers I don't really understand."

Cynthia laughed. "How did you meet him?"

"Was showing him condos. After he found one and the deal was done, he asked me out, and I said yes." She giggled like a school girl.

Although Cynthia was happy, when she heard Purvell talk about her carefree, unpredictable life, she was on occasion slightly envious.

"So how's the party planning going? How's Philip been?" Purvell asked.

"The party's coming along great. Going with a Packer theme."

"Oh, that will be so perfect," Purvell said. "He's going to love it."

"I don't know what his problem is lately. He sure won't talk to me about it. You know how even-tempered he's always been. Every time I ask what's wrong, he gets so worked up. I'm not going to ask anymore. I just hope things will improve after his birthday."

"He's probably just having a little mid-life crisis," Purvell said and chuckled. "It happens to the best of us. I wouldn't worry too much. By the way, about the party, I won't be able to come. I just can't get away, but I want you to start planning a trip here. It's been years since we did a girls weekend in New York. Christopher starts college in August, so no excuses. Time to do something for you."

She's so right, Cynthia thought. She had put a lot on hold over the years and was only now realizing it. "Okay. This fall I'm coming, so be ready."

"You know me, I'm always ready." They both laughed.

"Tell Philip happy birthday from me on the big day. I've got to run. Love you."

"Love you, too, Purvell." She hung up.

A trip to New York would be great. Maybe she could go this spring and not wait until fall.

She went back to her party planning until she heard the garage door open. Philip must have gotten off work early for a change. She put her folder back in its hiding place between the cookbooks.

Philip walked through the door looking exhausted and agitated.

"Sweetheart, what are you doing home so early? Everything okay?" Cynthia asked him.

"I'm not feeling well," he told her.

She put her arms around him, smelling his cologne and the starch in his shirt as she laid her head on his chest and closed her eyes. It was comforting to her for some reason.

"I just want to take a shower and lay down for awhile," he said. He wriggled out of her grasp and walked past her and up the stairs.

Later when they were eating supper, Philip was back to his old self, goofing off with Christopher.

When they were done, Christopher took off upstairs to do homework and Philip helped clean up the kitchen, giving them some time together.

"So what had you so worked up when you came home today?" she asked.

"What do you mean?" He responded like he didn't know what she was talking about.

"Something seemed to be bothering you."

"Nothing was bothering me," he said firmly. "I don't know what you're talking about. I work very hard, you know."

"I know you do, but something seemed to be wrong, and I just want to help. I can't help if I don't know what's wrong."

"You can help by leaving me alone and letting me relax when I'm home," he said angrily. "I'm going to watch TV." He left the room.

What was up? There seemed to be something preoccupying

him. How could she help if he wouldn't tell her what was wrong?

She got two wine glasses down from the cupboard and then immediately put one back. She didn't want to be around him in his present mood. Philip had always been intense with his job, but lately he seemed agitated, even mean. Eventually it'll all come out and he'll get past it, she thought as she went upstairs with her wine to watch TV by herself.

CHAPTER 3

*C*ynthia was in an abyss of fog and blurriness, alone, wearing her nursing scrubs. There were shapes in the blurriness. She could tell they were people, because she could hear them laugh and mumble.

The fog began to clear, and she saw she was in a room a good fifty feet from the blurred people, and her clothes had somehow changed to a nice pair of black slacks, white satin top, and silver jewelry. She held a glass of white wine in her hand.

She wanted to know what the blurred people were doing, so she started across the expanse when, all of a sudden, she stumbled down a hole she hadn't seen in the floor. The sensation of falling through air felt good and unburdening, but then suddenly she became panicked and felt the urge to find something to grab onto, to prevent her descent into the unknown. She kept falling, falling, falling.

Somewhere between consciousness and sleep the alarm went off, her hand slowly reaching out from under the covers to feebly push the silence button while her mind slipped into gear.

The sun was shining through the bedroom window, giving the room a warm happy yellow glow.

She vaguely remembered dreaming something before the

alarm went off. Parts and pieces still drifted in her mind until they eventually evaporated into the subconscious secret part of her brain.

Her dreams were always the same, starting out with a fog and blurred mumbling people that never made sense to her. She softly laughed to herself.

Very rarely did she share her dreams with anyone but Purvell, who appreciated her vivid imagination.

"You need to go to someone who interprets dreams someday," Purvell had suggested once. "That could be interesting."

As she continued to slip into wakefulness, she remembered it was the day of Philip's birthday and surprise party. The day was finally here after all the planning, and he didn't know a thing about it. She had until seven that night, and there were so many things yet to do.

The dream was forgotten.

She rolled over to touch Philip, wanting to cuddle with him before starting their day, but he was gone, only a slight indentation where he slept, his side empty, but still a little warm. She was disappointed. She wanted to be the first to wish him happy birthday.

It smelled like someone was making breakfast so she rolled out of bed and padded downstairs to find Philip wearing her ruffled pink apron and standing in front of the stove, going back and forth between two pans. What a sight.

"Hey, birthday boy. What are you doing?"

Philip turned around with a big wide grin from ear to ear. "Making milady breakfast." He bowed like a knight from medieval times. He only had on running shorts, so when he turned to face her, it looked like he was naked under the apron. At fifty-five he was still a good-looking guy, even in a pink apron. It was nice to see him in a good mood for a change.

"It's your birthday. I should be cooking for you. What possessed you?" Truth be told, breakfast was the only thing Philip could make. Okay, hot dogs, hamburgers, and frozen pizza could be added to his culinary resume as well.

"I woke up and saw how tranquil you looked and thought I'd surprise you," he said, a big smile on his face.

Why did he say surprise? Did he know about the party? Impossible! There was no way he knew. She was being paranoid.

"You certainly have surprised me," she said. "I like surprises, how about you?"

At first she thought he didn't hear her, but then she realized that the cooking was taking his full concentration

"What?" he asked finally. "Oh, surprises... ah... I don't know. Don't get many of them I guess. I never thought about it."

Did he know, she wondered.

"Cynthia, are you okay?"

"Oh, yes, I'm just fine. I was thinking of... well, nothing, you know, just what a beautiful day it will be for your birthday." She needed to get a grip on herself, or she was going to ruin it. "Can I help with anything? How about if I get out some plates and silverware?"

"I think I've got this cooking thing under control. It's not so bad, really. Maybe I should try it more often," he laughed.

"Knock yourself out," Cynthia said. She remembered the last time he cooked something other than breakfast. It was the biggest mess she'd ever seen. He must have used every utensil, pot, and pan in the kitchen for the very simple dish he'd created.

"Since you cooked for me and it's your birthday, I'll clean up the kitchen" she said. It was easier that way, actually.

As she waited for him to finish, she went over the day's plans in her mind. She was going to run some errands in the morning, get the last of the party arrangements done, head to Joe D's in the afternoon, and then come home and get ready for the evening.

Christopher was taking his dad go-karting this morning, something they loved doing together, and this afternoon,

Philip was going to play golf with some of his buddies who were also invited to the party. This was kind of dangerous because any one of these guys could open their big mouths and spill the beans, especially after a beer or two, but Cynthia had threatened all of them, and she meant it.

"Cynthia? Are you listening to me? You seem to be off somewhere else."

"Oh, I'm sorry sweetheart. I was just thinking about the errands I need to do. What did you say?"

"I wanted you to know that I might have to be working late more in the future. I'm just trying to get ahead. They keep dumping more and more on us."

"Sounds like you don't have much of a choice," she said. She didn't like that he had to push himself so hard.

"I don't, not if I want to get ahead," he said. "Tada. Here's your omelet." He turned around, placing a plate before her, spreading his hands out like a magician.

For a moment, Cynthia was speechless. "Wow, Philip, this is very impressive," she said. The presentation was beautiful. The omelet rested on one of her soft jade-colored plates, slightly off from the middle, orange slices, blueberries, strawberries and sausage links completing the picture. It looked delicious.

She couldn't help but lean over to touch his face. She placed her lips on his and let them linger. He set the plate down and wrapped his arms around her.

"What's that for?" he asked.

"Just because I happen to love you, darling. That's all," she said with a smile and laughed. "Happy birthday."

They sat down together to eat and talk and enjoy a rare thirty minutes of quiet time together. Cynthia suggested he take his shower so he'd be ready for the day while she cleaned up the kitchen. After all, it was his birthday.

But that plan didn't last. He came over and gave her a passionate kiss, his hand lingering at her breast and then moving down to her behind, holding her tight.

They both took off for the bedroom, closing and locking the door behind them. The kitchen could wait, but they couldn't.

Christopher and Philip took off at about ten, Cynthia doing the same shortly after them.

She had to pick up the decorations from their friends, Ron and Sandra Benjamin, so she and the kids could transform the patio at Joe D's into Packerland. She still hadn't heard from Millie, who was driving home today from Rome, Georgia, where she went to college. Cynthia needed to give her a call to see when she'd arrive.

Millie was a junior at Berry College in the northern part of Georgia. Berry was a small liberal arts school, but at 26,000 acres, it was physically the largest college campus in the world.

Millie looked at several schools, but it was only when they visited the Berry campus that she fell in love. Cynthia would never forget the day they drove onto the property for the first time. After passing through the front gate and touring the school, Millie couldn't see herself going anywhere else. She was now in the Campbell School of Business working on a degree in accounting. One year to go after this and then on to get her MBA.

Because Millie was so focused and an all-around good kid, Christopher always said she made life hard for him since she never did anything wrong. He over-exaggerated a bit.

Cynthia dialed Millie's number. She answered on the third ring.

"Hi, Mom. How's it going? I'm about fifteen minutes away," Millie said. Cynthia hated it when the kids traveled and always worried until they were home.

"That's great. Can you meet me at Joe D's around three to decorate?" Millie was going over to a friend's house until the party.

"Sure," Millie said. "I brought a friend along with me from school, is that okay with you?"

"Of course it is. We love your friends, and all of them are always welcome," Cynthia said. One more at the party would be no big deal. College kids were always looking for a free meal. She could stay in Millie's room with her, not causing any disruption at home. They'd barely even know she was there.

"I knew you wouldn't mind. So do you think Dad has any idea about the party?" Millie asked.

"I don't think he has a clue. It's been fun to be able to pull one over on him. He's with Christopher for the morning, then going golfing with some of his buddies in the afternoon. I'm trying to get organized right now but wanted to find out where you were first. I'll see you at Joe's later."

"Okay, Mom. I love you,"

"Love you, too, sweetheart. Drive carefully." She hung up.

⚜

After running around like a crazy woman, she managed to accomplish everything on her list by one o'clock.

Christopher was in the driveway playing basketball when she arrived home. He helped her carry groceries in.

"So how was go-karting?" she asked.

"It was fun. I let Dad win a few times since it *is* his birthday," Christopher said with a cocky look. "I got kind of bored though while he talked to some woman."

"What woman?" she asked.

"I don't know. Dad didn't introduce us," Christopher said.

"Did he talk to her long?" she asked.

"About fifteen minutes. They were laughing and acting stupid."

"Maybe it was a client. Acting stupid how?"

"I don't know. You know how adults act sometimes."

She didn't have time for Christopher's observations on

how adults act. It was probably an acquaintance or client.

"Okay, finish up here so we can go to Joe's and get everything decorated for your dad."

She spotted Millie's navy Honda Civic as soon as she pulled into Joe D's. Millie was out of her car and across the parking lot.

Cynthia watched her 21-year-old daughter walk over to them. She was no longer a girl but a woman — and a beautiful one at that. She was a little taller than Cynthia, with curly medium-brown hair, tan skin and a healthy look. Her eyes were a blue-grey color that sometimes changed depending on what she was wearing. Every time Millie came home for a visit, Cynthia marveled at how much more mature and beautiful she was from the time before.

Millie gave Cynthia and Christopher hugs.

"Where's your friend, Millie? Cynthia asked.

"At Beth's house, resting for the party tonight," she said. "We just had some big exams."

"Well, okay. We need to get started so we can be back home before your dad finishes golf. Here comes the bakery van with the cake," Cynthia said as the van pull into the parking lot.

Joe met them all at the door, and they followed him out to the patio. The long table was set up exactly how Cynthia wanted it with a smaller table placed to the side for the cake. She put a green tablecloth on the small table so the delivery man could place the cake there.

Cynthia had to look away as the young man carried the cake in all by himself, until it was safely placed on the table.

The cake was a replica of Lambau football field in Green Bay. What a shame the work of art will be eaten, she thought. She thanked the young man and gave him a check for the balance.

They quickly went to work decorating the patio in Packer green and gold, complete with life-size cut-outs of Vince Lombardi and Bart Star.

"Mom, you've done a great job. Dad will love it," Christopher said.

She looked at her children with their big grins and felt an instant jolt of nostalgia. She could almost see the little kids they once were. Millie, with those eyes of hers always twinkling and changing colors, showing the deep intelligence she possessed like her dad, even at a young age. Christopher, who liked to play the tough guy but was really more like Cynthia, always caring for others. Two individuals coming from the same place, but yet so different and unique. It was amazing.

"Christopher and I are going to head home now, Millie, but we'll see you back here tonight for the party," Cynthia said.

"Hey Millie, is your friend cute?" Christopher asked.

Cynthia laughed at Christopher but didn't say a word. Millie's friend would be several years older and far more mature than he, but she admired his spunk.

"I think so," Millie said, smiling.

CHAPTER 4

*C*ynthia and Christopher managed to get back home before Philip arrived. Since it was such a nice day outside, she knew he and the guys were probably sitting around talking with a birthday beer out on the patio at the club. They better not let Philip drink too much. He'd come home wanting to take a nap, which could prove disastrous for the evening.

Finally, at about 4:45, Philip was dropped off sober but a little tired from his day.

"So has your birthday been good so far?" Cynthia asked, giving him a kiss and a smile.

"You're smiling like the Cheshire cat. What's up?"

She better get under control, or she could blow the whole evening.

"I'm just looking forward to a nice quiet evening at Joe's with you and the Benjamin's," she said.

Philip sat down in a chair with exhaustion and said, "Yeah, I was thinking about that. Why don't we order pizza and hang out here? It's just another birthday to me, no big deal. I actually would like to start forgetting them."

She'd anticipated this and was ready. "We promised Ron and Sandra we'd meet them at Joe D's for a birthday drink and dinner, remember?"

"But I just spent the afternoon with Ron and had a drink. I'm tired, and I bet Ron is, too."

She responded quickly. "But Sandra wasn't there, and we already had this planned. We haven't gotten together with both of them in awhile. Sandra and I have a lot to get caught up on. Why, they might even have a gift for you."

After thinking about it a moment, he responded reluctantly, "Okay, okay. I better hit the shower." He walked by her and smacked her behind ever so slightly and smiled very devilishly, "But promise me we won't stay too late, okay? You women sometimes get to talking and forget about time." And with that, he went upstairs.

She was beginning to stress out and went to find Christopher. "Hey I need you to get ready to go in about an hour," she said. "Nice jeans, shirt and shoes, okay? You have to help Millie greet guests."

"Okay, Mom. You need to relax. I'll keep it all under control when I get there."

She took a deep breath and exhaled as she left the room.

Cynthia took a shower and was dressed and ready to go by six thirty. She came downstairs to find Philip sleeping in his recliner with the TV on.

"Philip, wake up! We need to leave in 5 minutes," she said, thinking she was going to have a stroke.

Philip came to life, and without saying a word, picked up his car keys, and they were on their way.

They pulled into Joe D's parking lot at 7:04 by the clock on the car dashboard. Perfect, everyone should be there by now.

Cynthia was getting butterflies in her stomach as they got out of the car and walked in. Ron and Sandra were standing at the bar and waved when they saw them. The plan was for Ron to tell Philip that they already had a table in the back.

"Happy birthday, Philip," Sandra said, giving Philip a big hug. "I'm so glad we can celebrate with you."

Philip looked toward Cynthia, and she gave him a, *see, I told you so*, look.

"It's so busy tonight, we had to take a table out on the patio. We were just waiting for you to get here, so let's go sit down," Ron said as he led the way.

Cynthia's butterflies did double time.

And then there it all was.

"SURPRISE!"

The look on Philip's face was priceless, but his next words were the ones she wanted to hear. "I had no idea you were planning this. It's such a surprise," he said.

Philip immediately got pictures with the life-size Vince Lombardi and Bart Starr cut-outs, but when he saw the cake, he was in awe. "That's a cake? You mean we can eat it?"

Cynthia smiled to see how happy he was.

Everyone at the party meant something to Cynthia and Philip. She hadn't realized how many friends they'd made in Atlanta until she'd planned this party.

Where was Millie, she wondered? Christopher was visiting with guests, but her daughter seemed to be missing. She worked her way over to Christopher, saying hi to friends and accepting compliments on the party along the way.

"Hey, where's your sister?" she asked.

"I don't know, Mom. I haven't seen her."

"She's not here?" Cynthia was shocked. "Did you try calling her?"

"Yeah, but she didn't answer."

She would try calling her, but didn't want Philip to know her concern until she knew for sure something was wrong. This was so unlike Millie. She was starting to really worry, but as she headed toward the door, she spotted her daughter. Millie looked beautiful, calm, and collected, so everything must be okay.

"Sweetie, where have you been? When I found out you weren't here, I started to panic. Did you have car trouble or something?

You missed the whole surprise. I wish you would have called to let us know."

Millie had a sheepish look on her face, a very unfamiliar look for her. This was a girl always in charge and always doing the right thing. Just then, Cynthia's eyes landed on the young man standing next to Millie. Millie took his arm.

"Mom, this is my friend, Jimmy Skidmore. He goes to school with me at Berry."

She assumed Millie's friend was a girl, not a guy, as did Christopher.

"Hi, Jimmy. It's a pleasure to meet you." She extended her hand. "I'm so glad Millie's brought you to her dad's party," she said, trying to focus on the issue at hand. The boy could wait. She turned to Millie. "Darling, where have you been?" she asked her daughter again.

Jimmy cut in. "You have to blame me for delaying Millie, Mrs. Lewis. But first, might I say that you look lovely tonight in that color?"

Cynthia turned her attention back to the young man. He looked like he started shaving just last week. She ignored his forced compliment. "And how did you delay her, Jimmy?"

"Well, I recently finished some grueling exams, and in my exhaustion, I fell asleep this afternoon. Millie tried and tried to wake me up but to no avail," he said, as he turned and smiled at Millie, Millie smiling ever so sweetly back. This was not just a friend, Cynthia realized. A mother knows this when she sees it.

Cynthia forced herself to stay in control. She turned back to face Millie. "The important thing is you're here now safe and sound. Go find your dad and wish him a happy birthday, and introduce your friend. Get something to drink. Are you twenty-one, Jimmy?"

"No, ma'am, not till next year. I was bumped up a grade in elementary school, because I was bored and needed more intellectual stimulation..." Jimmy said, still talking as he walked away with Millie towards Philip.

Cynthia attempted to put Jimmy out of her mind and began canvassing the room, making sure to talk to everyone and thank them for coming to help celebrate Philip's birthday. She saw most of the guests on a regular basis, but there were a few that she hadn't seen in a while. She vowed to get together with them soon.

Gradually the guests moved to the long table for dinner, with Philip at the head, she sitting at his right, the kids and Jimmy Skidmore to the left. Cynthia looked around at the festive room and inwardly smiled as she squeezed Philip's hand under the table. He turned and mouthed a silent *thank you* and then winked, making all the work and planning worthwhile.

Everyone seemed to be enjoying themselves, so when the meal was done, Philip did the honor of making the first cut into the Lambau Field cake. It was marble, Philip's favorite — he could never decide between the two different cakes and this way, he could have both.

As they were eating cake, Philip's friends toasted and roasted him, telling stories about their adventures, many of which Cynthia was hearing for the first time.

Around ten, the guests started leaving and by ten thirty, only the family, Ron, Sandra, and Jimmy Skidmore were left.

"Cynthia, you did a fabulous job," Sandra said. "Will you plan my next party for me?"

Ron chimed in, "Yeah, and don't forget I like the Falcons, Cynthia." They all laughed.

It was just the two of them in the car on the ride home. Philip and Cynthia talked about the party and eventually got to Millie's "friend."

"What did you think of this Jimmy Skidmore?" she asked. "I was surprised. When she told me she wanted to bring a friend, I thought it was a girl."

"Well, no guy is good enough for my daughter," Philip said, laughing. "You know who that guy reminds me of?" Philip continued. "Eddie Haskell, from *Leave It To Beaver*. What do you think?"

"I don't know," she said. "I watched the way Millie looked at him. She thinks she's in love, I'm sure of it." Cynthia recalled the look in Millie's eyes when she introduced Jimmy. "By the way, I do recall my dad saying he didn't know what I saw in you after the first time I brought you home." They both laughed.

The kids beat them home. Philip went up to bed, and Cynthia went to ready the guest room for Jimmy Skidmore. This "friend" would certainly not be sharing a bedroom with Millie.

Christopher walked in the guest room as she was making up the bed. "I guess you and dad know that woman?" he asked.

Cynthia tugged on the fitted sheet. "What woman?"

"You know, the one I told you about earlier today. She was at the party tonight talking to dad for a few minutes, but then she left."

She tucked the top sheet in. "I have no idea who or what you are talking about. Was it the wife of one of our friends?"

"Maybe" Christopher said. "It was the lady at the go-kart place today. She didn't stay at the party with us. Just talked to dad and left. I think dad gave her something."

The bed was finished. She turned to Christopher. "Maybe it was someone who couldn't stay at the party, and they were giving your dad a gift."

"Maybe," he said, but he didn't sound convinced.

"Well, I don't know," Cynthia said. She was too worn out from the day to be bothered. "You go to bed," she said. "You must be tired."

And without another word, he left the room.

❦

Philip looked at himself in the mirror as he brushed his teeth. It had been a better birthday than he thought it would be. He still couldn't get over the fact that he never suspected a thing. Cynthia was good at keeping a secret.

He hoped he was as good at keeping secrets, too, because his could destroy all that he'd worked for his entire life. That damn woman. He should never have mentioned his meeting friends at Joe's tonight when he saw her at the go-kart place. He couldn't believe she showed up, but with all those people around, he was sure no one noticed her. He hoped he was done with her once and for all.

His thoughts drifted back to Cynthia. What did he ever do to deserve her? He loved her as much, if not more, than the day they were married. She was kind and trusting to a fault. He guessed that's why she was such a good nurse. She had so much trust in him. She would believe anything he told her. It killed him to have to lie to her, but keeping his marriage intact was important to him, even though he'd messed up. She would probably forgive him, because that's the way she was, but why put her through it if she didn't have to know? That's what he was telling himself, at least.

He crawled into bed feeling the stress ease slightly as he shut his eyes, his mind going over his rationale as he drifted off to sleep.

❦

The morning after the party, everyone was up by eight reminiscing about the night before at breakfast. Everyone except Jimmy.

Millie had this ridiculous story about how intelligent he was and how his brain needed more rest than most people. His SAT score was almost perfect, she told them, while wearing a silly look on her face, one that Cynthia hadn't seen on her since middle school.

Out of the corner of her eye, Cynthia caught Christopher suppressing a laugh.

"So Millie, tell us about Jimmy and how you met," Philip asked.

Millie beamed. "We were actually in the same dorm several years in a row but never really spoke until this year. Jimmy and I were in the basement doing laundry one Saturday when we both went to throw our clothes in the same dryer. Jimmy suggested we throw our clothes in together since we each needed them dry and could save time and money."

Christopher excused himself, no longer able to stifle his laugh.

"We've done our laundry together every week since," Millie told them. "Jimmy is also in business school but isn't sure what he's going to do with it. He's lived in Rome his whole life and went to Berry Academy as a kid, so he's very familiar with the school. His father is a pediatrician, and his mother takes care of the house. Jimmy's an only child."

Cynthia glanced at Philip to see if she could tell what he was thinking. His forehead was creased, a clear sign of his undivided attention.

"We have dinner with his mom and dad once a week, and they've invited me to go along with them on a cruise during our spring break," Millie continued.

A red flag went up for Cynthia. This was moving faster than she'd thought.

As if on cue, Prince Charming graced the room, complaining of a headache. He looked a little rough, confirming Cynthia's belief that Jimmy had been drinking last night. He also hadn't bothered to talk to any of the family when they arrived home and did go to bed awfully fast she thought.

Jimmy ate his breakfast, while the rest of them continued to chit-chat about the night before. As soon as Jimmy finished, he and Millie packed up their things and headed back to Rome.

CHAPTER 5

*T*wo weeks later, the hospital was shorthanded, so Cynthia was called in to work a 7-to-7 day shift. Although she loved her job, she also loved being home, especially when her long shift was over. Her cell phone rang as she walked into the house. It was Millie.

"Hi, sweetie. How's it going?"

"Good, Mom. I've got some tough finals coming up, but I think I'll be okay. I've been studying a lot."

Millie had some of the best study habits of anyone Cynthia had ever known. She was so focused, she seemed to be in another world altogether. Although it had certainly paid off, sometimes Cynthia worried that Millie put too much pressure on herself.

"Millie, Dad and I are proud of you whatever you do. But we don't want you to make yourself crazy and overdo it," she said.

"Oh, I won't, Mom. It's important for me to do my best, though."

"So to what do I owe the honor of this call?" Cynthia asked.

"I want to bring Jimmy home for Thanksgiving. His parents are going to visit some relatives in New York, and he would rather stay here and be with me."

Cynthia hesitated, wondering if Millie was moving

too fast, but then she decided it could be good. Cynthia's mother and Granny were coming from White Lake for Thanksgiving and staying through New Year's. The whole family could get to know Jimmy and check him out. "Of course he's welcome, just as any friend of yours is always welcome at our house," Cynthia said. "Just tell Jimmy to bring his appetite, okay?"

"Thanks, Mom. Jimmy will be so excited. He never has any family around, so this is a great experience for him. See you soon." She hung up.

Something about this kid bothered her, but she couldn't put her finger on it. Maybe because he seemed so much younger than Millie. More like he should still be in high school. She'd have to let it run its course. Millie was a young woman fully equipped to make her own decisions. Her job as a mother now was to support those decisions the best she could.

❦

The Sunday before Thanksgiving, Cynthia and Philip were waiting inside the busy Atlanta airport for her mother and Granny's visit.

"So where did you decide to put Jimmy this weekend?" Philip asked.

"He'll sleep in Christopher's room, and Christopher will use the blow-up mattress in the study. I decided I'm looking forward to getting to know Jimmy better, since I think Millie really likes him. We didn't spend much time with him the night of your party. We know very little about the kid."

"I guess that's true," Philip said. "I don't know. I always feel there's something wrong with any of the guys Millie has dated. Maybe I can make a Packer fan out of this one," he laughed.

Cynthia shook her head, laughing, as, out of the corner of her eye, she saw her mother and granny walking their way.

Her granny, Hazel Pearl Valley, had striking white hair that was still thick and wavy, a beautiful wrinkled face, and stood as straight and tall as any woman of ninety-four years in a Green Bay Packer shirt could. Cynthia was almost a clone of her mother, Grace Valley Westerly, the only difference being that Cynthia had her dad's hazel eyes, where her mother's were brown. Her mother looked at least ten years younger than her seventy-six years.

Granny was first to throw her arms around Cynthia with a big hug and kiss, quickly followed by her mother. The two older women always looked forward to their visit every year.

Philip went to get the car while the women retrieved the luggage, meeting him outside at the passenger pick up.

As soon as they walked through the door at home, Christopher sailed down the stairs.

"Granny, Grandma!" He was always so happy to see them.

"Christopher, go help your dad with the suitcases." Cynthia told him.

"Do we get our usual room?" Granny asked.

"Yes, you and Mom will have your usual room," Cynthia said. "Millie is bringing her friend, Jimmy Skidmore, home to spend the holiday with us, so I'm putting him in Christopher's room."

"Jimmy what? Did you say Skidmarks? What an odd name." Granny was a little hard of hearing. They all laughed.

"Let's go to the kitchen, and you can show us what you have planned for Thanksgiving," Granny said, not really sure what was so funny.

Cynthia showed them her turkey and the menu she'd planned. Her mother suggested a few more things but approved of what Cynthia had in mind. Cynthia made them all a cup of Earl Grey tea with milk and sugar while the three women sat at the table, thoroughly enjoying each other's company. The older women talked about the recent news from White Lake, relatives, and their busy lives. They spent the next hour smiling and talking away about nothing in particular but everything important to them.

❦

Millie indicated she and Jimmy would be arriving well before noon on Thanksgiving Day, but it was already two o'clock, and dinner was at three.

Cynthia was alone in the kitchen when Christopher walked in looking for something to eat. It had been an hour since Cynthia put appetizers out.

"I'm worried about Millie," she said. "Would you call her? Your grandmothers and I have so much to do here, and it would help put my mind at ease."

"Sure, Mom, I'll see what she and old Skidless are up to," Christopher said, breaking into a chuckle as he left the room.

Cynthia laughed, too. He was such a typical brother. Reminded her of how Arthur always teased her about any boy she liked. Her brother had almost made her afraid to bring them home.

A few minutes later, Christopher was back with an answer. "Millie and Skidrow will be here in forty-five minutes. I guess Skidrow had a situation or something."

"What does that mean, a situation?" she asked.

"I don't know, Mom. I'm just the messenger," he said, leaving to go watch some more football with Philip.

Cynthia could push the dinner back a half-hour, she supposed. It annoyed her that Millie and Jimmy were going to be late, and she felt they should have called earlier. Millie was raised to be considerate of others.

She told her mother and grandmother what was going on so they could be prepared to keep things warm until Millie and Jimmy arrived.

"What's this Jimmy like?" her mother asked.

"We don't know much about him. I met him for the first time at Philip's birthday party and didn't know he existed prior to that. Millie seems to like the guy, so we'll probably like him after we have an opportunity to get to know him better. That's all I'm going to say at this point, so you can decide for yourself."

❧

At exactly 2:50 the love birds arrived. Cynthia watched out the window as Millie pulled into the driveway and both of them stepped out of the car, unloading their suitcases as if they had all the time in the world.

"We're here," Millie shouted as she swung the door open.

Everyone came to the front door in anticipation as Jimmy met Millie's grandmothers.

"Granny and Grandma, I'd like you to meet my boyfriend, Jimmy Skidmore."

Boyfriend, now that was new, Cynthia thought. It was friend last month at the party.

They surveyed the gawky skinny guy in front of them not saying anything. Cynthia's mother finally broke the long moment. "We're so pleased to meet you, Jimmy, and to have you here to share this special meal with our family."

"Thank you ma'am," Jimmy said with a smile, his southern drawl thick. "The pleasure is really mine."

Gee, that wasn't so bad, Cynthia thought. She enjoyed seeing a bit of southern charm come out of Jimmy.

Jimmy continued. "Millie has told me all about the both of you, and I must say you are far lovelier than what I expected. Might I call you grandmother and great grandmother? You both look way too young to be carrying those titles, I should add. I'm really looking forward to getting to know you and can't wait to hear about your tranquil home in Wisconsin. Millie talks about it with such fondness. I can't wait till I have a chance to visit y'all."

The grandmothers stared at Jimmy, not really knowing what to say, which was very unusual for them. After an even longer moment than before, Granny spoke. "Well, it's a pleasure meeting you, too, Jimmy. We love Millie, and any friend of hers is someone we want to get to know."

"Well," Cynthia said. "Don't mean to rush anyone, but there's a turkey waiting patiently and dinner to be served, so Millie, you and Jimmy take your things upstairs, Christopher show Jimmy where he'll be, Mom and Granny, you know what we have to do, and Philip, carve that bird!"

Everyone went into action, and within twenty minutes, the family was sitting at the beautifully set dining room table, ready for Granny to bless the lovingly prepared meal so they could start filling their plates.

No one uttered a word while they took the first few bites of their meal, a sign of appreciation.

Granny finally broke the silence as she took a spoonful of jellied cranberry sauce.

"You know, this red cranberry sauce reminds me of a story," she said. Granny was known for the entertaining stories she told whenever a memory was sparked. The family was used to it and felt that, at her age, she was entitled to tell whatever came to mind.

"My niece, Hilda Hoffensburger, fed her son, Butch, some red Jell-O® for the first time when he was about three years old. The kid loved it, ate almost the whole bowl. Hilda sent him outside with his older brother to play, and I'll be darned if that little tike didn't wander over to the neighbor's house. The neighbor was painting and had gone into the house to answer the phone, leaving his small can of paint unattended. You guessed it. Butch found the paint, and when he saw it was red, just like the Jell-O®, he took a big drink of it. Came home with red paint all over his mouth and clothes crying. His older brother got Hilda, and they took him straight to the hospital to get his stomach pumped."

"Okay, Granny I'm going to ask the obvious. What happened to Butch and his brother?" Millie inquired.

"Well, Butch survived just fine. His brother got spanked for not watching Butch. In those days, we could do that." Granny said, very seriously. "Butch moved to Baraboo, where the circus was headquartered. Fell in love and married the girl who swung on the trapeze and joined up himself. Ran the ring toss game. Hilda bragged constantly about how he traveled for business and saw the whole country."

They'd heard several stories before, but this one was new. After the laughing died down, Cynthia's mother turned to Millie. "So Millie, what held you up this morning? Christopher said you had a situation. Wasn't car trouble, was it?"

"No, Grandma," she said, smiling at Jimmy. "Jimmy is just a big kid and has to watch all the Thanksgiving parades. It was fun since I hadn't watched them for years, but it made us a little late in getting started."

Christopher snickered.

Cynthia would have to have a little talk with Millie later about being more considerate of others. This was not making her like Jimmy. Then Jimmy opened his mouth.

"This is an unusual Thanksgiving meal," he said. "I mean it looks familiar, but it doesn't taste like what I'm used to."

What's the matter with this kid? Cynthia thought. Did his parents not teach him any manners?

"The dressing and gravy taste weird, and some of this stuff I don't even know what it is."

"Well, Jimmy," Philip interrupted. "A lot foods are different in the North and the South. I found this to be true after we moved down here from Wisconsin. We make our stuffing with regular bread, and true southerners use corn bread. Makes a totally different taste. We also like a thicker gravy, while you're probably used to something thinner. The point is, we have to keep an open mind to try new things and be appreciative of the people who created this meal. That's what Thanksgiving is all about and what our country has always been about."

Cynthia looked at her husband and couldn't have loved him any more at that moment. What a wonderful person he was. In his own way, he took up for her grandmother, mother and herself, putting Jimmy in his place in the process. She loved him for that.

Jimmy sat with a stupid look on his face, and Millie stared at him, smiling. Cynthia was having a hard time seeing what attracted Millie to him, but still, she would try.

The meal continued, everyone filling their plates a second time. Conversation flowed from catching up about the relatives they rarely saw to sports, politics, and Granny wanting to know what time the Packers played on Sunday.

Cynthia's mother brought them up to speed on her brother, Arthur, his wife, Ann, and their 16-year-old daughter, Samantha. They lived in England, so Cynthia and her mother didn't see much of them.

"So what are you going to do with your life after you graduate from high school, Christopher?" Cynthia's mother turned the conversation to Christopher, who'd been unusually silent throughout the meal.

"I'm looking at a couple of schools. I've got my applications all ready to submit and plan to visit them all with Mom and Dad after the first of the year. It's a hard decision, and I'm putting a lot of thought into it. As far as my major, I decided I want to do something medical."

"That sounds great," Cynthia's mother said, and then continued, "Any girls you're in love with?"

"In the area of the ladies, I feel I need to keep my options open. You know, play the field until I find that special girl. Someone like you, Grandma."

Nice touch, Cynthia thought.

His grandmother smiled at him. She loved her only grandson, and he loved her.

The family lingered at the dinner table, no one having to rush off anywhere, everyone relaxed and happy.

Finally, it was time for dessert if anyone had room. They had pumpkin and apple pie, a chocolate cake with chocolate ganache frosting, and a plate of various cookies Granny had made.

As they were passing the desserts around, Jimmy said, "I'll have some pound cake and pecan pie."

Cynthia cleared her throat. "We don't have either one of those, but I'm sure we have something you like."

Jimmy looked it over unappreciatively. "I don't like pumpkin at all, so I guess I'll have apple pie and some cookies."

Everyone but Millie looked annoyed at this self-centered young man. *Come on, Millie, wake up,* Cynthia thought. But Millie said, "You know what, Jimmy? I'm going to learn how to make both of those, and next year we'll have them." Jimmy smiled at her.

Dinner was over. The tradition had always been that the guys cleaned up, so with Jimmy reluctantly in tow, they cleared off the table and disappeared into the kitchen. Philip cracked the whip and said that if the women could put together this meal every year, the least they could do was act as cleanup crew.

Everyone did their own thing the rest of the evening. Christopher and Philip played video games, Millie and Jimmy watched a DVD of "It's a Wonderful Life," and Cynthia, her mother, and Granny planned their shopping trip for the next day.

The three women were not big shoppers, but they enjoyed doing Black Friday every year because they were together. Each made a list, and shopping strategies were laid out. They would depart the house at 8 AM, always leaving an open invitation to anyone else in the family to join them.

Much to their surprise, Philip and Christopher said they would come later in the morning and meet them for lunch. They were brave men to come out on the craziest shopping day of the year. For the first time, Millie opted to not shop with them since she and Jimmy needed to do some studying.

The day wound down and slowly everyone went sleepily to their rooms.

Once in bed, Philip cuddled Cynthia in his arms.

"I love knowing all our family is asleep under the same roof with me," she told him sleepily.

"Even Jimmy?" he asked.

"I'm working on it."

He kissed the back of her neck with a breathy laugh and held her closer.

After a few minutes, she spoke. "Christopher talking about college made me think about something I've wanted to do."

"What's that?" he asked.

"Get my master's."

Another breathy laugh into her neck. "Really? When did this come about?"

"I've always wanted to get it I've just never felt the time was right. I've told you before. You really don't remember?"

"Yeah, I do vaguely," he yawned. "I just don't understand why this has come about now at this point in your life."

He really didn't get it.

"Because I want to, and that should be enough," she said.

He didn't respond, and eventually she heard his soft snore. She slid out of his arms and moved to her side of the bed. *I am going to go back to school even if he doesn't get it*, she thought, as she slipped into her own deep sleep.

CHAPTER 6

*T*he women were up and out of the house before eight. They found a fairly decent parking spot at the mall and hit the stores on their list with great skill. Granny was fearless, never complaining or expecting them to make special accommodations for her, even at her age.

Christopher and Philip were going to meet them at the food court around one, so the women headed that way at 12:45. They found Christopher sitting at a table alone.

"Where's your dad?" Cynthia asked.

"He told me to save the table, and he went that way to watch for you." He pointed in the direction they'd just come from.

"Mom, you and Granny sit here with Christopher, and I'll see if I can find him," she said.

The mall was crowded with people, so Cynthia wasn't surprised that they hadn't seen him. She was scanning the crowd when she saw his familiar smile.

He was talking to a woman, she not seeing the woman's face, only the back of her head. When she was a short distance away, she abruptly stopped. The woman took her right hand and placed it on the left side of Philip's face, slowly moving it down his jaw and to his chin.

Cynthia turned on her heel and walked away, barely believing what she'd just seen.

She must have been mistaken about what she'd witnessed. The thought of another woman caressing her husband's face in public was absurd, and the thought of Philip allowing it was even more absurd. She would ask him about it, and then what she thought she saw would be put to rest.

She waited outside the food court where the family couldn't see her so she could confront him.

A few minutes later, Philip came up to her.

"Hey, I was looking for you. Where's your mom and Granny?"

"At the table with Christopher," she said. "I wanted to talk to you alone."

"Okay." He looked puzzled.

She hesitated before she blurted it out. "Philip, I saw you talking to a woman, and she put her hand on your face in a very familiar way."

Philip first looked shocked but then acted as if he'd heard wrong. "What woman?" he asked.

"The one you were talking to just a few minutes ago."

"Cynthia, I have no idea what you're talking about," he paused. "Oh, some woman was walking around with a bottle of cologne trying to get people to come into her store and buy, I bet it was her. She sprayed some on me. That had to be it."

"I didn't see anything in her hand except the side of your face as she stroked it."

"I don't know how you could see anything with all the people around here today. Nothing happened," he said with conviction.

She felt foolish now. It seemed like a logical explanation. "I guess that must have been it. It looked different from where I stood though," she said, reluctantly, knowing now was not the time to make a big deal out of it. "Okay, let's get something to eat."

When they were done eating, the guys decided to do a little shopping on their own while the women visited the last of the stores on their list.

"I don't know when we'll be home, but supper will be the Thanksgiving leftovers," Cynthia told Philip, giving him a kiss on his left cheek. It was the same cheek he said the woman had sprayed with cologne, but it didn't smell like cologne at all.

At about five, everyone arrived home hungry, so together, they quickly set the leftovers out.

Millie and Jimmy said they studied in the morning and watched movies all afternoon.

Cynthia's heart warmed a little as she heard Jimmy ask Granny if he could help her find a place to sit so he and Millie could visit with her since they didn't go shopping that day. Granny even asked him if, by chance, he was a Packer fan. It was nice.

Everyone helped clean up before they went off to do their own thing. Philip stayed at the kitchen table as she took two wine glasses out of the cupboard and filled them with some white wine. She decided to once again bring up the woman.

After handing him his glass of wine and sitting down next to him, he took her hand and planted a kiss on it with a smile.

"What a great day. I loved it didn't you?" he asked.

"More than anything," she said, pulling her hand away. "Philip. I'm still concerned about the woman at the mall today. You didn't seem to smell like any cologne when I kissed you earlier. You've been working so many more late nights at work, and after I saw what I saw today, it made me start wondering if all is okay between us?"

He looked surprised but not concerned or guilty. She couldn't quite read him. Was he hiding something?

"I stopped off in the men's room and wiped the stuff off. It stunk. I don't know what you saw, but I can assure you, you are the only woman for me. I love you, Cynthia, and I love what we have together."

Was that an answer or an attempt to avoid giving an answer?

"Enough of this," he said, taking her in his arms and kissing her. "You have nothing to worry about. You're stuck with me," he said laughing. He kissed her once more and then left to join the rest of the family in the other room.

While she put the last dish in the dishwasher, it came to her. Christopher talking about the woman at the go-kart place and the birthday party. She instantly felt sick. Another woman? But he was a good husband and father, and they even had an active sex life. She felt it was impossible. He was a family guy. If there was a problem, she would know.

So she turned the dishwasher on and joined the family, having convinced herself that what she was thinking was totally ridiculous. She had nothing to worry about.

❦

As always, the time between Thanksgiving and Christmas flew.

Millie came home after her finals without Jimmy, so Cynthia had her all to herself.

"How serious are you about Jimmy?" she asked her one day.

"He's one of the nicest guys I ever met," Millie said, eyes sparkling. Cynthia knew that look.

"My main concern is your education," Cynthia said, thinking briefly about her own master's degree. "I want to make sure you get all the education you want. Women today need their education, and if you don't do it now while you're young, you'll never do it."

"Don't worry, Mom. I feel the same way and plan on getting my master's. I've worked too hard for this."

Cynthia felt so much better. This was the sensible daughter she'd raised. "So how about the two of us go to a movie one afternoon?"

"Sounds like a great idea," Millie said with a smile.

"Okay, let's go help Grandma and Granny with the cookies in the kitchen. They have everything planned as usual. We need to find out what our jobs are."

They entered the kitchen to see mother and daughter flitting around like two honey bees from flower to flower, Granny in charge of the proceedings. She was fixing cookie sheets while Cynthia's mother mixed dough in the Kitchen Aid Mixer.

Cynthia had two big gas ovens — Granny preferred electric — and a fully equipped kitchen the two older women truly found luxurious.

"Cynthia I want you chopping these nuts and Millie, you roll these cookies in sugar," Granny said. "I tell you every time I cook or bake in this kitchen, I feel like I have died and gone to heaven. I hope the good Lord has one just like this for me when I see Him."

The four women laughed for a minute and then got to work.

Granny put a sheet of cookies in the oven and said, "I remember the gas ovens in the old days. There was a pilot light that occasionally could go out. Was always afraid my house could blow up. Will never forget what happened to Joan Pomeranke. Poor thing had her pilot light go out, so she opened the oven door and leaned in over the opening with a match to light it and, poof, the excess gas ignited and singed off her eyebrows, eyelashes, and the hair around her face. The unfortunate thing about it, other than her missing hair, was her daughter was getting married that Saturday. Being a good friend, I told her she looked fine, but she really looked bad. I felt guilty after I saw the wedding pictures. We kind of drifted apart after that."

"Now I understand why you don't like a gas oven," Cynthia said. "But you know they have improved over the years." They all laughed.

❧

Millie went back to school before Christmas to exchange gifts with Jimmy. She was giving Jimmy a watch, which Cynthia thought was too personal, but kept her mouth shut. Cynthia couldn't wait to see what Jimmy gave Millie.

That night at dinner, Christopher speculated about what Jimmy might give Millie.

"The old Skidmiester is too skiddish to give Millie something good. Millie will open her present from him and say, 'You've got to be skidding!'" Christopher predicted. "Yeah, the Skidinator will probably leave skid marks in his undies when he opens his present from Millie, because he'll be so skidcited," he continued.

Christopher was on a roll. You couldn't help but laugh when he got going, but the surprise came from Granny.

"If he doesn't come through with something good, Mr. Jimmy Skidless will be on skid row with Millie. She should skid his butt."

They all laughed hysterically. Cynthia felt a little guilty taking entertainment at Jimmy's expense — but only a little.

Christopher continued on. If Millie married Jimmy, they could have three kids and call them Love To Skidmore, Last To Skidmore and Long To Skidmore. Cynthia and the rest of them laughed until their faces hurt.

❧

The next day when Millie came home, she was wearing a silver necklace with a diamond hanging from it. Jimmy did good. *Too* good. They'd been dating only a few months. Was it more serious than Cynthia thought? The answer appeared to be a definite yes.

"Are you still planning to go on the cruise with Jimmy?" Cynthia asked, trying to get more information.

"Oh, yes. I can't wait to spend a whole week with Jimmy on the boat," Millie said.

"So what are the sleeping arrangements?" Cynthia asked.

Millie looked at her shocked. "Mom, please. You don't sound like yourself when you ask stuff like that. Don't worry, my 'virtue' will be respected."

She didn't say *how* her "virtue" would be respected, but Millie was old enough to make her own decisions. Cynthia would say no more.

❦

Between Thanksgiving and Christmas, Philip seemed to have relaxed. He told Cynthia it was because things slowed down in his line of business that time of the year. He said he would make it up to her and the rest of the family by spending more time with them, which he did. She felt her husband was back and soon put the idea of another woman out of her head.

❦

When the New Year rolled around, it was time to send the grandmothers back to the north. Cynthia would miss them, but before she knew it, the summer would be upon them, and her family would be going to White Lake for a visit.

Cynthia and Philip delivered them to the Atlanta Airport, Cynthia slightly concerned about them arriving at their departure gate on time. The women really could take care of themselves, but they always allowed a little fussing by others. Off they went to their airplane, chattering to each other and smiling. The two couldn't wait to get home to share this latest adventure in their life.

As they walked to their car, Philip turned to Cynthia. "You know I was thinking about your upcoming birthday in March. Let's go somewhere just the two of us. How about I surprise you?"

"That would be wonderful," she said, smiling. "Where were you thinking?"

"If I told you, it wouldn't be a surprise."

As they drove home, she thoughtfully looked over at Philip. He was a good but not perfect husband. Were either of them perfect? He probably had complaints about her. Marriage was about accepting a person for who they were and not trying to change them into someone you wanted them to be.

She speculated on the upcoming year and how it was going to be a year of good changes for them, she could feel it. Christopher would graduate in June, they'd visit White Lake as a family in July, and in August, Millie would start her senior year, and Christopher would be a freshman in college. She and Philip would begin the next chapter in their life as empty nesters. This was the way life progressed. They would all learn to adapt.

CHAPTER 7

*I*t had been a quiet February day in the ICU where Cynthia worked. Her current patient was a young woman who had been in a car accident that morning. She found it emotional when her patients were so young — she could never help thinking of her own kids. As she was changing the IV bag, she saw her nurse manager from the corner of her eye outside the door, waiting as if she wanted to talk.

"Listen, Cynthia, the patient census is low today, so how would you like to leave after you get your patients medicated and comfortable?"

"Sure, I can manage that," Cynthia responded happily.

Cynthia was out of the parking lot by 6:05. While driving home, she decided she'd eat whatever the guys made, jump in the shower, put on her nightgown, crawl in bed, and watch TV until she fell asleep, which would be about five minutes after her head touched the pillow

Philip's car wasn't in the driveway when she got home, but she knew Christopher was there because every light was on in the house, something he was notorious for. She parked and went through the garage door into the kitchen.

It was a wreck. There were about five empty plastic containers piled in the sink, along with three pans on the stovetop containing macaroni and cheese from a box, sautéed mushrooms, and an unrecognizable mixture. Various plates, glasses, bowls, and utensils were strewn everywhere — no Christopher.

Cynthia headed up the stairs, calling his name, when she heard a noise coming from Christopher's room. She proceeded cautiously and discovered the sound was coming from the bathroom. She found him in there, his head hanging over the toilet.

"What's going on?" she asked with alarm.

"Oh my God, Mom, I'm so glad to see you. I've been puking my brains out with bad diarrhea and the worst smelling farts ever." Christopher let one loose, and she became a believer.

"When did this start?" she asked. "Where's your father?"

"My stomach started getting upset about ten minutes after I finished eating, and Dad doesn't usually get home until right before you do on the nights you work late," Christopher said.

"Every time I work late?" she asked.

"Every time," he said with certainty. Then he threw up again.

Cynthia sat on the side of the tub looking at her son. He was sitting on the floor, head resting sideways on the toilet seat with his eyes closed. Poor kid. She started running her fingers through his hair, and he looked up at her so pathetically.

"I remember you doing that when I was a little kid. Don't tell anyone, but it really makes me feel better."

She continued to run her fingers through his hair as he lay with his head on the toilet seat.

After about fifteen minutes, things had quieted down, and she helped him crawl into bed and under the covers. She tucked the blanket around his big limp body and gave him a plastic container in case he needed it.

She went back down to the kitchen, surveyed the mess,

and saw the time on the clock was 6:48. So much for her after-work plans. Meanwhile, where was her husband?

Her mind immediately started in with the thoughts about another woman. Christopher said he was late whenever she worked. Was it someone he worked with? Was she being played a fool? She pulled a wine bottle out of the refrigerator and started pouring, polishing off the first glass and pouring another. Where was he?

She was ready for him when he entered the kitchen from the garage. He looked tired, but so was she.

He smiled when he saw her. "This is a surprise. How come you're home so early?" He took in the disaster area formerly known as their kitchen. "What happened here?"

"Apparently Christopher was hungry and went through the leftovers experimenting with a little cooking. He's spent most of the evening hanging over the toilet." There was more anger in her voice then she'd intended.

"Am I in trouble over this?" Philip asked. "I mean, I was working trying to provide for this family. Isn't that what I'm supposed to do? I don't enjoy working late, but sometimes I have to."

"It sounds to me you come home late only the nights I work late. Are you trying to hide something from me?" Cynthia asked, all the feelings coming out that she'd so expertly been keeping inside.

Philip just stared at her. He was still holding his brief case, and his jacket was over his arm. Was he hiding something? She wasn't sure.

"What?" he asked, turning away and looking down. Now *her* stomach felt sick.

He went on, "I'm going to change, and then I'm coming back to help you clean this up. I know you're exhausted from the past three days," he said, looking at the empty wine glass. He put one hand on her shoulder, taking her chin in his other hand so she had no choice but to face him.

He looked her directly in the eyes. "Cynthia, I love you and the kids more than anything. I mean that."

And without another word, he left to change.

She sat in the nearest chair going over the past few minutes. What had just happened? Was it her? She *was* very tired, and maybe she overreacted. She started to doubt herself.

Philip came back. Without saying a word, they worked together to clean up the kitchen. When it was all done, he took her in his arms and held her close for a good while, then pulled back so he could look into her eyes.

As if he knew what she was thinking, he said, "There is no one but you in my life. I love you more than anything. I'm working late because I'm concerned over all the expenses coming up. Two in college, then graduate school for Millie, a wedding for her someday, and our retirement. We're talking a lot of money here."

"I can go back to school myself and get my master's," she said. "I can work full time and make more money with it."

He brushed her hair from her face and kissed her, long and hard, running his hands up and down her body. It felt so good. She loved him with all her heart. She felt him become aroused.

"You don't have to go back to school and work more. I'm taking care of everything for us," he said, turning away. "I've got a few things to do still, so why don't you check on Christopher, get a shower, and crawl in bed and wait for me?"

He walked away, and she stood by herself thinking about what had just happened. Maybe the real question here wasn't whether there was another woman. Maybe it was, where did she fit in? She wasn't being taken seriously. She felt as if she didn't matter.

Philip came back, breaking her thoughts. "Hey, do you think Christopher will be well enough to go on our college tour of UNC Charlotte later this week?"

At that moment, she could have cared less about any of them or what he had to say, but she forced herself to come around. "I'm sure he'll snap back," she said, and she turned away, not wanting to look at Philip. She decided to check on Christopher.

"Hey, Mom, I'm feeling better. I'm actually hungry," Christopher told her as she walked into his room.

"You must be better if you want to eat," she said, laughing as she tenderly ran her fingers through his hair. She wondered where the time had gone. "Let's plan on you staying home tomorrow, okay?"

"Well, okay, but I'm feeling better."

"Get some sleep, sweetheart," she said as she left the room.

She headed to her room, took a shower, put her nightgown on, and climbed between the sheets. The tension seemed to melt off her body as she settled in. She was not in the mood for sex, so if Philip came to bed before she was asleep, she would pretend she was, never having done that before. Right now, she wished she were alone somewhere else so she could make sense of what she was feeling. She slowly drifted off.

❦

When Philip came to bed, he stood for a moment looking at his wife sleeping soundly. He gently kissed her on the forehead so as not to wake her, climbed between the sheets, and cuddled up next to her.

The hospital was hard work — both physically and mentally — and yet she was still able give so much to their family. Sometimes he wondered how she did it. He remembered feeling the same way about his mom after his dad died. His mom had held everything together just like Cynthia did.

Feeling anxious, he rolled over to his back and stared at the ceiling, his mind reeling. What was he going to do?

He felt like a rock tied to the end of a rope hanging over a cliff. The more effort he put into fixing his life, the worse it became. The rock only got heavier, and the rope only stretched longer, inch by inch, taking him further from his family and farther down the cliff. He wasn't sure how much longer he could do this.

Last week, he had gone to see his doctor and golfing friend, Tom, for a physical. He was feeling tired and not right. Tom ran a bunch of tests and said he would give him a call with the results in a week or so. It was probably just stress, and he should think about slowing down, eating better, and doing more exercise.

But it wasn't possible for him to slow down at the moment. The extra money he'd been making was being funneled into investments he was sure would bring big rewards and free him from his problems. He hoped it would allow him to slow down and take care of the secret life he'd been leading. Cynthia could never know. He needed money to end what he'd so foolishly started.

At times, he was so stressed he was afraid he would drop dead. As he lay there thinking, his thoughts went to when he was ten and his dad died. Philip will would never forget the day.

It was the fall, and he and his dad were in the back yard raking leaves, laughing and goofing off while they worked. All of a sudden, his dad put his hand to his chest and fell to the ground. Philip thought he was kidding at first, but when his dad didn't move or start laughing, Philip sunk to his knees next to him and asked, "Dad, are you okay?" Not wanting to believe something was wrong, but realizing his dad needed help, he ran into the house to have his mom call an ambulance. It was no good. His dad was gone.

Seeing his dad die before his eyes was the single most traumatic thing that had ever happened to him, and he didn't want his kids to experience the same.

After he got through all this, he'd do a better job of taking care of himself. He'd learned a lesson and would never go down this road again. His dream was to see his kids finish college, get married, and give him and Cynthia grandchildren, maybe even great-grandchildren. But you didn't know when it was your time, did you?

Cynthia would never understand what he was doing right now or why.

CHAPTER 8

*C*ynthia hadn't talked to Purvell since Christmas. They seemed to play phone tag a lot, but she needed to talk to someone she could trust about Philip and her suspicions. She knew that Purvell would be honest. She dialed Purvell's number on her phone.

"Hey, Cynthia, I was just thinking of you. We must be psychic," she said, laughing, "What's going on? Please don't tell me about how warm it is, I'm freezing up here."

Hearing Purvell's voice made her instantly feel better.

"Oh, it's not that warm here but better than where you are. We're looking at colleges for Christopher, in fact we're going to look at one in a few days. Millie is doing fine. Don't hear as much from her now that she has a boyfriend. Philip works a lot. You know how it is. Mom and Granny are not able to do much with all the snow they have to deal with."

"So what about *you*?" Purvell asked. "Are you okay?" Purvell must have noticed something in her voice.

She hesitated, but then blurted it out, "Purvell, do you think Philip would have an affair?"

Judging by the long pause, Cynthia could tell she'd taken her friend off guard.

"I know you've been a little concerned about him, but an affair? What makes you suspect that?"

Cynthia proceeded to tell her about the woman Christopher saw, the mall, the late hours, Philip's behavior, and their recent exchange when she'd had a suspicious feeling. She told her how he had answers for everything and made her feel like she was overreacting.

"How does he act toward you?" Purvell asked. "Is he unkind or mean? How's your sex life?"

"No he treats me like usual. Our sex life has been no different. It's more of a feeling."

"Well, I'm never one to discount someone's feelings, but Philip? I never thought I would hear those words come from you about him. I've seen enough to know anything is possible, but Philip…" her voice trailed off.

"Purvell, you're the only one I can talk to about this. He said he loved me, and I was the only one for him. Maybe I'm being paranoid. That's why I had to ask you."

"I'm not the one living it, and there isn't enough evidence to convince me, but all I can say is, I never would have expected that from Philip. I wish I could be more help."

"You've listened to me, and that helps. I needed someone to talk to. Thanks."

"You've listened plenty to me," Purvell said. "Many times you were *my* voice of reason."

They spent the rest of the time talking about other things in their lives and soon Purvell had to run off to an appointment. Even though Cynthia didn't come to a conclusion about Philip, she felt better than she had in weeks.

Christopher recuperated from his food poisoning and was ready for his college visit to UNC Charlotte at the end of the week.

After getting to Charlotte and checking into their hotel just across from campus, they explored the city on their own, checking out the campus and the downtown area. Friday they were going on an official tour.

Christopher was the first one up the next morning, eager to go.

"I'm hungry, and the man at the desk said they had a breakfast buffet, so do you guys mind if I go down and start?"

"Go ahead," Philip said. "Just leave something for us," he laughed.

Christopher eagerly headed down, leaving them alone.

Just as Cynthia was taking her nightgown off to change, Philip came up behind her, putting both hands on her hips.

"Hey, mister, what do you think you're doing?"

"Christopher is gone, and I thought maybe we could take a little time for ourselves."

"And he can come back at any minute. Wouldn't that make for a memorable college visit?" They both laughed.

They continued with a little hugging and kissing. Cynthia couldn't help but think that if he was in love with another woman, there was no way he could do this. Philip ran his fingers through her hair and down her back, caressing her body. She worried they wouldn't be able to stop if they went much further, so she laughed and pulled away.

"We need to get dressed and meet Christopher, remember?"

Philip gave her one last kiss and then laughed along with her.

On the way down, Cynthia looked at their reflection in the shiny elevator doors.

If she went purely on his actions after their tense conversation when Christopher was sick, she'd have to say she overreacted, but on the other hand, there was the look in his eyes while they argued and when he turned away from her. An action that only took a second but spoke volumes without words. But now, so much passion and interest. She was lost. Was she over thinking all this when she really needed to let it go?

"Cynthia, Cynthia," Philip was saying. "Where are you? You look a million miles away. Are you feeling okay?"

"What? Oh, yes, I'm fine. Sorry. I guess I was daydreaming a little."

He smiled. "Let me guess. You're thinking about what life will be like without the kids. Like everything, we'll adjust to it together. Don't worry. I'll be right next to you holding your hand."

She didn't tell him that's not what she'd been thinking about at all and worried if she kept up with this train of thought, she might drive a wedge between them. Somehow she needed to get past it.

All Christopher could talk about on the way home was how much he liked the college. Soon his voice and the movement of the car lulled Cynthia into a soothing sleep.

She was back at her college in Madison as a student with Purvell, only they were the ages they were now, Purvell dressed as a New York realtor, Cynthia in nursing scrubs. They were at the Kollege Klub, a favorite bar they used to frequent. Looking around, she saw the familiar tables, chairs, and jukebox in the corner. It was softly playing "Looks Like We Made It," by Barry Manilow. Everyone around them was blurred and mumbling like it always was in her dreams. Everyone except the bartender, a chubby middle-aged man with a bad comb over and bloodshot eyes. He put two beers on the bar, turned away, and disappeared.

She and Purvell sat alone at the bar and drank the beers until their glasses were empty.

Purvell turned to her and spoke. "Be prepared."

"Mom, Mom, *Mom*," Christopher said. "We're almost home."

For a second, Cynthia wasn't sure where she was.

"How about we stop and pick up supper unless you had something else in mind?" Philip asked.

"What?" She asked groggily.

"We need to eat something. I'm starving," Christopher said.

"Oh, we'll pick something up," she said, a little more awake now. "Any suggestions?"

"Burgers," Christopher said with excitement. Philip agreed.

Back at home with their burgers in front of them, the conversation turned to the current college visit and Christopher's decision. UNC Charlotte was now officially in the running. The campus was a nice size with many new buildings. They even had a new football team. She could see him there. It would be a tough choice, but he needed to make it soon.

Cynthia was cleaning up the kitchen, thinking about the day, when she vaguely remembered her dream in the car.

She remembered Purvell had said something, but what was it? It starts with a *p*, she thought. Pre... pretend... present... presume. It was coming... oh, she couldn't remember. Maybe it would come to her later when she wasn't trying so hard to think of it.

CHAPTER 9

On the morning of her fifty-fifth birthday, Cynthia woke to a kiss on the forehead from Philip.

"Happy birthday, darling."

After a stretch and a yawn, she opened her eyes fully and smiled.

"I've got a pot of your favorite coffee and some warm cinnamon rolls downstairs. Christopher's gone to school, and I'm leaving for work, so relax and enjoy your day."

"You made homemade cinnamon rolls?" she said, surprised.

Philip laughed. "No, it's from the can." He continued to laugh, shaking his head as he left the room.

The house was quiet. She kind of liked it.

After having coffee and a roll, she got dressed for her run.

As she started to run down the street, her mind went to her surprise birthday trip later in the week with Philip. She had no idea where he was taking her. He told her to bring some lighter clothes, so she knew it had to be south of Atlanta. Maybe Florida or Alabama. She was looking forward to wherever they ended up.

Her concerns over Philip had been pushed to the back of her mind. He was still working a lot of hours, but his stress level was so much better. She felt comfortable in the belief it all stemmed from his birthday. She didn't share the same crisis over turning fifty-five, but she was sure her own mid-life crisis would come, and she hoped he would be as understanding with her when it did.

Christopher still hadn't decided on a college. The deadlines were coming up. He told her he was thinking about going into nursing. She was so proud of him and his career decision.

The rest of her run, she zoned out and took in the hint of spring popping up all around her. Even though she frequently ran the same route, it always looked different since nature was always changing — she loved that about running.

It was late morning by the time she was showered and dressed. As she went downstairs to the kitchen, her phone rang. It was Purvell.

"Happy birthday," Purvell shouted into the phone.

"Thank you," Cynthia said.

"So how does it feel? Do you feel old? You know I have mine coming up in a few months."

"It's not bad at all, in fact I don't feel a thing," she said.

"You're just trying to make me feel better, admit it."

Cynthia couldn't help but laugh. "No, really, I feel the same."

"So has Philip slipped at all about where you're going?"

"No, his lips are sealed."

"Can't wait to hear about it when you get back. So it seems things have gotten better? Are you still worried about another woman?"

"I think it was because of his birthday, worrying about paying for the kids to go to college, and our retirement. He seems to have worked through it, so I'm not bringing anything up to rock the boat."

"Well, good. Give me a call next week, and tell me all about the trip, and I mean all of it. Love you."

"Love you, too. Bye."

She was so grateful to have Purvell. They were so different in their careers and lifestyle and yet so alike. Maybe it was from their upbringing in Wisconsin.

Throughout the day, she received calls from her mom, Granny, Millie, and even Arthur in England.

Christopher arrived home from school at the usual time and told her to get a glass of wine and go put her feet up with a good book and relax. He had some things to take care of in the kitchen. She gave him a worried look, but he assured her nothing bad would happen. He was under strict orders from his dad and had a job to do.

She said it was too early for wine on a weekday and made a cup of tea instead.

Philip came home at four thirty with a bouquet of pink roses and joined Christopher in the kitchen. At about six, they called her to the deck for her birthday dinner. Since it was a nice day, they cleaned off the patio table and chairs and moved them into the sun. Philip got the grill going with hamburgers, and Christopher set the table with everything else.

When they went inside to have cake and ice cream, Christopher said he had an announcement. He had decided to go to UNC Charlotte in the fall. It was the best present she could have asked for.

Later that night as she fell asleep, she thought about what a great day it had been and looked forward to her trip at the end of the week. Being fifty-five really wasn't so bad.

❦

"I wish you would tell me where it is we're going," Cynthia said as they headed down I-95 on Friday. "It's probably one of those no-tell motels, isn't it?" Philip laughed, and he grabbed her hand, giving it a kiss before letting go.

"I think you'll be happy with my choice, and if not, I don't think I could ever please you. Just a few more hours, and your suspense will be over," he told her with a big smile on his face.

"I haven't heard from Millie, have you?" Philip asked.

"She's leaving for the cruise with Jimmy and his parents tomorrow. I hate that we won't see her till the end of the semester, but we'll have plenty of time this summer while she's home doing her internship, and there's our trip to White Lake this summer. She asked if Jimmy could come along so we could get to know him better."

"I would kind of like it to be just our family," Philip said.

"I feel the same way, and I told her so. This may be our last trip as a family up there, you know, with the kids both in college now."

"So how did she take it?" Philip asked.

"She sounded disappointed, but I didn't give in. I'm sure I haven't heard the end of it."

"So have you guessed yet where we're going?" he asked, excited as a little kid.

"I really have no idea. A beach in Florida?"

He laughed. "I thought you might think that, but we're not even leaving Georgia."

"It can't be Savannah, since we already passed the exit."

"It won't be long," he told her, and they continued on.

After a few more miles, they took the Brunswick, St. Simmons Island and Jekyll Island exit. Which one is it? she wondered.

She saw a huge bridge from a distance. It was so fragile and delicate looking. Cynthia knew nothing about bridge construction, and she wondered how those hammock-like strings of metal kept the bridge stable. Would it sway as they went over it? She couldn't wait to find out.

"Nice looking bridge, huh?" Philip asked.

She laughed. "I was admiring the bridge, too. It's so beautiful and fragile-looking from afar. I wonder if you could run across it?"

He laughed and took her hand, kissing it again before letting go and putting his hand back on the wheel. "I'm sure *you* could."

She wondered how it would feel to run across the bridge. It would be so open, wind whipping around, like running on air. And the view would be breathtaking.

She always brought her running clothes and shoes wherever she went, just in case. She hoped the opportunity might come up on this trip.

As they proceeded down the road, they didn't go on the bridge that led to Brunswick and St. Simons, but veered to the right where a sign announced Jekyll Island Causeway.

They were going to Jekyll Island! How wonderful. Jekyll Island. She'd heard about the island and had always wanted to visit. Philip was grinning ear to ear.

"This is it. Are you ready? We're staying at the Jekyll Island Club Hotel, where the Robber Barons of the late 1800s stayed when they came south for vacation. They felt as if they were roughing it down here," he laughed.

She was so excited to think for the next three days she would be alone with Philip on this island, transported back to a time when fine living was taken to a superior level.

The causeway onto the island was long. Marsh grass patches lined either side of the road, waving in the wind like little islands scattered along the way. Seagulls, pelicans, cranes, and smaller birds dotted the marsh among the grasses and water.

"We'll be there soon," Philip informed her.

They drove through the historic area, winding their way to the Jekyll Island Club Hotel.

A well-appointed turret greeted them as they traveled up the drive, giving the massive structure the look of a castle. The hotel was made of white stone, with balconies and porches emerging along the facade.

They pulled under the carport up to a valet dressed in khakis and a navy golf shirt.

Philip rolled down his car window. "Hi, we're here to spend the weekend. I have reservations for Philip Lewis."

The young man leaned down to Philip's window. "My name is Tony. I'll unload your luggage, park your car, and be waiting for you by the elevator. Step into the building at the top of the stairs and check in." Tony went around to Cynthia's side to let her out.

This wasn't any "no-tell motel," Cynthia thought with a smile and an inward chuckle, as another valet opened the door for them, welcoming them to the little inner building used as the lobby.

They found out the little lobby building was once used as a billiards room for the men back in the club's heyday. Cynthia imagined the ladies having a cup of tea and visiting in the parlor while the men played pool, smoked cigars, and drank their whiskey, making financial deals in the very room where they were standing.

After giving them their room key and a little overview of the club, the concierge directed them to the elevator, where they found Tony and a cart with their luggage. After taking their room key, Tony led them to the presidential suite, located on the top floor in the turret that had welcomed them as they drove up to the hotel.

The room was like a step back in time. The valet went in first, holding the door for them as they entered the outer sitting room, which was decorated in a very traditional style. Tony then showed them into the bedroom, where he pulled the drapes open with drama and flair, flooding the room with sunshine and exposing the turret. Off to the right in the turret was a winding metal stairway that led to the very top, which held a telescope and balcony — no doubt the best view on the island.

Cynthia imagined how many important and famous people must have stayed in this very room. Wait till she told Purvell, her mother, and Granny.

Tony gave them their room key, told them about dinner times, and wished them a wonderful stay. As soon as Philip tipped the man, he was gone and they were alone.

"So what do you think?" Philip asked.

What did she think? "Philip, this is unbelievable. Did you have any idea how fabulous this place was?"

"Honestly, no. I had seen what was online and thought it was pretty nice, but being here in person makes me really appreciate the place. Let's go exploring."

"Sounds great," she said. "I'm just going to change first."

She opened her garment bag and hung her clothes in the closet, Philip doing the same with his. While she arranged the clothes Philip came from behind placing his hands on her hips.

"Am I in your way, sweetheart?" she asked.

"No, change of plans," he said and started to tenderly kiss her neck and back. She turned around to face him.

She loved him and loved this weekend away together. How could she have ever doubted him by thinking he was involved with another woman?

He led her to the bed, and they started undressing each other. After all these years, he still did it for her. His once-athletic body, now that of a middle-aged man, potbelly, salt-and-pepper hair on his body, face, and head. Laugh lines around his eyes and mouth, receding hairline. He looked great.

When you were young and starting a life out together, you never thought of a day you would be married almost twice as long as you had been single. During that time the family you create, the tragedies you survive, and the good times you enjoy are what hold your relationship together. What you grow to love during this time is not the person you see on the outside but the one you uncover on the inside in the course of your life spent together.

They pulled the bed open at the same time and quickly laid down on it, arms around each other. He began running his hands over her breasts and nipples tenderly. She thought how good it felt and never wanted him to stop.

Wrapping their arms around each other again, she slowly moved her hands down his back to his buttocks. They looked into each other's eyes at the same time. "I love you, Cynthia," he said.

"I love you, too," she responded, as he moved to other parts of her body with familiarity. She let go and trusted him with her love. Any thoughts of another woman were ridiculous to her now, and she realized how foolish she had been.

❧

"Cynthia, we fell asleep. We should get ready for dinner."

It was Philip's voice, but where was she, and what was going on? Then she remembered. They were at the Jekyll Island Club and had just made love. She smiled at him. He was dressed like he was ready to go somewhere.

"What time is it?"

"It's almost six. I don't know about you, but I'm hungry. My plan was for us to go down to the Grand Dining Room, but it's formal, so maybe we could just find a place around here, more relaxed for tonight? What do you think?"

"That sounds good. I'm pretty hungry myself." She was in a happy, satisfied state of mind, quite content after her lovemaking and subsequent nap.

"Okay, so you get dressed, and I'll go down and ask for some restaurant suggestions. Sound good to you?"

"Sounds great," she said smiling.

She went into the bathroom and surveyed herself in the mirror before getting in the shower. Not too bad for a 55-year-old woman. Her breasts were no longer perky, and she had a tummy, but what could she expect after giving birth and breast-feeding two children? She had laugh lines around her eyes and mouth and although her hair was light brown, only her hairdresser knew where the grey was. She took in a deep breath, smiled, and got in the shower.

She chose a casual pink skirt and a new little white shirt

with black polka-dots she'd purchased especially for this trip. Even though the day had been warm, the nights were cool once the sun went down, so she grabbed a lightweight sweater to bring along. After a quick touch-up of her hair and the little bit of makeup she wore, she was ready to go in no time.

She sat in one of the sitting room chairs, waiting. Philip hadn't come back yet, so she called him on his phone. No answer. Where could he be? She couldn't remember — did he say he was coming back, or was she to meet him downstairs?

She decided to try and find him downstairs, when he walked in.

"Was I supposed to meet you downstairs? I tried calling you, but you didn't answer."

"Ah… no. I didn't really say. So let's go," he said, sounding rather agitated.

"Is everything okay?" she asked.

"Why do you ask?" he responded, something definitely on his mind.

"You seem to be bothered by something."

"Are you going to start that again? Nothing is wrong. I'm hungry."

"I hope you would tell me if there was something, Philip. Anything."

He took a deep breath and calmed down. "I would Cynthia, but right now, let's go eat." They headed to the elevator.

Something had bothered him. What happened? It could have been something simple. She was jumping to conclusions and needed to calm down and enjoy the weekend.

The concierge recommended a restaurant on the water called Latitude 31. It was located on the historical wharf pier just a short distance from the hotel with a great view and food.

They went down the elevator and across the covered porch to the circle driveway. Cynthia noticed how still and peaceful it was, the evening air pungent with the smell of earth waking up for another season.

She was grateful that the agitation Philip had displayed minutes before seemed to dissipate while going down the elevator as he took her hand in his. She didn't want this weekend to be spoiled.

As they progressed down the drive, they could see Latitude 31 on the pier.

"So what do you say? Let's walk over there and have dinner," Philip asked, smiling at her.

The sun was hovering over the rooftop of the restaurant with a warm yellow and pink glow, the bridge visible across the expanse of water in the distance.

Cynthia thought how romantic this was. She put her arms around her husband and said, "Let's go," with a kiss and a smile.

When they reached the wood planks of the pier, she turned and looked over her shoulder for a view of the hotel and towering turret before continuing towards the restaurant. Latitude 31 was a nice indoor white-tablecloth restaurant with a great view of the Jekyll and Brunswick Rivers. A hostess at the door greeted them.

"Hi. Do you have a table for two at a window where we could watch the sunset?" Philip asked.

"If you don't mind waiting fifteen to twenty minutes," she said.

"We don't mind at all."

They went back outside to the pier and found a spot where they could see the bridge stretching over the glowing horizon.

"This is the life," Philip said, looking out over the water.

He looked her in the eyes, kissed her, and smiled. It made her melt inside. "You doing okay?" he asked.

She took a deep breath and looked around at where she was. "Never been better," she said with a smile.

His arm went around her shoulders as they looked out over the water and the descending sun's brilliant threads of color. They were together but alone in their dreamlike thoughts. The hypnotic power of water and a beautiful sunset could have that kind of effect on a person. It was as if time stood still for a brief moment.

"We have your table ready," the hostess said, breaking the spell with her words.

There was a moment's hesitation from both of them as life naturally moved forward again. *I don't want to leave this moment*, Cynthia thought as she reluctantly followed the hostess into the restaurant.

"Hi, my name is Edward. I'll be your server tonight," their waiter greeted them. He proceeded to list off the evening specials and answered some questions about the menu, taking their request for a bottle of wine.

He came back with the wine and took their order for dinner. Cynthia ordered sea scallops and Philip decided on shrimp.

The wait for the table was worth it for the sunset alone. Cynthia speculated that no sunset was ever the same on this island as they slowly watched the last bit of light sink down past the horizon. Since Edward had been an excellent waiter, Philip made sure to tip him well.

They slowly walked back to their room, talking about the day and how nice it was to get away together like this. Before they went to bed, they went to the top of the turret to take in the incredible night view.

"Can we stay here forever?" she laughed, Philip behind her with his arms tightly encircling her upper body keeping her warm and safe. She felt him kiss her shoulder and then the back of her neck.

What a wonderful birthday gift, Cynthia thought. She had two more nights of this before they went home.

❦

She was in the turret alone by the telescope in her nightgown as she looked out over the heavy fog. Through the telescope, she saw an old-fashioned sail boat containing Philip and her children when they were elementary-school age.

She decided to go out to the water and brave her way through the fog to find them, taking another look through the telescope first. They were middle-school age now. How strange.

Once she went outside the hotel, the fog cleared a path to the pier, where she saw the boat. It had become larger and now looked like a pirate ship. She jumped in the water and swam out to it.

When she reached the boat, she climbed up the side to the deck where she found her family and Jimmy Skidmore, the children now their current ages.

Looking down at her hands, she saw a large gold sword in the right one. Lifting the sword with little difficulty, she swung it back and forth to keep the pirates away.

Just then a storm came up, and they were all washed overboard by a huge wave.

Everyone except for Cynthia.

CHAPTER 10

*T*he next morning, they took the original wood winding staircase down to breakfast in the Grand Dining room.

They found out from the hostess that the dining room was built in the late 1880s but was expanded over the years to accommodate the popularity of the club. The room was bright and cheery, with a traditional style throughout. To the left was a round sunroom also for dining, which reflected the shape of the turret. They decided to have breakfast there so they could enjoy a nice view of the grounds.

After breakfast, they took a tour of the historic area surrounding the hotel to discover more about this place where the wealthiest people in America created a grand retreat they could visit in the winter. The club was founded in 1886 and survived until 1947 when it was bought by the state park system of Georgia. In 1950, still owned by the state of Georgia, it was taken out of the park system and developed to be self-sustaining, as it is to this day.

Cynthia and Philip spent the morning visiting the so-called "cottages" that people lived in during their stay. To Cynthia, cottages were the little structures surrounding White Lake, not these massive homes with appointed guest rooms and servants' quarters. Several of the "cottages" were renovated into hotel rooms for guests to stay in, and others were restored for tourists to visit and see how these Americans "roughed it" on the island. They took their time, enjoying the walk and taking it all in.

Cynthia noticed Crane Cottage was being set up for a wedding.

"Wouldn't it be lovely to have a wedding here? I mean, how elegant and special would it be to have it in such a historic area," Cynthia said to Philip.

Philip stopped all of a sudden and looked at her.

"What?" she asked.

"Do you know something you're not telling me?"

"Like what?" she asked.

"Like anyone in our family getting married? Millie?"

"Oh my God, Philip. How could you let something like that come out of your mouth? Millie and Jimmy Skidmore. No! They've only been dating a little while. I'm just talking generally. We women love weddings. Any wedding."

They walked along in silence, both contemplating the same thing. What if Millie married Jimmy Skidmore? It could happen.

❦

They spent the rest of the day exploring the island.

Since it was still too early in the spring to swim or sun on the beach, they'd have to settle for a walk to the pier.

The pier was a surprise to them. The long T-shaped structure was built out of cement, more like a bridge then a pier with a large scalloped metal roof. Cynthia thought it had been built this way so it could withstand hurricanes. Lots of people were fishing — she almost wanted to drop in a line herself.

"This would be a great place to fish," Philip said, echoing her feelings. "It seems to be in a great location, I just don't know much about salt-water fishing." He looked around and then turned to her. "I loved going fishing with my dad and friends as a kid."

She had the same memories. "Well, you know I did a lot of fishing on White Lake with my dad, too."

She started thinking about those lazy days spent fishing for their supper as a kid. Her dad was such a committed fisherman. If you went out in the boat with him, you never knew when you were coming back to shore. Many times she'd had to use a bucket to go to the bathroom, because if the fish were biting, they were staying.

Being around the water again also made her recognize how much she'd missed it. "Philip. Do you ever miss the water?"

"What do you mean, miss it?" he asked.

"I don't know. Just knowing it's there. I spent so much time swimming and fishing as a kid and haven't done any of it as an adult. Most of my fond memories as a child involved water, and I miss it."

"Now that you mention it, I do, too. Being here around all this water seems to rejuvenate me. Does that sound crazy?" He looked at her with a spark she hadn't seen in awhile.

"No, sweetheart, I understand exactly what you're saying."

They sat for a good hour on the pier mostly in silence, taking in the peace and watching the world go by. For some reason, nursing came to mind, and she made her decision. Without even thinking about it, she spoke.

"Philip, I decided this fall when Christopher starts school I'm also going back to school to get my master's."

He looked at her. "Really? I guess if you want it that bad, go for it. I won't pretend to understand why you feel the need to do it at this point in your life, but go ahead. Having schoolwork to do doesn't sound like fun. I have enough to deal with at work."

"It does sound like fun to me. I'm not you, and I've always wanted to get it."

She felt good having made her decision. She was getting her master's.

He stood up and put his hand out to her. "Let's go back to our room and hang out for awhile before getting dressed for dinner. Figured you would want to get showered and all fancy for me."

"I do," she said, smiling at him and taking his hand.

❦

The next morning after grabbing a quick breakfast at Cafe Solterg, a little delicatessen located in the hotel, they drove over to St. Simons Island.

Cynthia was looking forward to driving across the bridge. She asked one of the valets if he knew any of its history. He knew nothing other than that it was called the Sidney Lanier Bridge. She made a mental note to find out more about it.

The bridge was very similar to the one going into Savannah, simply suspended over a body of water. Taken by the beauty of it, she looked at the huge string-like cables as they drove across. The sky above them was the bluest blue with the kind of clouds you could find Snoopy, Mickey Mouse, or a snowman in.

The bridge led to Brunswick, where they headed towards the island.

They were going to Christ Church and Fort Frederica. Both of these places played a big part in early American history. In the afternoon, they were going to visit the light house and Maritime Museum.

"This looks so different than Jekyll Island," Cynthia said to Philip, as they turned left towards the church. It was more populated with homes, in addition to places for shopping and eating. It was more like a place to live year-round. There were restaurants, apartment buildings, stores, banks, and houses that looked like homes, not weekend getaways.

"I really like this island," Philip said. "We'll have to stay here next time we visit."

They continued down Frederica Road and then there it was: A quaint white wood church tucked in between moss-covered oak trees.

Cynthia walked slowly up to the church so she could take in the beauty and appreciate the moment. It was so peaceful. After stopping at the church door to look around at the churchyard, she turned to a patient Philip. "Let's go in."

The entrance into the church was nothing special, just two old-fashioned looking doors, painted white like the church, with a peaked overhang that added charm and protection from rain. The church's three-story steeple loomed above. A kind lady stood inside the door offering tourists a tour of the church, which Philip and Cynthia gladly accepted.

They walked through the door into the dark wood-paneled interior, smelling an old musty scent. Like many churches from that era, it was built in the shape of a cross, with the ceiling resembling the bottom of a boat with all its exposed beams. The walls were filled with beautiful stained glass windows. Cynthia's favorite was one in the back of the church titled, "The Confession of Peter."

According to the woman giving the tour, the original church was left in shambles after the Civil War, so in 1884, Anson Dodge, Jr., a business man, financed the reconstruction in honor of his late wife. It still conducted services every Sunday.

When they'd seen enough, they stepped around to the back of the church to find a cemetery. Gnarled and knotted trees covered with moss surrounded the old graves. The trees that bent and curved around old headstones had been there for decades, maybe even centuries.

"Let's head over to Fort Frederica and then go have lunch," Philip suggested.

"Okay, let's go," she said. She guessed he'd had enough of looking at graves.

They picked up a pamphlet at Fort Federica and began the self-guided tour. Not much had survived the past 280 years other than the foundations of the buildings. The fort was built to protect the colony of about 500 people. It was hard to imagine the thriving little town by looking at the ruins today.

After spending over an hour walking through the remnants of the colony Philip said, "I'm hungry."

Cynthia laughed and said, "Me, too."

They drove back towards the entrance to the island and parked by the lighthouse and walked to Mallery St., where they had spotted several shops and restaurants.

"Philip, this is where I want to go. Barbara Jean's. I like the name," she said.

Philip started to laugh. "Okay, it's your weekend."

The menu at Barbara Jean's was southern home cooking. They both couldn't resist the crab cakes, which Philip thought were the best he'd ever had eaten. Cynthia vowed to come back to this place if they ever visited again.

With lunch finished, they walked leisurely along the beach back to the lighthouse. The lighthouse was built in 1872 to help guide ships into St. Simons Sound. After looking through the museum, they climbed the spiral stairs to the top, where they saw a breathtaking view of the area.

Cynthia noticed Philip was very quiet while they were at the top. He seemed thoughtful, so she walked around alone feeling the same, wanting to take in the view without conversation.

On the way down the stairs, she said, "I love this place, Philip. I wonder what it would be like to live here."

They drove down to the Maritime Museum, which Philip seemed to enjoy more than she did.

"One of the people working here told me that's a public beach over there where most people come to sit and walk around. Since it's such a beautiful day, let's kick our shoes off, take a walk on the beach, and pretend we aren't two old married people but a pair of young lovers smitten with each other," she suggested.

"I won't have to pretend about the smitten part," he said, laughing.

They went down to the beach and started walking hand in hand.

Philip had been very quiet since they left the top of the lighthouse so she asked, "What are you thinking about, sweetheart?"

He turned and looked at her, hesitating before he continued to speak and then stopped. It was the worried look she'd seen before in his eyes. What the heck was going on?

"I was just thinking about something you said. You wondered what it would be like to live here. Why not live here? We should do it now."

"We have jobs and a life in Atlanta. We have children and responsibilities," she said.

"Maybe it's time for a change. I don't know. I'm just thinking out loud, I guess." He looked at her, leaned over, and planted a kiss on her lips.

After walking for about an hour, they went back to where they were parked at the Maritime Museum.

"I'm going to run in and use the bathroom before we leave. Do you want to wait here?" Philip asked.

"Yeah, it's so nice, I would rather be outside," she said.

He went in, and she thought about what he'd just said about moving there. Could they really pick up and move? They were too young to retire, and according to Philip, they still needed to save for it. Then there was college tuition for the kids. Maybe someday, but not now.

It seemed like Philip had been gone a long time, so she went in to see what happened to him. She walked over to the men's room, where she could hear his voice coming through the vent in the door.

"I'm on vacation with my wife. Why are you calling me?"

"I don't always have all the answers."

"Miss you? Are you serious?"

"No, she doesn't know about you. There's no need for her to know. This is business."

"When I get back, we'll meet and I'll look it over. I've got to go."

Cynthia quickly went back to where she'd been waiting so he wouldn't know she overheard his phone call. Who was he talking to? He said it was business. She only heard one side of the conversation, so she shouldn't jump to conclusions.

"Ready to go back to the other island?" he asked.

"Everything okay? You seemed to take a long time."

He looked surprised. "I had a message from a client that I had to return." He looked down. "Sorry. I shouldn't be handling business on our trip. I just don't want to turn the phone off in case one of the kids needs us. Hey, that reminds me. You haven't called to check on Christopher since we got here," Philip said.

She dialed Christopher's number.

"Hi, Mom. You guys having fun? I'm not doing anything but hanging out. Nothings messed up. Everything's fine," Christopher babbled.

Suspicion set in. "What are you up to?" Cynthia inquired.

"Mom, please. I'm an adult now. I'll be going away to college and fending for myself in August. Everything is good," he said. "Just enjoy yourself. I've got everything under control."

"Okay, but if anything is wrong, I will eventually find out about it."

"I know. See you tomorrow. Bye."

"Bye," said Cynthia, still slightly suspicious.

When they arrived back at the hotel, they showered and got ready for their last night in the dining room, where there would be a small band for dancing.

Cynthia forced herself to erase Philip's phone call from her mind. Tonight they would have fun, and tomorrow they would go home and back to reality.

CHAPTER 11

"Hey mom, when will Millie get here?" Christopher hollered from the family room.

It was officially the last day of high school for Christopher. If all went well with his math exam, Friday was graduation.

"Millie is coming home on Wednesday," she responded.

Millie had an internship for the summer at an Atlanta accounting firm that started the following Monday.

He came into the kitchen and grabbed his book bag.

"Before you leave, I need to know what's going on with you for the next few days. Grandma and Granny will be coming on Thursday, so don't make any plans. It would be so nice if you picked them up at the airport. Can you imagine the look on their faces to see you there?"

"I'll go to the airport, just tell me when. Maybe Millie will go, too. Is she bringing Ole Skidless with her?" he asked, chuckling to himself.

By this time, Cynthia had thought Jimmy Skidmore would have been history, especially after Millie spent a whole week with him and his parents on the cruise during spring break, but it appeared they were as tight as ever. Millie had always been picky about the guys she dated. She'd never settled down with one as long as she had with Jimmy though.

"I don't think we'll be seeing Jimmy. Are you disappointed?"

"No, but the guy is kind of growing on me. Got to go, Mom, the last day of high school is calling." He glanced at the clock and ran out the door.

She looked at the empty doorway. Where did the time go? She still remembered the first day of kindergarten.

She decided to go for a run to lift her spirits.

Running always helped her gather her feelings and thoughts. You could only do three things when you ran. Run, breathe, and think. So that's what she did.

When her children were born, Cynthia would never forget the look they gave her as she held them in her arms. All trusting and totally devoid of any worry about whether they would they be fed, clothed, and loved. All of their trust was in her. They knew she would care for them. But now, they trusted no one but themselves.

When did that happen?

She started thinking about her recent trip to Jekyll Island with Philip. Life seemed slower and more relaxed there than in Atlanta. A person could get used to it.

Since their vacation on Jekyll Island, Philip talked more and more about moving to St. Simons Island. She *was* starting to like the idea. Their life was going to change now that Christopher was starting college, so maybe they should start considering a move.

❦

It was 12:15 when she heard the familiar sound of Christopher's Honda in the distance. She prayed all had gone well with the test.

The kitchen door flew open, and in he walked straight for the refrigerator, grabbing a bottle of juice, and then going to the pantry for some chips, not noticing her in the doorway smiling.

"So how did it go? Are you officially done now?"

He turned around, slightly startled. "That test was hard, but I did great. Some kid was caught cheating, though. Mr. Smith walked over to him, tapped him on the shoulder, and said, 'Come with me, young man'. Mr. Smith is a cool guy, but don't mess with him. The kid never came back. I wish I knew how he did it."

"Why would you need that kind of information?" Cynthia asked.

"Just so I don't ever accidentally do something like that and have it mistaken for cheating," Christopher said, looking as innocent as he possibly could.

❦

Millie showed up on Wednesday. When she arrived, Cynthia was shocked by her appearance as she walked through the door. Her daughter looked like she'd lost weight but not in a good way. She was pale and wore a tired look. It was probably from finals just a few weeks ago, Cynthia told herself, but this somehow seemed different.

"Millie, I'm so glad you're home. Are you feeling okay?" Cynthia wrapped her arms around her. Millie seemed to melt into her as she hugged her mother back. With a slightly stifled sob, she said, "It's good to be home."

"Are you sure you feel all right?"

"It's just exams. A good night's sleep will do me good. I'll be okay."

"Did you ever think you would see the day your brother would graduate?"

They both laughed, and the Millie she knew came back, if only for a moment.

"Mom, who says he grew up? That's an impossibility." They hugged again.

Christopher walked in the room.

"Hey, sis, when did you get here? I didn't think you would be coming until later."

"I was able to get away sooner than I thought. Could you help me carry my stuff in? Just the heavy things." Off they went to Millie's car.

As Cynthia watched them walk out to the car, her thoughts went to Millie's appearance and demeanor. Maybe she and Jimmy had a little spat. It would all come out eventually when the time was right, she thought as she headed into the kitchen. It was better not force it.

Both kids came down the stairs after putting Millie's things in her room.

"Hey, how was your cruise?" Christopher asked. "While you, Mom, and Dad were off having a good time, I had to sit at home doing nothing. Maybe I can live vicariously through you."

Millie looked at him and laughed. "Oooo, an SAT word. I'm impressed. Maybe you did learn something in the past twelve years." And just like that, everything was back to normal.

"The cruise was fun," Millie told them. "It's basically a floating hotel with everything you'd want to do and more. I've never seen so much food in one place. My favorite thing was the ice cream machines they seemed to have in every corner. Good thing the cruise was six days, because anymore, and I would have to run twice a day to get back in shape."

They spent the next hour at the table eating lunch, talking, laughing, and reminiscing about whatever came to mind. Millie seemed to have perked up from the conversation and lunch.

"Millie, remember last summer when I freaked you out at White Lake? I went out in that old rickety boat Grandma had sitting around. The one she said Grandpa built when Mom was little?" Christopher started.

"I would like you to know the boat was named after me," Cynthia informed them with pride in her voice.

"Sure, Mom."

"It was. My father named it Cindy. All great boats are

named," she laughed. "I have pictures of myself as a child sitting in the boat and it says "Cindy" as plain as day."

"Back to my story," he gave his mother a side-glance and continued on. "I rowed out to the middle of the lake after Millie told me the boat was a death trap since it was so old. It did start to take on water, so I played it up and capsized the boat but went under into the pocket of air and stayed there long enough to let Millie think something happened. She freaked out when I didn't come out of the water. That's how I know she really loves me deep down inside." They all laughed at the thought of a distraught Millie.

"Listen, you. I was getting ready to call 911 and jump in myself to try and save you."

Cynthia loved listening to her children's banter. She was looking forward to the next few weeks with her mom and Granny there, along with Millie home for her internship, and, of course, Christopher. Nothing could happen to spoil this summer. Life was good.

❦

"Can I trust you children to behave in the back seat and not mess with each other?" Philip said with a laugh and a devilish smile.

They were going to Joe D's for dinner like old times. The last time they were there together was Philip's birthday party. The four of them piled into the car.

"Millie, could you go with Christopher tomorrow to pick up the grandmas?" Cynthia asked, turning around to the back seat. "Seeing the two of you at the airport would make their day."

"Sure, Mom. Besides, somebody has to keep an eye on him," Millie said, pointing a finger at her brother.

"What's that supposed to mean? I have matured since you were home last," Christopher said with dignity, sticking his nose in the air. They all laughed except Christopher.

Joe D's was busy that night. They spent a little time visiting with several of their friends at the bar before sitting at a table. Once they were seated, Joe came over to see how they were doing and sent them an appetizer on the house.

Philip felt they should tell the kids this weekend how they were thinking about the move to St. Simons Island, even though Cynthia hadn't exactly agreed yet. Cynthia liked the idea, but she thought they should take it slow.

Philip broached the subject after they ordered their food.

"Your mom and I are thinking, just thinking, about doing something we want you kids to know about, especially before your grandmas get here," he said. He had their attention. "We think occasionally about what we're going to do when the two of you are gone and off living your lives. We loved it down on the Georgia coast when we visited in March and are thinking about moving there. We're kind of exploring it to see what it would take."

The kids stared at them. Millie was first to say something. You could see the emotion rising up in her.

"How can you do that? What about us? I mean, we might need you for something."

"Like what?" Christopher asked with a blank look on his face. "Mom and Dad should have some fun now before they get real old."

"Where do you want to live?" Millie asked.

"The beach on St. Simons Island," Cynthia said.

"The beach! Like right on the water?" Christopher asked, as if he couldn't believe his ears. "Sweet."

"How soon were you thinking about doing this?" Millie asked, almost tearful.

"We don't know, sweetheart." She turned and gave Philip a concerned look. "We're going to explore it, that's all. Dad and I realized when we were down there how much we miss being close to water and thought about what we wanted to do with the rest of our lives, that's all."

"We just want you kids to know what's going on. We may do nothing," Philip said and wisely changed the subject. He could see how upset Millie was getting.

"So when is your orientation for UNCC, Christopher?"

The conversation took a different tone, thank God. Christopher went on and on about school and graduation. Philip was going with him to orientation at the end of the month. Maybe then Cynthia could spend some time with Millie.

"I'm going to step into the men's room for a moment," Philip announced as he left the table. He wasn't gone more than two minutes before their food came.

"Go ahead and start eating," Cynthia told the kids. "Your dad will be back soon."

It took him a long time to finally come back.

"Everything okay?" she asked him.

"What? Oh yeah, everything is fine," he said, and he silently dug into his dinner.

On the car ride home, Christopher's voice came from the back seat.

"Dad I've been meaning to ask you something. Who's the woman we saw the day of your birthday at the go-kart place?"

Cynthia froze. Why would he bring that up now?

"I'm not sure I know what you're talking about. That was awhile ago," Philip responded. The car was dark and Cynthia couldn't see his face.

"I also saw her the night of your party at Joe's and she was standing at the bar tonight. I was just wondering. You must remember."

"Not really sure, son. Could have been a client."

"I don't think it was. I'll point her out next time I see her."

And they rode silently the rest of the way home.

Later when they were alone in their room, Cynthia got up the nerve to confront him.

"Philip, I was wondering who was the woman Christopher was talking about?"

"You're not going to start that again, are you? It's all a coincidence. I assure you I have no idea what Christopher is talking about. Why would I want to move to St. Simons if there was another woman? Seriously, Cynthia." He sounded angry.

"I'm only wondering. Who is she?"

"I have no idea. Cynthia, I love you and only you. You have to believe me."

He was convincing. There weren't any other signs he was seeing someone. He wasn't working as late as he had been and treated her decently. They'd had no real arguments except about this. Why did Christopher have to bring it up?

"Okay, I believe you, but the same thing keeps coming up. You understand my concern?"

"There is no need for concern. Please, trust me. You and the kids are my life," he said, and he came over and kissed her.

"I'm going to bed," she said and crawled in, facing away from his side.

All the answers he gave her made sense, but this woman kept coming up. Was she overreacting? Maybe so. She was tired of every few months getting a little reminder of her.

He crawled in his side and scooted over to her.

"Not tonight, please," she said, pulling away. She wanted to be left alone.

She soon slipped into sleep tired from the day.

CHAPTER 12

*T*he kids were on their way to the airport, and Cynthia was taking advantage of the time and empty house to do a few last-minute things before her house guests arrived. She was preparing a surprise dessert for graduation night — red velvet cake, a favorite of Christopher's.

She had made the cake layers a few days before and had hidden them in the garage refrigerator. Once the cake was assembled and decorated, she put it back in the garage.

While working on the cake, her mind went to Millie, who hadn't mentioned Jimmy once since she arrived home. Millie could hardly wake up this morning but went to bed at about ten. Kids. If it wasn't one concerning her, it was the other.

Then there was Philip wanting to pick up and move. He wanted to move more quickly then he let on when telling the kids about it. She had mixed feelings. He told her they could afford it, but they would both have to work at least until they were sixty-two, maybe a little older.

She had no problem with working, since she liked what she did, but why was he so determined to make the move this quickly? When she asked him, he never gave her a straight answer.

They would make a lot of money from the sale of their house, and he said he'd made some really good investments. She knew about nursing, not investments, so she had to believe him.

But she had a gut feeling. What if he just wanted to sell the house and never buy anything else? STOP! She was being ridiculous and needed to quit the speculation.

She vacuumed the living room and then went into the kitchen with her to-do list. Today, Thursday, pick the grandmas up and have a nice family dinner at home. Friday, Christopher needed to be at the school by one thirty for the three o'clock graduation ceremony. She was going to send Philip with him so he could save some seats for the rest of them. She didn't want her 94-year-old granny to have to sit and wait all that time.

Later in the evening, they were going to celebrate with dinner at Buckhead Diner, where they had a 6:15 p.m. reservation. She would surprise Christopher with the red velvet cake after dinner when they were back home.

They were having a party for Christopher from three to seven Saturday afternoon at their house so all his friends could stop by. She was getting barbeque catered from a local restaurant. Everything was set.

❦

The kids were supposed to call her once they had the grandmas safe and sound.

She started working on getting her dinner together when her cell phone rang.

"Hello," she said.

"Mom. We got 'em. They sure are funny." Christopher was on the other end.

"Oh, good. Do you have their luggage yet?"

"Yeah. I'm standing here with them while Millie pulls the car around. Oh, forget about fixing any lunch. Granny has already said she wants to stop by Chick-Fil-A and buy lunch for everyone, no argument. She's been waiting since Christmas for this." He was laughing. Granny loved the fast-food chain. She would probably want breakfast and lunch from there tomorrow as well.

"Okay, sounds good to me. Surprise me with something, okay?"

"Here's Millie. Got to go." He hung up.

An hour later in walked her mother, Granny, and the two kids with three white paper bags and two drink trays. They sat at the kitchen table talking all at once, laughing and telling stories, when out of the conversation came Granny's voice:

"My neighbor, Bob Jankowski, recently got a big bite of bratwurst stuck in his esophagus. He'd just taken it off the grill and put it into a bun slathered with butter, ketchup, mustard, relish, onions, and sauerkraut. Apparently all those condiments made the thing slick, so when he took the first big bite, the whole piece went down his throat like a slippery slide lodging itself in his esophagus. He could still breathe somehow. His wife took him to the little satellite hospital urgent care over at Kelly Lake. No one could believe it. Every time the doctor went down his throat to grab the brat, it slipped away. Finally the doctor went down his throat carefully, cut the brat in half, and pulled each part out individually. It's a true story."

When they were done, Christopher retrieved the luggage out of the car and took it to the room the two older women were sharing. Both decided after the long trip to take a little rest so they would be fresh for the evening. Millie said she was tired and headed to her room for a nap.

That left Cynthia and Christopher.

She looked at her son. He was no longer a boy but a young man with the whole world before him, although he had no idea. She remembered she'd had no idea either at that time in her life. Everything going on this week was making her sentimental.

"You know how proud Dad and I are of you, don't you?" she asked. "You're a great kid."

"Well, you and Dad are great parents. I always feel like you're behind me a hundred percent, right?"

"Right," she choked up a little and took a deep breath to help get the next words out. "No matter what."

The tears started, and she couldn't stop.

"Geez, Mom. I didn't mean to make you cry."

She stood up and put her arms around him as she cried. He put his arms around her and picked her up in a bear hug, both of them laughing.

"Put me down. I've got work to do," she said, feeling better. "Since I'm such a great mom, how about helping me out? I need you to set the table for tonight, and when you're done, I may have something else."

"Sure, Mom, whatever you want."

He ran into the dining room, and she heard clanging of her china and silverware. She couldn't wait to see how he set the table.

❦

Dinner went well. The table was the most eclectic thing she'd ever seen. Christopher went Martha Stewart and mixed and matched the dishes and glasses. It was unique and original, to say the least.

"All we're missing is Arthur," Granny said.

Cynthia wished Arthur could be there, but he only came home to visit once a year if his family could swing it.

"Are they coming to visit this year," she asked.

"Yes, sometime this summer. I'm not sure when yet, your brother is trying to coordinate it with business so it won't cost as much," her mother explained.

"Let me know as soon as you find out so we can try to plan our vacation around them."

"That would be so nice," her mother said, a big smile on her face.

"Yeah, and maybe next year they can come to the island where Mom and Dad are moving," Christopher said.

His statement silenced the table.

"What island?" Cynthia's mother asked.

"When we went on our little trip this spring we got to thinking about what we might do in the future, you know, since the kids are on their way. We loved St. Simons Island and thought, well, could we afford to live there? We're just looking into it, that's all," Cynthia explained.

A distraught look appeared on Millie's face, and her mother and Granny stared blankly in her direction. All of a sudden, Granny found her voice.

"Do it."

Cynthia turned to her and said, "What Granny?"

"You should do it. You'll enjoy it more if you go now. I think it's a great idea. Millie, get that look off your face. In my day, you all would have been cut loose at eighteen years old and told *good luck*. Kids are babied today. Why, I was married and having children when I was Millie's age."

Millie started crying and left the room.

"I guess Millie doesn't like the idea," Cynthia's mother said.

"No," Cynthia said looking in the direction where Millie just left. "It appears not."

"I'll go talk to her," her mother suggested and left the room.

The rest of them continued eating and soon Millie and her grandmother were back at the table, all was well again and Millie back to her old self.

❧

The next morning, Cynthia sent Christopher to get Chick-Fil-A for breakfast, knowing Granny would love it.

Since it was so pleasant outside, everyone had breakfast

on the deck except Philip. He had to go into work for a little while that morning, but he would be home by eleven to get ready and go to the school with Christopher.

"Cynthia, you are such a sweet girl to indulge me so," Granny said with the biggest smile as she put away her fifth chicken mini.

"You deserve it, Granny."

"There sure are a lot of bees out today. A friend of mine named Gertrude Krueger once had one crawl into a pop can she was drinking. She took a big gulp and swallowed the bee. It got caught in her throat and stung her. Gertrude didn't know it, but she was allergic to bees, so she had to be rushed to the hospital. Almost died but through the fast work of the doctors, they saved her."

They all sat in silence as they listened to Granny's story almost in disbelief. "Is the woman okay today, Granny?" Cynthia asked.

"Poor thing, no. She's dead," Granny said with the most sympathetic look.

"What did she die from?" Christopher asked. They were all interested.

"Was going for a walk one afternoon and was hit by lightning. Fried her." Granny lowered her head.

They laughed and then Christopher spoke: "Granny, you should write down all these stories you make up."

"Young man, I would like you to know they are all true stories and not made up. Every detail and don't you forget that."

No one dared continue to laugh, but they all had wondered at times if the stories were accurate.

❧

The next day, Cynthia dropped Granny, her mother, and Millie at the door of the auditorium and told them where to find Philip. He'd called earlier to tell her where he'd gotten seats.

After parking and saying hi to some friends, she found her family, settling in next to Philip who was smiling broadly.

"You sure are happy today," she said.

"I'm thinking about how we're going to sell our house and move to an island," he said with great pleasure.

"I haven't said yes yet," she replied.

"But I have Granny on my side now," he replied with one eyebrow raised.

She laughed and shook her head.

Philip took her hand like he so frequently did and kissed it.

Just then the lights dimmed and the ceremony began. It was the usual graduation ceremony, young faces full of hope, promise, and expectation as they waited for their turn to walk across the stage.

What a bittersweet day this was for Cynthia. Watching Christopher walk across the stage affected her in a way she didn't expect. She hadn't had the same feeling when Millie graduated. Millie was easy. Christopher was work. She was constantly staying on top of him: Did you get this done? You did what? Why did you wait so long to start? What do you mean you left the book at school? How long did you know about this?

Hopefully college would be a little easier.

Christopher's name was called, he walking straight and tall across the stage. It was as if she saw into the future. His first job, marriage, a home, children, and friends — a life built on a foundation she and Philip had helped lay. Her eyes stung as she fought back tears.

After speeches from the valedictorian and salutatorian urging their classmates to make an impact on the world, the principal and other local dignitaries extolling the virtues the young people should strive for, and all the new graduates taking pictures after the ceremony, Cynthia and Philip somehow managed to find Christopher.

"Are you ready to go?" Philip yelled to him above the crowd of people trying to leave the auditorium. "We have reservations for 6:15 p.m. at the Buckhead Diner, and I know you wouldn't want to miss that."

"Yeah, but I have one more picture to get," he said. Just then a cute girl walked up and hugged Christopher. The family watched in silence taking it in.

"Okay, Dad, if you would do the honor." Christopher handed his dad his phone.

"Just exactly who was that girl?" Granny asked as they walked to the car. Cynthia was paying close attention.

"No one special, Granny. Just a girl I know," said Christopher. Typical evasive Christopher, Cynthia thought.

❀

The Buckhead Diner was a funky retro place with upscale food. After Joe D's Sports Bar, it was Christopher's favorite place to go.

Since this was not the kind of food they were used to having at a Wisconsin diner, Cynthia made a few suggestions to her mother and Granny. They ordered the Warm Maytag Blue Cheese Chips and Mac & Cheese Tots for appetizers. Granny chose the diner's famous Veal and Wild Mushroom Meatloaf and her mother thought the Braised Beef Short Ribs sounded good. The place was packed and added to the festive atmosphere.

"So, Mom, are we ordering dessert tonight?" Christopher asked. The kid had devoured his New York strip and finished off half of Granny's meatloaf.

"No, I have a special dessert at home for everyone," she said and left it at that.

By the time they arrived home, everyone's food had settled and they were ready for something sweet. Cynthia set the dining room table with her nice china and silver before they left, so all she had to do was pull out the red velvet cake.

Alone in the dining room, she set the cake on the table while she listened to the voices of her family in the next room.

Memories of parties and holidays went through her mind when suddenly she felt a cold flush go through her body.

"Is that what I think it is, Mom?" Christopher interrupted, bringing her attention back. "You are one awesome woman. Red velvet cake!"

Christopher was given the honor of serving up the fare, which he did in a Julia Child voice. What a ham. He had two huge pieces of cake, which meant it was a big hit.

❦

The next morning, the whole family pitched in to get things ready for the party. Philip was going to cut the grass and get the deck and yard set up while the women fixed the food. Millie was going to pick the barbeque up at eleven.

They were expecting about fifty friends, so Cynthia was glad to have her mother and Granny's help. They fixed all the usual Southern staples: baked beans, hush puppies, macaroni and cheese, slaw, banana pudding, and, of course, sweet tea.

"I have some mint growing in an area behind the garage that would be nice to use in the tea. I wonder if one of you wouldn't mind cutting some for me?" Cynthia asked.

"We'll both go, honey," her mother volunteered. She and Granny went out the door.

Cynthia was making the banana pudding when her mother came in the kitchen door with a troubled look.

"What's wrong mom?"

"I think there's something you need to see behind your garage," she said.

"Okay," Cynthia said, wiping her hands on a towel.

She followed her mother and stopped dead in her tracks when she saw it.

"Mom, go get Philip, please," Cynthia said.

Philip came around the corner, stopped and said, "Where did this come from?" He looked at Cynthia. They both looked towards Christopher's bedroom.

Philip took off for the house with Cynthia behind him.

He opened Christopher's bedroom door. "I want to see you downstairs right now."

Christopher sleepily came downstairs and sat on the couch.

"Your grandmothers went behind the garage to cut some mint for your mom, and guess what they found?" Philip quizzed him.

Christopher had a puzzled look on his face.

"I have no idea, Dad," he bravely answered.

"Follow me," Philip ordered.

The three of them headed back to the mint garden where the grandmothers were silently waiting, not wanting to miss a minute of this excitement.

"What do you have to say about this?"

It was about six feet tall with full green leaves cascading down to the base. This was one healthy-looking plant.

Christopher answered, "That's a marijuana plant, Dad. You know, pot, Mary Jane, grass, dope, weed, reefer, cannabis, hash..."

"I know what it's called. I grew up in the 1970s, not the 1870s, Christopher," Philip said, obviously angry.

"This isn't mine, Dad. I don't do that stuff. I know kids that do, but..." Christopher's voice trailed off as if something had dawned on him. "I think I know what happened, but first you have to know that I wasn't involved, and thought I was doing the right thing." Philip crossed his arms and waited for Christopher to continue. "It was the weekend you went to Jekyll Island. Some guys stopped by for a little while to hang out with me. Turns out, they had some pot and went out on the deck to smoke it. I freaked out as soon as I saw them and told them to leave. I found what they hadn't smoked of their joint and so I buried it out here with the mint 'cause I didn't want to get in trouble. I thought that was the best place since no one ever goes back here, but I guess there must have been a seed in it. What are the odds of that happening? Dad, I didn't do it."

"Go get yourself cleaned up, and help your mother and grandmothers with your party. I need to get rid of this plant before your guests arrive," Philip said, furious.

Cynthia had never seen her husband this angry with one of the kids before. They all gladly left Philip to his task and went in the house.

Cynthia filled Millie in when she arrived back with the barbeque. Millie's only comment was, "Why did I have to miss that?"

"Cynthia, do you remember your kindergarten teacher, Belinda Schneidewend?" Granny asked.

"Why yes, Granny," Cynthia said, wondering what Mrs. Schneidewend had to do with anything.

"Well, she happens to have been a friend of mine for years. She smokes pot every day. Says she does it for medicinal reasons, but I think she kind of likes it," Granny said thoughtfully.

Medicinal marijuana for her kindergarten teacher. Before she could comment, Philip came in the house and pulled Cynthia into the family room.

"I cut it down," he said.

"Where did you put it? We could get arrested if someone found it."

"We won't be in trouble," he pointed at Christopher, "but he might if it's found." Christopher was out on the deck setting up.

"Oh, Philip, you don't mean that?" Cynthia responded.

"I'm not going down. This is our house, and we asked him not to have friends over when we were out of town. He did. End of it," he said.

"Don't ruin the party. We've all worked hard on it, and he

isn't a bad boy, you know that, he just made a bad decision. We have all done that," she responded.

"I won't ruin the party, but I'm having a man-to-man talk with him before it starts. That should do it." He went back to finish the yard, and Cynthia went back to the kitchen, her kindergarten teacher and the medicinal marijuana still on her mind.

True to his word, Philip went to Christopher's room before the party for about forty-five minutes. No voices were raised, and the two came out with smiles on their faces. Cynthia was relieved.

Guests started arriving promptly at three o'clock.

Christopher was charming as usual. He worked the back yard like a pro, making sure he spoke to everyone and thanked them for coming.

"Cynthia, this is the nicest party. You should go into the catering business," her friend Alice from work complimented her.

"Thanks, but no thanks. I'll stick to nursing." Both women laughed.

It did look nice. She had big white plastic tubs on the deck filed with ice and drinks a long table for the food in the garage and a short table for desserts. With Philip's hard work, the yard looked good — it was the perfect backdrop for the party.

This is it, she thought. Christopher starting his next stage of life, Millie's last year of college, and no reason she and Philip couldn't make a change. She looked around at the house, her friends, and family. Could she leave this and go somewhere she didn't know a soul? Atlanta was a great place to live and had been good to them. Many of their friends would probably be considering the same thing since they were all so close in age. Why not? She would tell Philip they should look into it. See what it might take to sell their house and buy a house on St. Simons Island. As long as she had Philip by her side, she could manage anywhere.

CHAPTER 13

A soft shade of yellow slowly developed where the sun was peeking above the horizon. The emerging sunshine reflected off the canopy of scattered clouds above, mingling with the shades of pink and blue. The sky was a canvas of color.

Cynthia began her run in the silence. Since it was Sunday morning, the quiet would last a little longer until people lazily woke to retrieve the newspaper and set out for church.

Currently her family didn't belong to a church. When they first moved south, she found the social network of the church was where she made most of her friends, but their lives became busy with her working at the hospital on Sunday sometimes. Mostly she didn't feel called to a certain church and so she drifted away. She didn't drift away from God, though. For Cynthia, being outside running and taking in what God created was better than any church.

Last night, after everyone left the graduation party, she told Philip she wanted them to explore the idea of moving.

He looked at her with surprise and something she couldn't quite put her finger on, almost like relief. "Okay," he said enthusiastically. He gave her a big smile, embraced her, and kissed her soundly on the mouth.

"Maybe we should start with a realtor here in Atlanta to see what the market would be for this house and what we might expect to make on it. Then we'd have a better idea of what we could purchase on St. Simons. Do you want to use Larry Lambert or someone we don't know?" he asked. Larry had originally sold them the house.

"I think we should use Larry," she told him. "He'll do a better job than a stranger. I could be wrong, but let's start there."

Philip agreed and said he would give Larry a call on Monday.

The ball was in motion, and she had to admit she was a little excited. Okay, a lot excited. To be at their ages and starting a new life was exciting, to say the least.

She was coming to the end of her first mile and could feel her breathing and body relax. This was her favorite part of running — she felt like she could go on forever, like she could do anything.

Her thoughts drifted to yesterday's party. With the exception of what they found growing behind the garage, it had been a good time. Christopher was his usual self but had a maturity and charm about him that convinced her he'd do well on his own.

Then she thought of Millie, who was starting to concern her. She wasn't as outgoing as Christopher, but since she'd arrived back home, she was far quieter than usual. It must be because Jimmy wasn't there. Now that they'd all be settling into a summer routine, she'd try to spend more time with Millie and do some things they enjoyed. Maybe Cynthia could draw her into looking at houses on St. Simons to make her feel better about the eventual move.

She was still determined to start her master's in nursing this fall and had been looking at several online courses. Moving to St. Simons Island wouldn't happen overnight, so she could easily start in the fall.

When she got home and headed inside, she smelled coffee brewing.

Her mother was sitting at the kitchen table in her nightgown and robe, with a cup of coffee, staring out one of the windows as if she were a million miles away.

"Hi, Mom. What got you up so early?" Cynthia asked.

"Oh, Cynthia," her mother replied as she slowly turned to face her. "Did you have a good run, dear?"

"Yes, it was beautiful out there. Is Granny still asleep?" Cynthia opened the refrigerator and poured herself a glass of orange juice. She sat down next to her mother.

"I'm so glad. It's good you like to exercise the way you do. It'll keep you young," she said in a woeful voice as she patted Cynthia's hand. "Granny is still asleep. She wore herself out yesterday, but it's good for her." She seemed a little distracted.

"Mom? Is there something wrong you haven't told me about? You and Granny are okay, aren't you? You seem… I don't know… distracted a bit," Cynthia replied in a very concerned tone.

"What? Heavens no, dear. Granny and I are both very healthy. Why, I wouldn't be surprised if Granny lived to be 100 years old," she said with a smile on her face. Cynthia's mother was such an attractive woman for her age and did look young herself. Cynthia hoped she had the same genes.

"I've decided we're going to take it easy today," Cynthia said.

"Sounds good to me. Why don't you go take your shower? And how about a cup of hot coffee to take with you?" Her mother got up, pulled a mug out of the cupboard, and poured her some coffee. Cynthia added some creamer and went to a still silent upstairs to take her shower.

Philip was gone when she finished in the bathroom forty-five minutes later, and she realized that others must be up since she could hear several voices downstairs. As she was heading down the hall to the stairs, Millie came out of her room looking pretty rough.

"Sweetheart, are you okay?" Cynthia asked, wrapping an arm around her daughter.

Millie started to cry.

"Is it because Jimmy wasn't here yesterday? Why don't you see if he can come down this weekend? Things will be much calmer then."

Tears rolled down Millie's cheeks, but Millie hugged her mother and said, "I love you, Mom."

Cynthia smiled, and the two walked downstairs together, arm in arm, into the kitchen where everyone was gathered at the table.

Cynthia's mother was the only one who saw them walk into the room and must have noticed Millie's disposition. "Let me have a little talk with her darling," her mother said. She went off with Millie to the deck outside.

Millie came back with her grandmother trailing behind a few minutes later with a smile on her face.

"Just so you all know, today you're fending for yourself when it comes to meals," Cynthia announced.

"I have to do that every day. It's a jungle out there," Christopher said, laughing at his comment.

"Your grandmothers and I are going to relax out on the deck. Anyone else is welcome to join us."

"I will, Mom," Millie said with the familiar smile still on her face.

They all found a chair on the deck and settled in. The deck was shaded most of the day, making it a favorite spot to relax before the summer humidity invaded. Even Christopher decided to join them, probably thinking he was missing something.

One of the things Cynthia's mother and grandmother enjoyed doing when they came to visit was to go through old *Southern Living* magazines. The two were hilarious, going through the pages and discussing recipes and "southern culture," which was so different from Wisconsin.

Cynthia thought about giving the women their own subscription to the magazine as a gift but realized the fun of reading them when they came to visit would be spoiled.

Millie stayed with them awhile and then said she was going to call Jimmy and take a nap in her room. Exam time at school was rough, but why was she still so tired?

Soon Christopher realized he wasn't missing anything and said he was going to watch TV, leaving Cynthia alone with her mom and Granny.

Granny was reading a story on Charleston, a place neither women had been to visit.

"Next time we come, I want to go to Charleston," Granny said.

"That would be fun, Mom, but Cynthia and Philip will probably be living on St. Simons Island by then," her mother said. "We'll want to explore that area, I'm sure. What's it like, Cynthia? I can't imagine living on an island."

"Me either, Mom. The area is beautiful, and the island itself is not real beachy looking, although I'm sure tourism is their main business. There's a lot of history, not only on St. Simons but also on Jekyll Island, where Philip and I stayed when we were down there. You and Granny would love it."

She looked over at her Granny who was passed out. She and her mother smiled at each other and gave a little laugh at the older woman who they both loved dearly.

"I know she'll never admit it, but I believe time is catching up with your Granny. I've seen her slowing down, but at ninety-four, she can still run circles around me some days."

"Everything is okay with her, isn't it, Mom?" Cynthia asked, dreading the day when the sweet woman would no longer be with them.

"Oh yes, dear. At her last physical, the doctor said he couldn't find a thing wrong. She takes no pills other than a few vitamins to keep up her energy. I hope when the time comes, she painlessly falls asleep. If we could all go that way," she smiled at Cynthia and then changed the subject.

"What I really want to talk to you about is how you feel about moving. This is a big change, sweetheart, and all of a sudden. What made the two of you decide? You don't think you should settle into the empty nest first and then think about changing your life?" Her mother asked.

Having her mother ask the same questions going through her mind brought back some of her feelings of reluctance she had when Philip first proposed the move. She again thought of the impulsive craziness of it all, but she reminded herself that Philip really wanted to do it.

"I know it sounds like it's all of a sudden, and it is, but I've grown to realize that if we do this now, we'll have so much more time to enjoy it, like Granny said. It's an adventure. Since we're already changing our lives with Christopher going off to college, Philip figures, why not, and I agree."

"But is it what you want?" Her mother asked, looking at her with the eyes of a concerned mother who knows her daughter.

"I do, Mom, because Philip wants it so bad. And think about how much fun it will be visiting us there. All your friends at White Lake will be so jealous when they hear about your visits. The history on the island goes back to before our country was formed. Imagine living there," she said convincingly, although inside she had the same gut feeling she couldn't shake. "Besides it's going to take time to get it all together — it won't happen overnight. I think in the long run leaving Atlanta will be good for us."

Just then she thought about Philip and the other woman she'd been concerned about. Why did it pop into her mind? Is that why she was going along with this? Because they'd be away from Atlanta? Was she running away from her fear, or did she really want to move?

As if her mother could read her mind, she said, "Things are okay between you and Philip, aren't they? I mean, sometimes when kids leave the nest, you find your life maybe isn't what you thought or wanted. The kids were the ones holding it together, and you don't realize till they're gone it's all you had in common. Anything you want to talk about?"

Inside she wanted to say, "Mom, do you think Philip could have an affair or love another woman? Tell me he would never love anyone but me," but she couldn't. She didn't want to share it with anyone. It made her feel embarrassed, like a failure. Maybe in time she could talk about it, but right now it was too much.

Instead she said, "There is something I wanted to tell you. I've decided I'm going to get started on my master's in nursing this fall. I've always wanted to do it, and now seems as good a time as any."

"That's great, Cynthia. I'm so proud of you. Lots of changes. Well, as long as you're going to be happy. I'll love coming to visit St. Simons; just don't jump into things too fast, you know, before you have time to think about it is all I'm saying."

"I love you, Mom," Cynthia said. She got up from her chair, slid onto the lounge chair next to her mother, and gave her a kiss on the cheek. "Let's look at some of these magazines together. I've turned down the corner of the pages I like. Maybe we can find some ideas for decorating a beach house," she said as her mother scooted over and smiled at her.

❦

Later in the evening, they all were visiting and watching TV in the family room. Millie would start her internship in the morning, Philip was back to work, Cynthia had the rest of the week off to spend time with her mother and Granny, and Christopher would start working at a golf course in the afternoons, where in addition to a paycheck he was able to golf twice a week for free.

"I'm going to Charlotte in a few weeks for orientation with Dad," Christopher told the grandmothers. "Maybe you'd like to visit me there sometime?" They all laughed at the thought of the two women on a college campus with Christopher.

"And then we'll be coming to see you at White Lake. I can't wait to go fishing and out in the boat. I guess mean old Mrs. Deen is still alive," Christopher added.

Mrs. Deen was in the cottage two doors down. She wasn't really mean, just loved her lake and was the equivalent to a neighborhood watchdog. She had the Department of Natural Resources on speed dial so she wouldn't waste time. Mrs. Deen fussed at Christopher for driving his boat fast and making too much noise, but she actually enjoyed watching him. No one knew how old she was, but she had to be close to Granny's age. She spent nice days sitting on her dock watching the lake and the world go by. One of the highlights of her summer was when the Lewis family came for two weeks.

"Mrs. Deen is indeed still alive, and she is not mean at all," their grandmother informed them. "She likes you. She told me herself."

"Grandma, you haven't heard her yell at me. I'm telling you, she's mean," Christopher said, and they all laughed.

"When I was a girl, I knew Mrs. Deen as Ethel Fahrenkrug. Her parents had the dairy farm down the road from us. She was a beautiful young woman," Granny said.

"No way, Granny. That mean old woman could never have been beautiful."

"She was, and it's a sad story. Ethel was considered the beauty of the county. Not only did she look beautiful, but she painted, did exquisite needlework, and wrote poetry and sonnets. I will never forget the day Ethel married Wilfred Schultz.

"Wilfred had gone to college for engineering and could speak German and French. He was also one of the most handsome men I had ever seen. Being younger than Ethel, I was quite enamored with the nuptials and listened to everything being planned. I wanted to be Ethel. Her father was very well off, not only a dairy farmer but also president of the bank, so Ethel wanted for nothing.

"She and Wilfred had a beautiful storybook wedding and lived on the farm with Ethel's parents after coming back from their honeymoon in Canada. Wilfred joined the Army like all the young men at that time. After boot camp, he got himself shot the first day out on the battlefield. Poor Ethel, and she was pregnant on top of it all. She had a son she named after Wilfred and when Wilfred Jr. was about two years old, she met Jim Deen and married him. He was not that good looking or smart, but she made a life with him and had three more sons. He died about twenty-five years ago."

Cynthia had known Mrs. Deen her whole life as the old lady on the lake who yelled at them, not as a woman who'd suffered love and loss. Maybe that's what caused her to yell.

"Ethel now stays on the lake in the summer and in Walden Falls during the winter. One day when we were sitting on her dock reminiscing, she told me how she dreams of Wilfred every night. He comes to her and tells her how much he loves her and how some day they'll be together again. That's true love." Granny finished her story and closed her eyes for a moment.

The story touched Cynthia, and she looked over at Philip, wondering what he was thinking. She couldn't imagine a life without him. Just then, his eyes met hers, and he smiled at her. Was he thinking the same?

Then Granny broke in. "Can't wait until you come to visit this summer," she said, bringing them back to the present.

Cynthia saw her mother look over at Millie, catching her eye. Millie's eyes went to the floor, her face so sad. Was it because she knew Jimmy wouldn't be coming along to

White Lake? Maybe Granny's story about Mrs. Deen had made her think of her relationship with Jimmy the way Cynthia had just thought about her own with Philip.

Christopher soon took off with several of his friends and left the rest of them alone.

Something was up. Cynthia could feel the electricity in the air. Her mother was holding Millie's hand smiling at Millie the whole time.

"Mom and Dad, I have something to tell you, but once you think about it and accept it, you will come to be happy for me, I hope." Millie looked at her grandmother and then back at them after her grandmother gave her an encouraging smile.

Millie took a deep breath. "I'm pregnant."

Cynthia was stunned.

Granny was the first to find her voice and speak. "Millie, you're going to be a wonderful mother." It was the right thing to say. God bless Granny.

Pregnant. How could that be? What about Millie's education? They'd had such big plans for her. She was so smart and had so much potential. She now wished Jimmy was there so she could lash out at him. She knew he wasn't good for Millie. She should have made her feelings known. Why had she kept silent?

And then she stopped. She was only thinking about herself and not about Millie and how hard it must be to tell them this. Millie knew they weren't crazy about Jimmy, but a baby was a person, a new soul coming into this world. Her grandchild. Millie was looking at her with wanting in her eyes. She wanted, no, she *needed* her mother right now more than ever. She needed to know her mother was there for her in this scary uncertain moment of her life. She found the words.

"Sweetheart, come here. My little girl is having a baby." Millie went to her open arms and cried, as did Cynthia. When they separated, Philip gave Millie a hug and kiss, as did both the grandmothers.

"We're all here for you, dear," her Granny said. "We love you so much. I'm going to be a great great granny," she laughed. "What are your plans? Does Jimmy know?"

They all gave Millie their undivided attention.

"Jimmy and I want to get married as soon as we can. We don't expect much. The baby will come in December, so I should have my exams done by then. I fully plan on finishing school, and I might have to put off getting my master's a year maybe. We can live with Jimmy's parents. Since his mom doesn't work outside the home, she's more than eager to watch the baby for us, and Jimmy's dad is a pediatrician. We told them the day before I came home. Jimmy wanted to be here with me to tell you. Now he'll be part of our family."

Cynthia somehow found the words. "Starting tomorrow, we'll begin planning your wedding. How fortunate that your grandmothers are here to help us get started."

Millie's tears and worry were erased from her face, replaced by the glow only a happy pregnant woman can wear. Cynthia choked back the tears teetering on the edge when she saw the transformation in Millie. Jimmy Skidmore was going to be her son-in-law. She guessed it could be worse. At least he was standing up to his responsibility toward Millie.

Although Philip hadn't uttered a word, she saw the hurt and confusion expressed in his eyes when she glanced his way. Finally, he spoke.

"I hope it's a little girl just like you. I can't wait to be a grandfather. Grandfather. That sounds weird doesn't it?"

And they all laughed.

As Cynthia got ready for bed, the events of the evening ran through her mind. Millie pregnant, planning a wedding, Christopher going to college, wondering if Philip was interested in another woman, selling their current house, buying a house on St. Simons Island, finding and starting a new job, living in a new area, making new friends... her head was spinning. Could she even consider going to school for her master's? It was overwhelming, to say the least, and she'd be the one expected to hold it all together. She was fifty-five years old and didn't want the job anymore. They all had a piece of her, and there was nothing left. When did this happen? How did she allow it to happen?

She started crying, not wanting Philip to see, because she knew he was as devastated as she was by the news. Fathers and daughters have a different kind of bond, as mothers and sons do.

Cynthia was sure Philip wanted to take Jimmy out back and beat the living daylights out of him for what he'd done to his daughter. Truth be told, Cynthia would have liked to get in a few punches herself. But Millie was so excited and happy about the baby. She would try to give her daughter the wedding she'd dreamed of, determined to make this the special occasion it should be.

The wedding would have to be the end of July or the beginning of August, just as Millie started showing. Millie said she wanted it that way, and Cynthia was in full agreement. Very small, but as nice as they could make it. She hoped Millie would be up for the whirlwind planning this wedding was going to be. The first three months of a pregnancy were so unpredictable with your first baby. Cynthia hoped Millie would have minimal morning sickness.

She looked at herself in the mirror and wiped the tears away before she came out of the bathroom.

Philip was already in bed, so she slid in next to him as close as she could get. He rolled over, wrapping his arms around her, burying his face in her hair. She heard his staccato breaths and knew he was crying. Her sadness immediately became her strength. She loved this man more than life at this very moment.

What a blow to know the little girl you've been protecting for all these years is unmarried and pregnant. She imagined he felt a little guilt thinking there should have been something he could have done. He lifted his face to hers and gave her a long, passionate kiss.

"I love you, Cynthia. What would I do without you? Tonight you handled this whole thing with Millie perfectly. I didn't know what to say, I was so angry. You held it together as always. How do you do it?"

You held it together as always.

She wanted to tell him to go ahead and take a turn. Instead, she said, "I don't know what you mean. I love my daughter, and being angry isn't going to change the new life growing inside her. The only thing to do is accept it and move forward. What choice do we have, Philip? She's our daughter, and she needs us."

"You're right, and I need to hear it daily so I don't strangle Jimmy next time I see him," he said, and they both laughed.

"I have something else to tell you," he said. " I hope you'll look at it as good news, but it may add some pressure. I've been checking out available jobs with the bank in the St. Simons area. I discovered a guy is retiring, and it looks like I'm a shoo-in for his job. It's even more money. Isn't that great news? It's like all the pieces are falling into place."

She couldn't believe he'd already been looking for a job and brought it up now after Millie's announcement. Talk about adding pressure.

"This is moving faster than I thought, Philip. We were only going to check into it to see what was possible. Sounds like you have it all worked out, and I have no say. What about my plans for my master's and now a wedding?"

"You can postpone your master's another year. What's another year compared to the change we're planning on making? The wedding shouldn't impact anything."

He was clueless and could only see what he wanted to

see. He kissed her again and rolled over, settling in for the night. She lay for an hour staring at the ceiling, running everything through her mind. There was so much change going on in her life right now. Could she do it?

First, they would get through the wedding and Millie's pregnancy. What a wonderful mother Millie will be, Cynthia thought. And herself a grandmother.

In the morning, four generations of women — great grandmother, grandmother, mother, and daughter — would begin preparing for Millie's special day. As for St. Simons, she'd have to wait and see how things progressed. The move could easily be a year away.

CHAPTER 14

*M*illie and Jimmy came up with the idea to have their wedding at Berry College where they were attending school. The school served as a venue for many current and former students' weddings and would help them keep the event low-key like they wanted. The location made the most sense and was meaningful to Millie and Jimmy.

Cynthia was presently driving up to Rome for two reasons. First, to work on wedding plans with Millie and second, to go with Millie to her doctor's appointment and hear her grandchild's heartbeat.

The news of the baby was a surprise at first but the family was adapting. Christopher couldn't wait to become an uncle, telling Millie he would take his job very seriously. Cynthia had no doubt, be it a boy or girl, the child would love their uncle.

The week after Millie's big announcement had been frantic with decisions. Cynthia was so happy her mother and Granny had been there with her. They were a source of strength.

Jimmy sheepishly showed up at their house mid-week, like the cat that ate the canary — not sure what to expect. She wished she could say she liked Jimmy, but she kept her feelings to herself as they all warmly welcomed him into their family — what else could she do? She would never share this with Millie or anyone else. What purpose would it serve other than alienating her daughter? She hoped over time she'd understand what Millie saw in Jimmy. He had no idea the jewel he was getting with her.

Jimmy and Millie were able to secure the last Saturday in July at the college for the wedding due to a cancelation — it made them feel as if it was meant to be. They'd have a simple ceremony and reception at the school.

Sadly, the wedding meant there would be no White Lake visit that summer, and the grandmothers would come back to Atlanta for the wedding, which was fine with both of them. The whole family was excited when they found out Arthur and his family were coming. Even Philip's sister, Cathy, who they rarely got to see, was coming in from Texas. Since Philip's mother passed away, Cathy was all the family he had.

They decided they wouldn't say anything about the pregnancy before the wedding and find a wedding dress that could camouflage the baby bump. Most people would suspect, since the wedding came on so suddenly, but, they'd never ask.

Much to their pleasure, they found *the* dress the first day out shopping at a small bridal shop in Atlanta. Millie tried on several dresses that were very pretty and flattering, but none felt like the one. While Cynthia was waiting for Millie to come out in the next gown, she watched some of the other young women in the shop. She heard someone in the store say, "oh my" and the woman sitting next to her loudly inhale and say, "oh". Cynthia turned in the direction the women were looking and saw it was Millie they were reacting to in a dress that made her glow. They always say you know it's *the* dress when you try it on, and in Millie's case it was true.

In the few seconds it took Millie to walk over to her, Cynthia had a flashback to Millie as a child playing dress up and mother to her baby dolls. For those few seconds, it was as if Millie was transformed into a little girl standing in front of her saying, "I want to be a mommy like you someday, and I'm going to marry someone like Daddy."

By the time Millie reached her, Cynthia was back in the present. She felt a warmth in her heart, and she imagined something else, as well — a woman embarking on the next chapter of the story of her life, a story yet to be written and open to so many possibilities.

Finding the dress made it all real — her daughter would be a married woman and a mother. And then the thought came, about who she was marrying. Jimmy Skidmore! Millie would always have an extra child with Jimmy, for he was helpless and clueless.

He came across as self-centered and lazy. According to Millie, he was smart, and Cynthia didn't doubt it. But she knew many smart lazy people. Jimmy had made his bed and now needs to lay in it by getting a real job after he graduated to support his family. She was going to have to work on keeping her mouth shut. This was a done deal with a baby coming, and her job was to be there for Millie.

All this was going through her mind as she drove up to Rome. Today Cynthia would be meeting Jimmy's mother for the first time. She was picking Millie up at Jimmy's parents' home, Millie's new home. She should be grateful that Jimmy's parents were willing to help out because otherwise Millie might not be able to finish her education.

It hadn't occurred to her before but it was possible that Jimmy's parents felt that Millie had trapped their son. Surely they could tell that, for whatever reason, Millie loved this guy and was in no need of trapping anyone.

The GPS system announced the turn into the Skidmore's neighborhood, which wasn't that much different than her neighborhood in Atlanta, with the same Georgian brick homes and neatly manicured yards.

As she pulled into the driveway, her stomach churned, but she ignored it and closed her eyes, praying for the strength to be supportive.

Here goes nothing, she thought, as she climbed out of her car and walked up to the front door.

A petite, tastefully dressed blonde woman answered the door. "Cynthia, we finally meet. I'm Melanie Skidmore," the woman said in a thick southern accent. "I've heard so much about you from Millie. She is quite the fan of yours. We just love her to death and can't wait until we're all family."

The woman threw her arms around Cynthia and hugged her. Cynthia immediately liked Jimmy's mother. Go figure.

"I'm glad to finally meet you, too," Cynthia said with a relieved smile. She walked into the house, following the chattering Melanie to the family room where they found Millie.

"Mom," Millie said, jumping up to hug Cynthia. "I'm so excited about today."

Cynthia took Millie in her arms and held her tight."Me too," Cynthia said sincerely.

They visited with Jimmy's charming mother for about twenty minutes, talking about family and the wedding, when Millie suggested they set out to make the most of their time.

When they were in the car on their way, Millie finally asked, "So mom, what did you think of Jimmy's mom? She's very nice and caring, but she's not you. She's been loving and supportive, but, well, I don't know..."

Cynthia knew where she was going without Millie having to say another word.

"Millie, don't worry. We're not far away, so I'll be in my car on my way to you whenever you need me. I'm your mom and will always be there for you. Melanie will never take my place, so don't worry."

Millie looked at her with relief and smiled a little-girl smile, not the one of an adult woman expecting a child.

Cynthia would be there every step of the way.

Their first stop was at the college to talk about the wedding.

Cynthia loved driving onto the Berry Campus. She may not realize it now but someday Millie would look back and understand how fortunate she was to have attended school in such a special place. It seemed to Cynthia that you never fully appreciated your college days until you were working in the real world and wished you could go back.

They were meeting a woman named Ana at Frost Memorial Chapel where the ceremony would be performed. Cynthia knew Ana would be like a new best friend since the wedding had to be planned so fast.

Frost Memorial Chapel was very quaint looking. The flagstone building had a castle-like structure on the side and a peaked arch doorway, which gave it a gothic look.

Ana was waiting in the alcove at the front entrance.

"Hi, I'm Ana. You must be Millie and Cynthia? We have a lot to talk about, but first I want you to see the inside of the chapel," Ana said, right to the point. Cynthia was glad they wouldn't be wasting any time.

It took Cynthia's eyes a few minutes to adjust to the darkness inside the church. Ana disappeared into a corner and flipped the lights on.

The ceiling was covered in dark wood trusses and cross-beams. The walls were flagstone on the outside with diamond-shaped windows that complemented the arched door. There were three stained-glass windows in the altar area, in beautiful jewel tones that depicted the life of Jesus.

Cynthia thought of her own wedding back in the day as she looked at the chapel. Wisconsin weddings were so much different than in the South. She was married in an old musty-smelling rectangular white church with a short steeple where the floors and pews creaked and the minister's wife played the organ. Her reception was a sit-down dinner at a hall where the open bar consisted of a keg of beer and a few mixed drinks. The live three-piece band was well versed in polka music for dancing after dinner. She and Philip thought it was great.

"I love it," Cynthia said. She could envision Millie's wedding here.

Next Ana took them to the dining hall where they'd hold the reception. The front door had the same peaked arch and gothic style as the chapel door but on a much grander style and scale. Without a doubt, this place would make for a lovely reception.

After an hour and a half, they had a folder full of information and lots of decisions to make. Arrangements still needed to be made for a minister, flowers, seating, catering, and a whole host of other things. They left the school with their minds swimming.

"We have our work cut out for us, Mom," Millie said after getting into the car.

"It seems overwhelming right now, sweetheart, but before you know it, the wedding will be planned," Cynthia said, trying to be as upbeat as she could. "Now we need to have lunch before seeing the doctor. You don't need to be skipping meals."

❦

Dr. Alice Rosewood was a young energetic woman who appeared to love what she was doing.

Millie was now far enough along to hear a heartbeat. Immediately after the doctor put the monitor to Millie's bare stomach, the constant beat started thumping away, very strong. Cynthia became emotional and hugged Millie. "We're having a baby," she said, and the three women laughed.

"Have you been sick at all?" Dr. Rosewood asked Millie.

"No, but I'm so tired all the time. It seems like I need ten hours of sleep every night and still could go for a nap."

Dr. Rosewood smiled and said, "Perfectly normal and

what you should be doing. This little person growing inside you is sharing your body and everything in it until it arrives. Don't think you need to eat more, just eat healthier and make wise choices so you and the baby stay healthy. I want you to start taking some vitamins to help with your energy level. Do you have any questions for me?"

"No, you've answered everything, but I'm sure by my next visit I'll have a whole list for you."

They said good-bye to Dr. Rosewood, Millie made her next appointment, and they were on their way back to Atlanta.

"So what's Jimmy's dad like?" Cynthia asked as they drove down the interstate.

"Jimmy looks like him, but that's about it. Being a pediatrician, his dad is very patient and soft-spoken. Dad will like the fact he golfs and loves football."

"What's his dad's first name?"

"Don't laugh. It's Ashley," Millie said, laughing.

Cynthia looked at her in disbelief.

"You're telling me his mom is Melanie and dad is Ashley. Like in *Gone With the Wind*?"

Hardly being able to speak, Millie answered through her laugh. "Yes."

"Thank God your brother has never seen the movie or he'd have a field day with this. I'll have to warn your dad and grandmothers. How in the world did they find each other?"

"In Atlanta when they were in college. I think it's hysterical, but Jimmy doesn't, so don't say anything around him. He's kind of sensitive, because he was teased about it as a kid. His mom is really into the movie and its trivia. She knows everything about it and has a *Gone With the Wind* area in their study filled with memorabilia. It's actually some valuable stuff."

"We all have our obsessions," Cynthia said with a chuckle.

"Jimmy's parents are really nice to me, Mom. I think his mother always wanted a daughter, and now she feels like

I'll fill that void for her. The name Melanie fits her. We're so lucky to be able to live there and finish school. It'll all be okay, don't you think, Mom?"

"Yes, sweetheart, it will," Cynthia replied, and she meant it. Now that Cynthia met Jimmy's mom, many of her concerns had been put to rest. Although Melanie would never take Cynthia's place, she could tell Melanie loved Millie like a daughter, and Cynthia was relieved Millie would have an added source of support during her pregnancy.

Cynthia had just poured herself a cup of coffee and sat at the kitchen table with some of her wedding notes when Philip walked in.

"I thought we'd have time this summer to go down to St. Simons and start looking at houses. I found a realtor for us," Philip said.

Cynthia looked up from the piece of paper she'd been reading, "Philip, I can't think about looking at places or moving until this wedding is over. Don't we have to sell this place first?"

"No, we should be able to make the move if we find the right place for us. Maybe we can move before Thanksgiving and spend Christmas with the whole family there. You know, with our newest member," he said with a big grin.

The baby. Imagining the baby always made her happy. After hearing the baby's strong, steady heartbeat in the doctor's office a week ago, she was loving the idea of being a grandmother more and more. It was sweet of Philip to be thinking about them all together for their first Christmas, but she still had too much going on to think about moving.

"I thought we were just collecting information at this point to see what it would take?"

"I'm thinking if things start falling into place, we should go with it. After all, there is the guy retiring soon in the area."

"I can't think about moving until this wedding is over," she said again.

"Well, think about it when you can." He kissed her with a smile and was gone.

Back to her task at hand. She resorted to a big calendar for the months of June and July so she and Millie could stay organized and not forget anything. It was the last week in June. The wedding was four weeks from Saturday.

She smiled to herself. Imagine Philip thinking she could take a few days away from this to go to St. Simons Island. *Men!*

She reviewed the calendar. The grandmothers were coming from Wisconsin two weeks before the wedding. Cynthia and Philip's good friend, Sandra, was giving a shower for Millie the Sunday after they arrived.

Jimmy was coming down this weekend to pick out tuxes and go with them for the cake tasting. Cynthia was trying to keep his involvement to a minimum but felt they needed to include him in something so she could try to get to know him better.

Millie chose colors for her wedding right after they found her dress. All Cynthia could think was thank God Millie had classic taste. She picked royal blue with accents in pastel shades of pink, yellow, blue, purple and green. There would be two bridesmaids. Her best friend, Patti, from high school was her maid of honor, and her sixteen-year-old cousin, Samantha, would be the other. They had to guess on Samantha's size, since she was in England, but would be getting in early enough to alter the dress if needed. According to Arthur, Samantha was very excited to be asked. The wedding would be at four o'clock with the reception right after.

Philip and the boys were all wearing tuxes, and Cynthia would be in a beautiful soft pink long dress. She'd found her dress two days earlier at a little shop in Atlanta. Melanie was wearing soft green, so it all worked out well.

The invitations went out as soon as the date was decided on, with responses already rolling in steady. She felt 100 was a good number to expect. So much for a small wedding.

After looking over the calendar again, it occurred to her that everything really was set. She only had the cake and program to settle. Everything else was done. Why not go down to St. Simons for a few days? She would tell Philip. It might be good to get away from wedding life for awhile.

❧

Cynthia was sitting on a wooden park bench outside of Tara's Bakery, the cake shop they'd chosen for the wedding. She'd been patiently waiting for Millie and Jimmy for more than fifteen minutes, but who was keeping track? This should be fun, and Cynthia hoped she would see a different side of Jimmy.

She watched as they finally pulled up, parked their car, and walked up to the shop. As they came toward her, she asked herself what made her dislike him so much. The thought of Millie spending the rest of her life with him and having his child — she didn't want to think about it. It was up to Cynthia to find out what Millie saw in him and focus on that.

"Hi, you two. Ready to try some cake? I think this is going to be my favorite part of wedding planning," Cynthia said, greeting them both with a hug.

"Oh, Mom, I hope you haven't been waiting long. Jimmy wanted to finish watching a show on TV, and I told him you wouldn't mind waiting," Millie said, smiling at Jimmy and then back at Cynthia.

Had he not heard of DVR? This was the kind of stuff that added to her dislike.

"Let's eat cake," Cynthia said with a laugh and opened the shop door.

An old-fashioned glass case along the back wall holding

three shelves of bakery items greeted them as they walked in. She closed her eyes and took in the smell, remembering the fabulous bakeries back in Wisconsin. She and her mother would get a plastic number from the rack before they took their place in line, Cynthia practically salivating at the bear claws, French crullers, and Danishes boxed up neatly with string. She wondered how they all stayed so thin back then without worrying about carbs and sugar.

As they walked up to the glass case, two people working behind it greeted them with big smiles. "We're here to see Tara," Millie told them. One of the people went to the back, and a tiny woman with red hair came out.

"Hi, I'm Tara, and you must be Millie," the woman said. "And I'm guessing you're the groom, and you're the mom," she said, turning to Jimmy and Cynthia. "Follow me to my tasting room."

The room they entered contained a glass-topped wrought-iron table in the middle with life-size pictures of cakes around the perimeter.

"I want a traditional three-tiered square layer cake," Millie told Tara, "with a little scroll work on it and real flowers."

"That makes our work easy," Tara said. "Let's try some cakes."

Tara left them and came back with a tray of cake pieces on three plates. She handed them each a plate and explained what they were about to try. Millie liked the traditional wedding cake with a raspberry filling and butter cream frosting.

Jimmy is behaving rather well, Cynthia thought, and then he did like he always did when she started to feel good about him. He opened his mouth.

"Do you really want to pick that? I mean it's so ordinary and boring." He looked at Tara, "Let's do something like cookies or cupcakes. That would be so cool."

"Jimmy," Millie laughed, "I've always wanted a cake like

this. For me it's not boring but a dream come true." Millie seemed to know how to handle him.

"What are you doing for your groom's cake at the rehearsal dinner?" Tara asked, obviously she was used to mediating when there was a difference of opinion.

"I get to have a cake for that? Cool. I'll talk to my mom about it," Jimmy said, as if he were a five-year-old getting a cake for his birthday party.

They worked out the logistics, and all was set. Afterwards, Jimmy and Millie stopped by the tux rental place to get Jimmy fitted for his tux before he headed back home.

Two more things were crossed off the list.

CHAPTER 15

*A*fter Cynthia told Philip she would make a trip to St. Simons before the wedding, he called the realtor and made plans to go the following Sunday.

They met with a nice young man named Brad Davies on Monday. Brad had lived on the island his whole life with the exception of when he went to college.

"I want to show you a few properties so I can have a feel for what you like. It'll help me when I watch for what comes on the market. Now do we have to wait until your place sells in Atlanta?"

"No. We'll be taking a mortgage out on this new place, but our house in Atlanta is paid for," Philip told Brad.

"Okay, let me get my car, and we'll check out a few areas," he said.

"I didn't realize we would have to take a mortgage out on this place," Cynthia said to Philip with surprise in her voice while they waited for Brad to pull his car around the front of the office.

"Think of it this way," he explained, "the new place will cost more, and we can afford a house payment, so why not take a little of the money we currently have in the house, invest it and make it work for us. It'll also give us a tax deduction. We'll eventually put it on this new mortgage. You trust me, don't you?"

"Well, of course, Philip. I had to ask so I know what's going on. I don't want to be overextended, and this makes it sound as if we will."

"Don't worry. We'll be just fine. I have it all worked out."

Brad took them to three very different houses, but the one they liked the best had something they never thought of. On the lower level was a separate little apartment. The raised area under the first floor in most beach homes was to protect the structure from water damage in the case of a hurricane or tide surge. Brad told them that the people who have these little apartments built under the raised first floor rent them out or use them as a mother-in-law suite. They're not really concerned about storms since the last time a hurricane did serious damage to the island was in the 1960s. The apartment would be perfect for company or her mother and Granny when they visited.

"Do you see many beach houses with the extra living space?" Philip asked Brad.

"Not a lot, but many do. Do you want me to let you know when places with a separate space like this come on the market?" Brad asked, notebook in hand.

Philip and Cynthia looked at each other and said, "Yes," at the same time and laughed.

Brad seemed to have a good handle on what they wanted. They spent the rest of the day driving around and walking the beach looking at the houses facing them, hardly believing they might someday own one.

⚜

Looking out the window of the car as they left the island, Cynthia had to admit that coming down here was a much-needed escape from all the wedding planning. Now that she felt a little more energized, she was ready for the events of the next four weeks.

Spending a few days looking at houses got her excited about the move in a way she hadn't been so far. As they crossed the bridge connecting Jekyll Island to Brunswick, she thought, *The first thing I'm going to do when I move here is go for a run on this bridge.*

She smiled to herself.

❦

The dining room table had become her mission control. It was the Saturday two weeks before the wedding; the grandmothers were arriving at the airport in the afternoon.

She was sitting at the table in a comfortable office chair that she had moved into the dining room, since she was spending a great amount of time there. After coming back from their trip to St. Simons, Philip had been busy. She didn't mind since she was living and breathing wedding planning and didn't want to be bothered with anything else.

Philip was to make the airport run for her mother and Granny. She was looking forward to the two women arriving for many reasons but mostly because they were always ready to help out and pick up the slack.

On her list for after the wedding was getting Christopher ready to start college, moving toward putting their house on the market, and finding a new house on St. Simons Island. Cynthia's head was swimming. How had she done this to herself?

Her cell phone rang. It was Millie.

"Hi, sweetheart. What's going on?"

"I was wondering if you needed me to stop and pick anything up before I get home?"

"No, I'm good. I'm sure I'll think of something later, but I can send your brother or your dad."

"I just talked to Jimmy, and he was wondering if there was enough room for him to come down this afternoon and stay the night. He's kind of excited about the shower tomorrow and would like to see Grandma and Granny."

Cynthia knew it was the right thing to include Jimmy. After all, he was soon to become part of their family. "Of course he can come. I should have included him from the start. Tell him we'll have a place set for him at supper and look forward to him staying the night." She hoped she sounded convincing.

"Thanks, Mom." Millie hung up.

Just then, Christopher walked by the door.

"Hey," Cynthia got his attention. He had very wisely taken on a low-profile persona during the wedding planning. Plus, the golf course was keeping him busy.

"What's up, Mom?"

"Do you realize you start college in four weeks?"

"Yeah."

"We haven't had a chance to get anything together."

"It shouldn't be that big a deal."

"Have you communicated with your roommate at all about how you want to do things?"

He looked at her as if to say, "Really?"

"Mom, we're guys. We don't care about what matches. We'll make it up as we go along and get what we need when we need it. Relax, and do your wedding thing. It's under control," he said as he went to his favorite room: the kitchen.

❦

The grandmothers arrived in one piece very excited about the wedding and their new grandchild. Both had new dresses and wanted to make hair appointments for the morning of the wedding. Cynthia delegated Millie in charge of their needs.

Jimmy showed up with his bag at about five o'clock, not too early but in time to eat. The kitchen was crowded with people talking and laughing. It was possibly their last time in this kitchen with all of them together.

Since it was a fairly pleasant evening for that time of year, after supper they all sat outside on the deck visiting.

"Do you know when I was a young woman, the backyard was used for a sand box, swing set, and a clothesline. Nobody seems to use a clothesline at all anymore. Why I used to even hang clothes out on winter days." Cynthia's mother reminisced. The kids laughed. "Your mother remembers, don't you, Cynthia?"

"Do I ever? I used to get the job of taking the clothes down and folding them when they were dry. I'll take my dryer any day."

"I had a friend by the name of Flo Gullickson that had something funny happen to her at the clothesline." Everyone turned and looked at Granny, who had been fairly silent until that moment.

"Flo had a daughter named Mary with a vivid imagination. I'm sure that little girl became a writer, because she came up with the most amazing stories. The problem is, you can't tell stories all the time. One day, she told her mother that their neighbors, the Shukoskis, bought some pigs and were keeping them in their dog pen. The Shukoskis were a little different, but that was the wildest story Mary ever told Flo, so she was punished. She sent a sobbing Mary to her room, but Mary never backed down on her story. Flo went outside to the clothesline to hang some clothes when she heard a strange noise. She couldn't figure it out, so she walked in the direction she thought it was coming from. You guessed it, the Shukoskis house. Flo followed the noise to their backyard and couldn't believe her eyes. There were pigs in the dog pen! She knocked on the Shukoskis' front door, and Bertha Shukoski answered. 'You have pigs in your dog pen,' Flo said. 'Yes,' Bertha replied. 'We didn't have a dog, and thought we could use the pen to raise pigs and then eat them.' Flo went home and apologized to Mary. She never punished her for a story again."

"That was interesting," Jimmy said, "but where do you get this stuff?"

Granny turned and looked at Jimmy with the look no one wants to see.

"What do you mean, young man?" Granny asked.

"You make this stuff up, right?" Jimmy asked.

The look continued. "It's what you call life, young man. You can't make this stuff up," Granny replied with finality, Jimmy wisely realizing that at that point he should keep his mouth shut.

They all laughed hysterically. All, that is, except Jimmy.

❧

The bridal shower Sandra gave was beautiful, with about twenty-five guests. Millie received many gifts she would be able to use once she and Jimmy lived in their own place.

Jimmy hung around until after the shower was over before going back home. It warmed Cynthia's heart to see how excited he was when Millie showed him the gifts she received. It was a first.

Cynthia worked several days that week but was off the week before the wedding and the Monday and Tuesday after.

When she got home Wednesday afternoon after her shift, the house was empty. Odd, but nice. It had been a rough shift that day with two patients dying within fifteen minutes of each other. No matter how long she was a nurse, the passing of one of the patients she cared for was always heavy on her heart. She found it to be as intimate and emotional a privilege as witnessing a birth, only in a different way.

She made herself a cup of tea and sat in the recliner to relax but was soon asleep.

She was in a hospital, not familiar to her, wandering the dark halls. It must have been nighttime for there were no lights on in the rooms. She could hear the low mumbling noises, but she couldn't see anyone.

Down at the end of the long hallway, there was a flashing light coming from a single room drawing her to it. She started to run to the room — it seemed far away and felt she must hurry to it. As she ran, she looked down at the floor and could see a large tile pattern of white, light blue, and yellow tiles. The door was ajar, and she pushed it open to find a single bed with body covered head-to-toe by a sheet.

At that point, she started to feel uncomfortable and restless, wanting to run out of the room, but when she turned to leave, the door had disappeared. There was no way out.

She approached the bed. Who or what was under the sheet? The mumbling became louder and more chaotic. She had to know what was under the sheet, so she slowly extended her hand and started to pull the sheet down ...

She woke abruptly, her heart pounding. Christopher, her mother, and Granny were standing in front of her with shopping bags.

"Hey, Mom! Are you okay?" Christopher asked. "You don't have to worry about me and school. Dad gave Grandma his credit card and told her to take me shopping for whatever I needed for my dorm room. I actually had fun picking out stuff. You want to see it?" He didn't wait for a response. "I got a comforter that's red on one side and blue on the other and two sets of sheets. It was Granny's idea," her mother piped in. "We had so much fun, dear, and now you don't have to worry about a thing."

Cynthia smiled groggily. Her mother and Granny had gotten everything Christopher needed for his dorm room. She couldn't have been happier to hear what they had done.

What a relief.

At the end of the week, Millie finished her internship. She had another doctor's appointment on the Monday before the wedding, so she spent the weekend with Jimmy and his parents and saw the doctor before coming home.

Cynthia's brother arrived Monday, Philip's sister,

Thursday. She borrowed air mattresses from a few friends for all the kids and let the adults stay in the bedrooms — they had a full house. On Friday, the whole caravan would go to Rome for the rehearsal dinner and the wedding on Saturday.

❦

Finally, the day before the much-awaited wedding arrived and all ten of them headed to Rome.

After having lunch, they checked into their hotel and got settled. She knew Granny and her mother would need to rest before the rehearsal and so did Millie, although none of them would admit to it. She could use a little rest herself, but she also would not admit to it. A family trait, she guessed.

Cynthia lay down on the bed in the hotel room. Philip left, saying he needed to walk around a little after all the driving. There was a knock on the door. It was Arthur.

"I think Granny and Mom passed out as soon as they hit the bed," he laughed.

"They're so afraid they'll miss out on something. I admire their tenacity. We'd be fortunate to have half their energy and drive when we're their age," she laughed.

They sat in her room, catching up.

"When are you coming to visit us in England?" Arthur asked. "You've got a free place to stay as long as you want."

"Since we're planning on moving to St. Simons Island sometime in the next year, it might not be possible until after next summer. Philip's determined to move," she said.

"Oh, yeah. So what's up with Philip?" Arthur asked, "He was outside on his phone freaking out on somebody. He didn't see me, but I sure heard him. He was definitely agitated. I know agitated when I see it."

"I don't know, but I'll ask him. He said he wanted to go for a little walk to stretch his legs after driving," she was really bothered by this and hoped it wasn't work… or worse, her suspicions. They were just that, suspicions, and bringing them up this weekend was not good. If it was work, they needed to let him alone. His daughter was getting married. "What did he say?"

"I heard him say, 'It's all coming together,' kind of angrily at the person on the other end."

Cynthia sat with a puzzled look on her face. "I have no idea, Arthur, but it sounds like work bothering him."

She brought it up with Philip when Arthur had left and they were getting ready for the rehearsal.

"Sweetheart, was work bothering you today? I think it's so inconsiderate when they know your daughter is getting married. If they call anymore this weekend, just don't answer," Cynthia said.

"What are you talking about?" he asked. "I haven't talked to anyone from work."

"Arthur mentioned he heard you on your phone getting upset with someone. He was passing by."

"Arthur needs to mind his own business. Who does he think he is eavesdropping on my phone calls? What nerve, and then to come running to you. Unbelievable."

"It wasn't like that. He was passing by and said you were quite loud. He couldn't help but hear you."

"So what did he think he overheard?"

"Nothing, really. He just could tell you were angry. So who was it?"

Philip stood there with a blank face. "It was someone from work, and I told them to stop bothering me," he replied.

"But you *just* said it wasn't work."

"Not my office, just someone I've done some work with. Not a big deal, so tell your brother he doesn't need to be concerned."

"It was more he didn't want anything to spoil the wedding, I think," she replied.

"The wedding won't be spoiled."

"Tell me who it was then," she wanted reassurance from him not an argument.

"Just someone I've done work with. I already told you that. I'm not talking about it anymore," he was starting to become angry. "Now let's get dressed and go to the rehearsal. I can't wait to meet Jimmy's parents."

She let it go as she seemed to do frequently. He always had an answer and to continue arguing now *would* spoil the wedding.

❦

They arrived at Frost Chapel early so both families could meet. Everyone was well-behaved, which meant Christopher was being a gentleman. No jokes about Jimmy this weekend, though she was sure he would have plenty on the ride home.

Cynthia already met Melanie, so she was curious to meet Ashley. He was like Millie described him, soft spoken and Jimmy definitely favored him in looks. Cynthia didn't really see Jimmy's personality in either parent.

When the rehearsal was over they headed to dinner at the Skidmore's country club.

Huge brick pillars flanked the entrance to the club, supporting concrete pineapples, the symbol for southern hospitality. The doors were bordered on either side by two huge pots containing trees with flowers and ivy. Inside, a wood table held a breathtaking floral arrangement. The place was elegant.

"Wow," Granny said, her mouth agape. "Wait until Alma and Trudy hear about this place. Christopher, will you get a couple of pictures with my camera in front of these flowers?" she asked. Christopher, of course, obliged.

They were escorted to an elegant private dining room. Cynthia spotted the groom's cake and stifled a laugh, it was The Star Ship Enterprise, in all its glory.

"Cynthia," Melanie said in her sweet southern voice, "join our table with your lovely mother and grandmother. It will let us get better acquainted."

They all sat down except her mother, who stopped off at the ladies room. She came in the room shortly after with an excited look on her face. "Dear," she said to Cynthia quietly. "You should see that ladies room. I've never seen such a thing in my life. Each stall is like its own private bathroom, with its own sink, a huge mirror, a little tray of toiletries, and a winged-back chair — two of them even have showers! I've got to tell Granny."

"What was that about?" Philip asked Cynthia.

Cynthia laughed a little. "Just more for them to talk about when they get back to White Lake."

The groom's cake was cut, Jimmy taking full advantage of the moment and Cynthia finally seeing a different side of him. She could see he was truly excited about marrying her daughter, and he loved Millie as much as Millie loved him. Maybe she had been a little hard on him in the past and should have looked beyond the surface.

When it was time to leave, the grandmothers stopped in the bathroom to get a few last pictures to share with their friends at home.

The next day at Frost Memorial Chapel, Cynthia looked around her — she couldn't help but be proud of how wonderful her family looked in their wedding finery.

Both grandmothers were thrilled with their bouffant hairstyles, thanks to a local beauty shop. Cynthia's mother wore a long purple dress with lace overlay, and Granny a powder blue dress with a matching jacket. Christopher was so good looking in his tux.

Philip came over to her, also very handsome in his tux, and surveyed her long fitted V-neck dress. "You know, if you weren't already married, I would try to pick you up at the reception later," he said, and he winked at her. She laughed.

Millie looked beautiful and radiant. Her dress was a strapless champagne color with a sweetheart neckline and

A-line skirt covered in crystal and pearl beading throughout. Her something old was a delicate diamond bracelet Granny had gotten from her husband on their own wedding day all those years ago.

"Millie, I'm so happy I'm still alive to see this day." Granny told her as she hooked the bracelet around her wrist.

Suddenly, it hit Cynthia. In a little over an hour, her daughter was to be Mrs. Jimmy Skidmore… Millie Skidmore.

She remembered her wedding day and thought about her life and how it had unfolded. It was nothing like she'd dreamed that day. You have expectations, but life gets in the way — raising a family, dealing with grief and joy, keeping your head above water. Although it may not have turned out the way Cynthia had imagined, she wouldn't change anything.

❧

Cynthia and Millie were in Millie's dressing room, waiting for the wedding to start, when there was a knock at the door. It was Christopher.

"Mom, I found someone out here wandering around who you might like to see."

In walked Purvell, looking as beautiful as she always did. It had been more than a year since the two women were together, and the last time they talked on the phone was after the trip to St. Simons Island. Cynthia was so happy to see her best friend.

"Oh, Purvell!" They held each other tight.

"I wouldn't miss this for anything. I already talked to Philip and heard about all the changes going on. And I thought *I* lived a crazy life."

Purvell turned and looked at Millie. "What happened to the little girl I knew? Millie, you look radiant." She hugged her.

They talked briefly. Purvell had brought her boyfriend along to the wedding. Cynthia would get a chance to meet him later at the reception where she wanted to be brought up to date with all the details.

As Cynthia watched Purvell walk out of the room, she thought of how you knew when someone was your true friend. She and Purvell may not have talked and seen each other as much as they would have liked to, but talking to and seeing her right now was as if no time passed and they had last spoken only yesterday.

❦

Philip came in about fifteen minutes later. It was time to escort the grandparents and then the mothers down the aisle. Cynthia rose from her chair and went over to Millie, giving her a kiss while holding back tears. She pulled back, ran her hand over Millie's hair, then her soft glowing cheek, and smiled.

"I love you, sweetheart." Cynthia said simply.

"And I love you, Mommy." Millie responded like a child. Cynthia almost lost it.

Christopher walked Cynthia down the aisle with such tenderness. He leaned down, kissed her cheek, and smiled as if to say, "I know, but it will all be okay." How was she going to keep it together during this ceremony?

She watched the groomsmen and Jimmy take their places at the front of the church. Next, the bridesmaids came down, first Samantha then Patti. Then, the music played, and Cynthia stood up to watch Millie and Philip walk down the aisle, all smiles. As she turned to the altar, she was surprised to see Jimmy's face wet with tears.

Philip put Millie's hand into Jimmy's and said it was he that gave this woman in marriage and then came and sat next to Cynthia, taking her hand firmly in his smiling.

It would all be okay, she decided.

❦

The room was empty now. It was hard to believe that a few hours ago, it had been full of people.

The once perfectly set tables now could tell a story about

the people briefly inhabiting them: crumbs left from the food served, glasses with a little splash of champagne lingering in the bottom, a crumpled napkin with a lipstick smudge, a cake plate with the cake gone but the frosting still there in a perfect outline, someone's business card, and the once lit candles cold and still.

Philip walked over to her. "Are you okay?" he asked.

She slowly looked up at him and thought, *Is this all there is to life? You get married, raise a family, educate them, marry them off, and then what do you do next?*

"I'm fine. Just being sentimental. Seems kind of lonely."

Philip laughed and looked at her with surprise. "How could you be lonely after a wedding? You just spent an evening with about a hundred of your friends."

He sat down next to her and gently picked up her hand, lacing his fingers with hers.

"I'm going to get Christopher and start loading the car up. You sit here as long as you want." He kissed her, got up, and walked away.

She studied his back until he disappeared into the darkness. Why couldn't he understand? Actually, she didn't understand herself. She closed her eyes, trying to collect her thoughts.

Things were moving too fast. Christopher going to college, Millie was pregnant and married, and Philip was pressing her to sell their home and move. They all assumed she would follow along, but what about *her* life?

She told herself she was being ridiculous. She had her own life. She was a nurse, for Pete's sake.

She got up and walked around the room and over to a table arranged with pictures of Millie and Jimmy as they grew up.

She picked up one of Millie in a silver frame. Millie was about four in the picture. Where had the time gone? She ran her fingers across the glass and began to cry.

"Cynthia," Philip hollered, startling her. "Oh, great, after you finish putting those pictures in the box, come get Christopher to carry it to the car."

She kept her head down and retrieved the box from under the table. She felt like she was packing away a lifetime as she put each picture in it. All the planning and time creating this day for Millie, and it was over like a flash.

She surveyed the room and let out a sigh. She felt empty and alone.

CHAPTER 16

*I*n a mass exodus on Monday, all the family visiting returned to their respective homes.

Millie and Jimmy left on Tuesday for a honeymoon in the Bahamas, given by Jimmy's parents as a wedding gift. They'd be back the next week, starting school the week after. Christopher started college at UNC Charlotte in two weeks, moving into the dorms the weekend before.

Philip made an appointment with their realtor on Saturday to put their home on the market.

At eleven on Saturday, Larry Lambert rang the doorbell.

"Hi, Larry," Philip said as he answered. "Good to see you. How are Shelly and the kids?" He shook Larry's hand and let him in.

"The family is good, Philip. Thanks for asking. So, you've had a lot going on. Wedding, son starting college, and now moving. Y'all don't do anything in small doses, do you?" Larry laughed.

"No, it appears not," Philip said, shaking his head and laughing also.

Cynthia didn't laugh. It seemed too fast, and Philip had been putting on a lot of pressure these last few days. But she told herself to trust him. She always had before.

"Hi, Larry," Cynthia said, forcing herself to be cheerful. "You ready to sell our house?"

They took Larry for a tour of the house, and he gave them some suggestions about removing some furniture and personal pictures along with sprucing up the yard to make it more appealing.

The house was going on the market the upcoming Monday, with a tour on Tuesday by all the realtors in his office. "That should get things going," Larry told them.

Now, they just had to wait.

❦

The Saturday before Christopher's first week of classes, they loaded a rented van and Christopher's Honda with all his belongings. Of course, it had to be the hottest day of the summer to move in.

He was living in Moore Hall, a 12-story dorm. After checking in and getting his room key, they went to see if his roommate had moved in before unloading, but he hadn't.

"Dad. How about I go down to the drop-off area and scope out a parking spot for you while you get the van?" Christopher suggested.

"Good idea, son. You want to wait with him or come with me, Cynthia?"

"I'll wait with Christopher," Cynthia responded.

This was the moment she had been working towards since Christopher was born, but now that it was here, she felt a little apprehensive as she stood next to this young man she'd raised.

She briefly closed her eyes, asking God to be near him and trying to hold back tears.

Just then, Christopher put his arm around her and tickled her. He must have sensed her sadness.

They took Christopher's things to his room after Philip finished parking.

It was time to say goodbye.

The three of them walked down to the car together. The circle drive had calmed down, and there were only a few stragglers left unloading.

"It's time for your mom and I to get started home. I know we've talked to you your whole life about what we expect from you as our child. We pretty much expect the same as an adult, but the only difference is, now you'll do it on your own. I love you, son."

Philip extended his right hand. Christopher took his father's hand and then threw his arms around him and kissed him on the cheek. Cynthia lost it with a full flow of tears trailing freely down her face.

"Aww, Mom, I'm going to be fine. I'll be home for fall break before you know it. Make sure the fridge is stocked!" They laughed. She couldn't wait.

❦

Cynthia heard her cell phone ring in her purse as she walked into the kitchen after arriving home from work.

"Hello."

"Cynthia, it's Larry. Got some great news. Another showing tomorrow. Your house is on fire. Haven't had a house show this much in a long time," Larry sounded very happy. Their house had been on the market for just shy of two weeks with ten showings. It helped that they were in a good school district and a great location.

"Great, what time?"

"They want to come between one and two thirty. Is it a problem?"

"No, Larry, not a problem," she told him.

"I like that attitude, Cynthia. It's another agent in my office with a family from Ohio relocating with Coca-Cola. Keeping my fingers crossed. Bye!"

"Bye, Larry," and she hung up.

It was easy keeping the house in shape for all the showings, since it was only her and Philip now. They were going down to St. Simons in a few weeks to look at some places with Brad. There was no hurry until they sold their home. Even though Philip had confidence in their finances, she would feel better having their house sold before buying another.

She found Philip in the family room watching TV.

"Got another showing tomorrow," she told him.

He looked up, half asleep. "Great. We're going to sell this place soon. I can tell."

"I love your optimism, sweetheart. I'm going to heat up the spaghetti from last night and pour myself a glass of wine. Do you want some?"

"Yeah, sure," he smiled and went back to his TV.

She went upstairs and changed into her nightgown before going to the kitchen to warm the spaghetti in the microwave. While the spaghetti was heating, she opened a bottle of wine and filled two glasses, taking a long sip from hers. It was so good. Next, she fixed them each a plate of spaghetti with a roll and took them into the family room. They ate, drank, and talked about their days before going to bed so they could get up and do it all over again tomorrow.

⚜

"I've got great news," Larry said after the showing. "We've got an offer from the family moving here from Ohio. They loved your house." Larry was beside himself.

"That's great. Is it a good offer?" Cynthia couldn't believe it.

"Well, I think it is. I was wondering if you and Philip would be able to let me come by tonight and show it to you?"

"Sure, he'll be home by six thirty, so how about seven?"

"Perfect. See you then." Larry hung up.

An offer that quick. She hoped it was a good one.

꩜

It was. Larry came by at seven on the dot with an offer just $5,000 less than what they were asking. The family wanted to move in as soon as they could — they didn't want their children to miss much of the beginning of school.

They signed the papers with a mid-October closing date. Philip called Brad the next morning and told him they sold their home and were ready to do some serious looking.

By the afternoon, they'd made plans to drive down the first week in September to meet with Brad and find a house so they could start their new life on the island.

꩜

Several days before they were scheduled to make their visit to St. Simons, Brad gave them a call.

"Just wanted to let you know a great property has come on the market, and if you're interested, you better take a look at it as soon as possible, because it will sell fast. I think it might be perfect for y'all. Can you come a day earlier?"

They did, and the house was just what they wanted. Cynthia knew when they walked in that this was it. Twelve steps went up to the front door and foyer, which opened into the living area surrounded by tall windows wrapped around the room, giving the most extraordinary view of the water. Off to the left side was a gas fireplace. The kitchen had been remodeled, and even though it wasn't as big as the one in her house right now, it was very functional, bright, and cheery.

There was a nice-size dining room between the living area and the kitchen, a study, and a full bath on the first floor. Upstairs was a master bedroom suite in addition to two more bedrooms, each with their own bathrooms. The best part was under the first floor facing the water — a separate little apartment was built with a kitchen, dining area, living area, two bedrooms, a full bath, and a patio.

"Philip," she said. "I love it, but can we afford it?"

"We'll just have to negotiate it out. Depends on how much they want to sell." He smiled and kissed her on the forehead.

They went to Brad's office and worked out a deal they hoped the owner could not refuse. In the mean time, Brad had some more houses for them to look at, just in case, so they could find a back-up if their offer fell through. The other houses were nice, but they couldn't compare.

That evening, the owner came back with a counter offer. The deal was on if they would close before the end of October. They agreed, and by the weekend Cynthia and Philip were the soon-to-be owners of a house on St. Simons Island.

❦

Philip and Cynthia spent the morning of the next day with Brad signing papers before going back to Atlanta. They hadn't told anyone their news yet, since it was still sinking in.

Now that the move was a reality, Cynthia was getting excited and thinking about how she would decorate the beach house and the little apartment. She couldn't wait until her mother and Granny saw it.

They had been back in Atlanta for about two hours when Cynthia's cell phone rang, and she saw it was Jimmy. That was odd.

"Hi, Jimmy," Cynthia said, a little apprehensive.

"Mrs. Lewis," Jimmy said in a tone that alarmed Cynthia. "Millie needs you. We're at the hospital… something is wrong with the baby."

Cynthia dropped into a chair; the blood felt like it had drained out of her.

"What do you mean? Is Millie okay? Did she fall or have an accident or something? What's wrong with the baby?" Cynthia fired questions at Jimmy one right after the other.

"I don't know the answer to any of your questions. She went to the doctor today, and the doctor said the heartbeat couldn't be found, so she sent her to the hospital. They still can't find a heartbeat."

This wasn't good. Poor Millie. The fear and confusion she must be experiencing. Cynthia didn't want to think about. Her little girl.

"Mrs. Lewis, I need you, too."

Cynthia was stunned by Jimmy's request.

"Yes, of course, Jimmy. Let me get Philip, and we'll be on our way to the hospital as soon as we can. Call me if you get any more information, okay?"

"Yes, ma'am," Jimmy replied.

She hung up the phone, found Philip, and explained. They were back in the car thirty minutes later.

Jimmy called when they were fifteen minutes away, sobbing. Millie lost the baby.

It was a little girl.

❦

Philip dropped Cynthia off at the front door of the hospital so she could go in while he parked the car.

She found the waiting room, her eyes resting on Jimmy, who was sitting by himself, looking out a window into darkness. She stopped. Her disdain for him abruptly vanished as if something pulled it out of her chest. She felt nothing but tenderness as she compassionately observed the face she saw reflected in the window. She believed she was witnessing the evolution of Jimmy Skidmore from a boy to a man. His face had changed from one of a goofy-looking kid to one of dependability and strength. After a moment's hesitation, she found her voice. "Jimmy, have you heard anymore? Is she okay?"

Jimmy turned when he heard Cynthia, hurrying over to wrap his arms around her.

"I love her so much, Mrs. Lewis. I can't stand to know she's in pain. The baby was a girl. A little girl," he sobbed into Cynthia's shoulder as Philip walked in.

"Is Millie okay?" Philip asked with alarm.

"I believe so," Cynthia responded as she rubbed Jimmy's back.

After getting Jimmy calmed down, he relayed the story.

Millie hadn't been feeling well. She had a doctor's appointment the next day with Dr. Rosewood and felt she would talk to her about it then. Although Millie felt the baby moving frequently, it was not unusual for the growing child inside her to be quiet for a day, but when she saw Dr. Rosewood, the first question the doctor asked was about the baby's movement. The doctor could find no heartbeat. Millie called Jimmy, and they came to the hospital where an ultrasound was performed, determining the baby had died in the womb. Dr. Rosewood said they would do an autopsy and tests to establish if it could have been genetic, but in most cases, things like this happened because the fetus was not developing as it should. Millie would have to deliver the baby.

Jimmy said, "It was the hardest thing I have ever experienced. I sat there holding her hand the whole time. She cried out in pain as each contraction waved over her body. It seemed so cruel to go through the delivery, but the doctor said there was no other way."

The look on his face said more than words, Cynthia thought. Poor Millie, having labor induced to deliver a child she would never care for, nurture, and watch grow into adulthood.

"There wasn't a sound in the room when the baby came out. I'll never forget it. It was the longest silence I think I've ever experienced," Jimmy said, looking straight ahead and not focusing on anything. "The nurse took the baby aside and cleaned her up, wrapping her in a pink blanket and then asked if we were ready to see her. I wasn't sure I did, but Millie said yes right away. We held the baby; she was so tiny. Millie's resting now. They gave her a mild sedative to help her relax. I decided to wait here for you so I could explain without Millie hearing."

Cynthia was trying to let all Jimmy had told them sink in. It was too much, too fast.

"The baby is in the room with Millie. All Millie has been talking about is when you're going to get here. She needs her mom."

Cynthia felt a wave of anxiety pass over her. Oh, Millie. As a nurse, she had seen plenty of death, but not like this. Her own sweet little granddaughter. The thought was unbearable, and she started to cry. Jimmy held her hand and met her eyes, his also overflowing with unrestrained tears.

"You are our strength," Jimmy said.

There it was again. *I don't want this job anymore.* The thought stunned her.

"Okay," was all she could say.

Jimmy led Cynthia and Philip to the labor and delivery room where Millie was. When they entered the room, Cynthia saw her daughter lying in the hospital bed looking so small.

Millie stirred, raising her head and looking at each of them, finally sobbing at the sight of her mother. Cynthia took her in her arms, stroking Millie's hair and face ever so tenderly. A new mother always needed mothering herself, and even though Millie was not taking a baby home, she was a mother to this little soul who only briefly lived inside her. Cynthia never experienced a miscarriage, but she could feel her daughter's unbearable pain as if it were her own.

"Mom, I'm so glad you're here. My baby... what am I going to do? I feel so empty. We were just getting to know each other, and she's gone — why, Mom, why?"

Cynthia didn't know why.

"Darling, we never know." It was all Cynthia could think to say.

Philip walked over, kissed Millie on the forehead, and held

her hand, unable to utter a word. They looked at each other through their tears. Philip finally said, "I love you, Princess," a name he hadn't called her since she was a little girl.

Cynthia crawled in bed next to Millie and held her against her chest while Millie cried like a wounded animal, her pain tearing at Cynthia's heart. It was good for Millie to get it all out, painful as it was.

A nurse came in to see how Millie was doing. Millie asked her if she could have the baby, the nurse handing her over to her ever so tenderly.

Millie was so peaceful, as she looked into the little face. This little angel had a piece of all of them in her. How amazing. It was the strangest yet most natural thing at the same time. Millie opened the blanket to look at the body of her child. She was so beautiful in the way she was perfectly formed, just in miniature. The tiny face looked a little like Philip's.

Cynthia reached out and touched first the baby's head, cheek, and then hand. The little feet were so small as she took them in each of her palms. She loved this child she would never know with all her heart. She stifled a sob.

Millie held the baby against her breast, rocking her slightly as silent tears rolled down her cheeks. Cynthia marveled at how a woman always automatically rocks a child.

Philip and Jimmy had to leave the room. They couldn't handle it.

After some time, Millie asked Cynthia to put the baby back in the bassinet. Cynthia obliged, while Millie never took her eyes off of the little bundle.

"Why, Mom, why?" she asked again, looking like a little child, herself. Cynthia had no answer, so she lay next to her in bed, holding Millie until she fell into an exhausted sleep. Cynthia then slipped out to find Jimmy and Philip.

Walking to the waiting room, she felt so many emotions surging through her that she had never experienced before.

Jimmy and Philip stood up when she entered the room.

"It's going to be okay. Just give her time. Oh, Jimmy, where are your parents?"

"They're out of town, Mrs. Lewis. Won't be back for three days."

"Well, then I think you and Millie need to come home with us, and I think it's time you call us Cynthia and Philip."

"I was hoping you would want us to come home with you. I'm so worried about Millie… Cynthia." He looked at her and then Philip.

Things would be okay in time.

Millie spent the night in the hospital, Jimmy staying with her. Cynthia and Philip got a motel room, and the next day Millie and Jimmy came home with them. Jimmy went back to school a day later, Millie following two days later. She insisted she didn't want to miss school. *She's such a strong young woman*, Cynthia thought.

❧

The month of September was over before it started. Millie and Jimmy were mourning the loss of their baby, deciding to continue living with Jimmy's parents until they graduated. Cynthia thought this was a good idea since Millie would still experience some sad days and she knew Melanie had an eye on her. Melanie was a very sweet person, and after she and Cynthia talked about the lost baby, Cynthia knew Millie would be loved and in good hands with her.

CHAPTER 17

*C*ynthia hadn't seen Christopher since the day they dropped him off at college, so she couldn't wait for fall break. On the day of his arrival, she spent the morning in the kitchen, cooking up all his favorites.

Unfortunately for him, once arriving home, he'd be put to work sorting through his room and packing up what he could for the move.

The weekend after Christopher left, Cynthia was having a big yard sale to get rid of what she could. What didn't sell was going to charity.

Bittersweet as it was, two weeks earlier she quit her job at the hospital so she could dedicate more time to the move. She'd worked there ten years and loved what she did every day. Her plan was to look for a job at the Brunswick hospital intensive care unit after the first of the year to give herself some time to get settled in the house. She had already sent her resume, hoping for word of an interview after they moved in, since she knew it may take a while to get the type of job she wanted.

Although she didn't want to, she decided it would be better for her to postpone starting on her master's until after they were settled. She expected her life on the island to be slower, thinking it might be better for her to start school after she became used to her new job.

Cynthia heard the familiar Honda pull into the driveway.

The door opened, and Christopher walked in, carrying a suitcase and a laundry bag. In the two months since Cynthia had seen him, he'd changed. He looked different. More manly and confident.

"Mom!" Christopher came to her and picked her up in a bear hug. "What's there to eat?"

Now *that* was the familiar kid she knew.

"I have some homemade chocolate chip cookies in the jar, some leftovers in the fridge, and I'm making Grandma's chili and fresh bread for supper," she said.

Christopher took a deep breath and sighed, "It's so good to be home. Hey, can I do my laundry?" Without waiting for a response he went galloping up the stairs, just like old times.

❦

Philip and Christopher went the next day to have some fun at the batting cage while Cynthia stayed home to pack. She didn't mind being alone because she was able to get so much more done.

While packing, she thought about this time last year when she was planning Philip's birthday party, never imagining that a year later, they'd be headed to St. Simons. Philip's birthday was two days before the move. *Happy birthday*, she thought and smiled.

It was kind of nice going through all their belongings alone. Some of the stuff she came across was hard to settle on whether to keep or not, so she decided she'd pack it up to go through later when there was more time and she wasn't in such a nostalgic mood.

She had taken two trips to the island since their offer was accepted on the house. The beach house was empty, so Brad let her go in to measure and take pictures, which helped her decide what furniture to keep and what to get rid of. She really loved the place and couldn't wait for the move.

Philip would start his new job on November 1, giving him a little time to settle in. He seemed so happy about moving and a little more relaxed. She guessed his new job wouldn't be as high-pressure, so hopefully he wouldn't have as many late hours and as much stress.

The guys said they would be home around five, and it was already four thirty, so she stopped to have a quiet cup of tea before they came home. *It's weird seeing all the boxes stacked around the house*, she thought, as she peacefully sipped her tea and nibbled on a cookie.

True to their word, the guys were home at 5:02, breaking the silence in the house. Philip went immediately upstairs, saying something about a phone call, and Christopher began digging through the fridge.

"Oh yeah, Mom, remember how you told me to tell you if I saw that woman I thought you and Dad were friends with? You know the one?"

Cynthia's heart raced. She had put thoughts of the woman aside, but it was hard to do so now. "Yes, what about her?" she asked.

"She was at Taco Mac today where Dad and I had lunch. Dad spoke to her while I was eating. I thought he was probably telling her about you guys moving. When I asked him who she was, he said she was a client, so I guess you don't know her."

"Are you sure she was the woman you had seen before? She may have just looked like her."

"No, I'm sure it was the same woman. She was kind of good looking. I'd remember."

Later, Cynthia had to bring it up with Philip. "Christopher mentioned you talking to a woman at lunch. Someone he's seen you talk to before. Who was it?"

He looked surprised and hesitated, "Oh, just a client. I

told him that. Why would he tell you about her?"

"He's mentioned before seeing you talk to her, and I was wondering who it was."

"I hope you're not thinking again there's someone other than you in my life? We're starting this major change in our life on St. Simons. I've said it before, there's only you." He came over and kissed her.

She felt better and silly she'd even brought it up.

❧

Philip headed out of the garage with a few bags of trash. He couldn't believe that Christopher had told Cynthia about the woman. He was so close to solving his problem. He needed to relax. Soon, she would be off his back, and he and Cynthia would be starting a new life with nothing hanging over them.

After dumping the trash in the bin, he went to the deck and sat in a chair to think before he went back in the house.

Things always seem the worst before the end, he thought. A few more weeks and it would be history. He couldn't wait to put it all behind him.

❧

With fall break ended and Christopher back at college, the last few weeks were upon them to tie up the loose ends.

Their friends, Ron and Sandra, gave them a going away party at Joe D's. It was a chance to say goodbye to all their friends and invite them to visit down on St. Simons Island.

They quietly celebrated Philip's birthday on Sunday, which was fine with him since he said he wasn't counting them anymore.

The next few days were spent getting all the boxes and furniture ready for the movers so everything would be out before the closing and on its way to St. Simons.

The closing process would be like a well-rehearsed

football play, according to Philip. They would intercept the funds on the Atlanta home, make a deposit touchdown in the bank with the proceeds, and wait for the first down on St. Simons. Finally, the week was upon them.

On Wednesday afternoon, they were sitting in an Atlanta attorney's office with the Ohio couple who was purchasing their home. They reminded Cynthia of herself and Philip when they'd first moved to Atlanta. Truth be told, she'd love to do it all over again. They shook hands with the couple, wishing them luck and took the check to the bank in preparation for their closing on Friday.

The moving truck had headed down to the island with all their things the day before. Cynthia didn't want to think about it. According to the men driving the truck, they would make several stops along the way, dropping off and picking up other loads. She wondered what would happen if the men gave their things to someone else by accident. Philip said that's why they had insurance, but it didn't make her feel any better. Some things were too precious for insurance to cover.

Since they had no home at the moment and a couple of suitcases between them, they decided to stay at the Jekyll Island Club Hotel until they closed. It was where it all had started, after all.

The weather was warm — Cynthia felt as if the islands were welcoming them. They spent Wednesday walking the Jekyll Island beach and renting bikes to explore the nature trails. Thursday, they took the bridge over to Brunswick and the causeway to St. Simons to do a little exploring. Philip seemed to know where he was going, but she was totally lost. Give her a month, and she'd have the island memorized, she told herself.

"We're so predictable," she told Philip when they pulled into a parking place down Mallery St. and went for lunch at Barbara Jean's. After lunch, they walked through the shops and went to the Dairy Queen for an ice cream before stopping by Brad's office to see if all was okay for the next day. He assured them it was.

Just for fun, they ended the day by walking the beach in front of their new house, thinking that tomorrow they would no longer be tourists but residents of this island.

⚘

Cynthia was alone in the fog as if floating, yet stable. Soon the wind picked up, and debris was flying around her. She realized she was on the beach with only one blurred figure in a storm.

Soon Philip appeared, yelling to her but inaudible because of the storm. He motioned her to follow him, which she did, the blurred figure trailing at a distance behind her.

Philip led her to the front of their new beach house. The storm grew, and like in The Wizard of Oz, *their house was picked up whole and whisked away, leaving the beachfront empty.*

Soon the clouds evaporated, and the sun came out. Philip and the blurred figure had disappeared, and she was all alone on the desolate beach with the sand blowing around her feet.

She woke up with a start, her heart beating quickly, sweat covering her body. The dream was still real in her mind. All the change and stress had put her imagination in overload, her excitement getting the best of her. She rolled over, slipping back to sleep and thinking that tomorrow, after the closing, everything would finally be done.

⚘

"Philip, the truck just pulled in," Cynthia yelled to Philip, as excited as when they'd bought their first home.

"Whoa, that's a tight squeeze. I sure hope these guys know what they're doing," Philip said.

It appeared they did or else they were just lucky, because they backed right up to the door without a scratch. The men opened the doors on the back of the truck, pulled out a ramp, and started unloading into the house immediately. By the end of the morning, just as the last box came in the house, the rain started coming down. What timing, Cynthia thought. Today was their day.

Now they had the next task of opening boxes and finding a home for their belongings.

"Philip, I'm going to start on the kitchen since we'll need it the most. How about you? What do you want to start with?" she asked.

"I think I'll try to move all this furniture to where we want it and then start on boxes in here if that sounds okay?"

"Sure," she told him, and they got to work.

She had picked up some fruit, cheese and crackers, and other items to munch on if they became hungry. In one of the boxes, she found a plate and fixed them a snack after working a couple of hours. Philip was in the living area cutting open a box labeled television cords at the moment. Her priority was the kitchen; his was the entertainment. It made her laugh.

"Great. I was getting hungry. I actually could use a rest. I must be getting old," he looked at Cynthia and they both laughed.

He placed a winged-back chair and ottoman in front of the huge glass windows framing the view of the water. It was beautiful. Cynthia pulled up another chair, and they ate, talking about all the plans they had for their new life. It was fun to be at this time of their life knowing they made it through all the rough stuff together.

"I think I'm going to take a little power nap if you don't mind. I'll be all the more energetic when I wake up," he said and winked at her.

She walked over and gave him a passionate kiss on the lips. "How long should I let you nap?" she asked.

"Oh let's say about thirty minutes max."

"All right. I'm going to continue with the kitchen. Since the refrigerator is up and running, let's plan on stopping by the grocery store after we get some supper out tonight so we have something to eat around here." She went back to the kitchen.

She lost track of time and realized after an hour passed she should go wake Philip. There he was, sleeping like a baby. She was afraid they were both getting old, because she was tired, too.

Leaning over him, she ran her fingers through his hair and kissed his forehead.

"Sweetheart, time to wake up. We've lots more to do." There was no response.

Smiling, she kissed him again and said in a playful voice, "Philip, wake up." Nothing.

She shook him a little, but he was like a rag doll. His chest had no apparent rise and fall, and his face looked ashen. Her hand went to his neck, where she felt a faint pulse.

Immediately, she pulled him to the floor and started CPR. Never did she think she would be doing this to her own husband.

After numerous attempts of blowing air into his mouth and pumping his chest with no apparent response, she knew she needed help, so she called for an ambulance while continuing with CPR until the paramedics arrived and took over.

"Could you tell me what happened, ma'am?" one of the paramedics asked while the others continued the CPR, prepping Philip for travel to the hospital.

"We moved in today and were starting to unpack some boxes when he wanted to rest. I was in the kitchen and came to wake him up, and this is what I found," she responded, eyes never leaving Philip.

"You did a great job on the CPR. Have you done it before?" he asked.

"Yes, I'm a ICU nurse — well, I was. I'll be looking for a job here when we're settled," she said, knowing what he was doing. He was trying to keep her calm. She did it herself all the time.

"We have to get him stable for travel and then to the hospital. Looks like he may have had a heart attack. Your CPR helped. We'll know exactly what happened when we get to the hospital."

In minutes or seconds, she could hardly tell, they were wheeling him out to the ambulance.

"Would you like to ride with us or drive yourself? Is there a neighbor or someone you could call to take you or ride with you to the hospital?" the young man asked.

She thought for a moment. She had no one to call and would have to get back home, "No. I'll drive myself," she decided.

❧

Somehow, she found her way and parked by the ER. Someone met her as she entered the hospital, took the insurance information, and ushered her into a small private waiting room. She didn't like that. After all, she was a nurse and knew a small waiting room meant bad news. Soon, a doctor arrived and introduced himself as Dr. Carroll.

"Mrs. Lewis, are you here alone?" he asked.

"Yes. My husband and I were moving into our new house today. We just moved here from Atlanta. Dr. Carroll, I'm a ICU nurse. What's going on?"

"Mrs. Lewis" the doctor's head went down and then up to look her in the eyes, "I'm sorry to have to tell you this, but your husband had a massive heart attack," Dr. Carroll said slowly with feeling. "Thanks to your efforts, we were able to keep him with us for the trip here, but it was too severe an attack. I am so sorry but we couldn't save him," the doctor never lost eye-contact with her. "Is there anyone we can call for you?"

Cynthia sat in a daze, not believing what she heard. "No. There's no one." They sat in silence a few minutes. Not a tear came out. Nothing on the outside, but her heart was screaming inside her chest. "No, God, no. Take this away from me... turn back time... I'm not strong enough... what will I do? Oh please, God, not me... not me."

The doctor went on talking, but she didn't hear a word.

"Mrs. Lewis? Do you have any questions?"

She shook her head.

"Do you want to see him?" the doctor asked.

Cynthia shook her head up and down to signal yes. Her throat was closed up, and she couldn't utter a word.

She waited about fifteen minutes when she heard, "Mrs. Lewis," and looked up to see a nurse in front of her. "I'm Lisa, and I'll take you to see your husband if you're ready?"

Again, her voice wouldn't come out so she just nodded.

She followed the nurse out of the little room into a brightly lit hallway with sterile white walls. She looked down and oddly saw what appeared to be a vaguely familiar tile pattern of white, light blue, and yellow tiles on the floor. She kept her head down and followed the nurse.

They stopped outside an ER examining room. "Your husband is in here. If you're ready, I'll take you in, but if not, we can wait until you are."

Somehow, Cynthia found her voice. "No, I'm ready."

They walked in, and the nurse pulled open the curtain hiding Philip. There was her husband, the man she loved. He looked like he was still asleep.

"Thank you, Lisa. You have been most kind. I'm going to sit here and — " she paused again, trying to find her voice, "and just sit here." Tears started rolling down her cheeks, but there was no sound or feeling in them as if her body knew she needed to let something out, whether she was willing or not.

For a good while, she stood next to her husband, studying his face. The thick dark hair touched by grey, his high cheekbones, angular nose, determined lips, and strong chiseled jaw were so familiar to her.

She leaned over and ran her fingers through his hair, as she remembered doing earlier when trying to wake him. His face was bristly from an emerging mid-day beard. She touched his nose and ran one finger across his lips, noticing one of her tears on his cheek. She leaned over further, kissing him on the lips, then leaned back thinking how cold and unfeeling it all was. He'd been such an engaging and passionate man. This was so unnatural.

She sat down in the chair next and closed her eyes, starting to pray.

Dear God, you know what's in my heart right now. I'm not sure myself, but you always know. Why have you taken him away from me now? Have I done something to anger you? What do you want me to do now? I need you to guide me. I don't feel you at all. What do I do now?

Then it started. The sobs burst from her, and she couldn't stop. Lisa came in and put her arms around her. Cynthia leaned into her. She needed human touch so badly.

She was not sure how long Lisa's arms were around her, but the sobs stopped when the kids came to her mind. She couldn't call them yet, because she didn't know what to say. She needed to get strong for them first.

Poor Millie just losing the baby and now her dad. Christopher away from home on his own the first time in his life. Now the burden he would feel about being the man for her. She wouldn't let it happen. She would be strong. She had no choice.

It was late and had been raining steady. She knew she needed to leave so she could find her way to the house. Thank God for the GPS system on her phone. Her phone. She'd left it at the house. She felt so lost in so many ways at the moment.

Fortunately, Lisa lived on the island and was able to give her directions to her house. Cynthia was dreading going back there. This was not the big plans they had for their new life. She now was all alone on an island where she didn't know how to get around, had no job, no husband, and no friends.

With only what could be the grace of God, she left Philip at the hospital, walking through the ER doors alone to a new life. Not the new life she'd been planning for the past several months. Instead, she was starting a life she didn't ask for or want but would somehow have to live.

CHAPTER 18

The hymns had been sung, the scripture read, and friends had shared their anecdotes at Philip Michael Lewis's "celebration of life." The minister said "celebration of life" way too many times. Cynthia was mourning, not celebrating. She sat in disbelief during the service.

Her heart felt as if it was being ripped out of her chest, but she was unable to acknowledge the pain deep inside. Where was God? Why did He let this happen? How could this be part of His plan for her? Philip had so much life in him. Oh, she hurt so badly.

Once the service was over, the family walked down the aisle and out of the church to a room, her mother standing on one side of her, Millie on the other, each holding one of her hands, periodically giving her a hug, squeezing the hand they were holding, and speaking words she didn't hear.

Looking at Millie made her want to cry, but she didn't. She hadn't cried since the night Philip died.

Her mind drifted to that night when she'd wandered into a barbeque restaurant. At the time she told herself she needed to get something to eat, but mostly she wanted to run away from the reality hitting her in the face and what was supposed to have been her new life. That was where she met the woman who reminded her of an angel. What was the name of the restaurant? She couldn't remember, but the woman's name was Betty. Betty had taken her angel wings and wrapped them around her that night with love. She would never forget the woman.

Her mother was talking to her, but she tuned it out. Cynthia felt as if she were in a fish bowl full of water, one of the inexpensive round ones you put goldfish in. She was the goldfish living in the bowl, only observing, not participating, in the show around her.

They were going to place her at the head of a receiving line so the mourners could make her feel better with their comments on how Philip was a wonderful person and how his life was cut short.

She didn't think she could do it.

Millie and her mother were now talking to each other, Cynthia hearing her name spoken several times. This angered her, knowing she was the topic of their conversation as if she wasn't there. Out of the corner of her eye, she saw a figure emerging, realizing it was Granny's four-foot frame coming straight for her.

"Cynthia. Come, walk with me," Granny said sweetly, taking Cynthia's hand and leading her away, down a deserted hallway.

Off the hallway was an open atrium hidden in the middle of the church. There was a little pond and a columbarium, the final resting place for ashes of church members who had passed away. She would not put Philip's ashes there but keep him with her wherever she was.

She looked at the cross in the atrium, and felt warmth blossoming from the center of her chest. It both startled and calmed her.

Granny led her to a wooden bench in the corner. After sitting for several minutes, holding hands, and watching the fish swim in the pond, Granny broke the silence.

"Cynthia, I know how hard this is. I lost my husband when I was not much older than you. It happens so fast, and there is no time to absorb what is going on, and you're thrown into this 'celebration of life,' when you only want go back in time."

Cynthia looked at her with relief. Granny knew what she was feeling and completely understood.

"These people here today loved Philip, too," she said. "You have to look at it this way: Philip touched these people, and that's why they're here. What a beautiful thing. Whatever gifts God gave Philip were used to make a difference in their lives, and today they want to tell you how that happened. The world is a different place because he was here. Just look at your children."

As if on cue, Christopher stuck his head in the doorway.

"Hey, Mom, the preacher wants to know if you're ready to see people."

What Granny had said sunk in and brought her back to life. Cynthia was making this about herself, and it should be about Philip. Shame on her. She looked at Granny, leaned over, and kissed her on the cheek. "Thank you. I needed to hear that."

She stood up and walked over to the door where Christopher was standing and hugged him.

"I'm ready now," and she went to greet the mourners and celebrate Philip's life.

❦

Cynthia, the children, and the grandmothers stayed at Ron and Sandra's house while they were in Atlanta. What great friends they had always been to them.

Two days after the funeral, Millie, Jimmy, and Christopher headed back to school, as finals were coming up. It was hard for them, but their dad would have told them school was their first responsibility. Cynthia returned to St. Simons with the rest of the family.

Her mother and Granny were returning to Wisconsin the end of the week but would be back for Christmas. Millie said she was coming down to St. Simons for the weekend by herself, since the grandmothers were leaving, just so Cynthia wouldn't be alone. Cynthia was glad for that.

What she was really looking forward to was Purvell coming the following Monday to stay for a week. Purvell had been out of the country and couldn't make the funeral. Cynthia couldn't wait to see her.

At the moment, along with her mother and Granny, she had Philip's sister, husband and their kids and Ron and Sandra staying with her. Cynthia's brother and family weren't able to make the trip from England, since they'd just been there for the wedding in the summer.

They all pitched in and helped Cynthia make a big dent in unpacking the boxes, making the house less overwhelming.

Ron and Sandra were taking her mother and Granny to the airport on Friday when they went back home to Atlanta. Slowly everyone left, going back to their own lives, leaving Cynthia to start her new life alone.

Just before they left, Millie called to say she wasn't going to be able to come down and stay with her for the weekend because of a big project she had assigned that week in one of her classes.

"Will you be okay until Purvell comes on Monday?" Millie asked. Cynthia felt a little bit of panic.

"Of course, I'll be fine," she told Millie, thinking she would have to start somewhere.

Everyone left, and Cynthia was alone for the first time in her life.

❦

So far, so good. It was Saturday night. Cynthia had spent all day getting her house in order and taking a few walks on the beach. Having a lot to do and being in unfamiliar surroundings helped her keep from breaking down. Add to that the fact that she was still in denial.

She'd touched nothing of Philip's. Ron and Philip's brother-in-law had moved his boxes down to the garage under the house until she felt up to going through it, which could likely be never.

In the morning, she made a trip to the grocery store to get a few things and something to fix herself for supper. She decided on chicken.

Though she felt sad and empty, it was good to do some cooking. While the chicken was sizzling in the pan, she put together a salad. In the pantry, she grabbed the ingredients to make a quick vinaigrette dressing as well as a bottle of wine.

After searching through several drawers, she found the corkscrew, and soon the bottle was open.

She went to the cupboard, opened the door, and took down two wine glasses. She'd done it so many times. It hit her like a blow to the stomach. Her knees gave out, and she slid slowly to the kitchen floor, holding on to the two glasses but never taking her eyes from them.

Her ears hummed with a sound she could only describe as pure chaos. She raised the glasses over her head, closed her eyes, and threw them across the room at the wall. They smashed and shattered all around her, just like her life.

What she'd been so carefully protecting came out all at once. There was a feeling of loneliness, disappointment, and anger, gnawing at her soul.

A cry came from deep inside her she hadn't known she was capable of, like the first clap of thunder in the storm. It felt good to be angry. She was lost and scared. Scared to be alone, scared about how she would survive, and yes, still scared that Philip had been seeing another woman. Now, she would never know.

The room was starting to spin. Raising herself slowly from the floor, she walked to the stove where she turned off the sizzling chicken, went to the cupboard again, and took out a large water glass. She grabbed the wine bottle and went into the living room, sitting on the sofa, where she faced the moonlit beach.

She looked up at the mantel of the fireplace where the urn of Philip's ashes sat, hot tears covering her face.

She tipped the wine bottle, till the water glass was half-full and started drinking, tears flowing as the warmth of the drink trailed down her throat. She grabbed the first of many tissues to wipe her eyes and nose as she let the pain finally flow freely. Another half-glass of wine and another, until soon the bottle was empty, just like her heart.

❦

The next morning, the sun shone through the windows, waking her up to a new day.

As she raised herself slowly from the sofa, she shaded her eyes with her hand. The empty wine bottle and pile of used tissues on the floor brought back what had happened last night.

Never before had she done anything like this, but it felt so good.

Her eyes immediately fell to the urn on the mantel.

She chuckled to herself, knowing she had made a small step towards healing. "Good morning, Philip. I hope you enjoyed the show." She walked out of the room, her head pounding.

She went upstairs and took a shower, washing away the night before. While she was brushing her wet hair, she stopped and looked at her image in the mirror. Who was this woman she was looking at? Was she half a person now? Would she ever feel whole again?

She forced herself to think. The way she saw it, there were two choices at present. Stay here, or go back to Atlanta.

She would stay here for the time being. She always had

the option to change her mind in the future if she wanted, but what she needed now was time. Time to put the pieces back together, time to grasp what had happened and time to mourn her loss. It had only been a few weeks since Philip died. Would life ever be good again? She doubted it, but she had to try. She had no other choice.

⚜

Purvell was arriving from New York at the Jacksonville airport on a 1:18 flight. Cynthia parked and went in to wait for Purvell, first checking that the plane was on time. After looking at her watch, Cynthia realized she had about forty-five minutes to wait, so she found a chair outside the concourse.

She watched the people as they scurried here and there. You never knew what was going on in the lives of others. Where were they going? Was it for happy or sad reasons? Business or pleasure?

If an alien wanted to study a good cross-section of Earth in a short period of time, this would be the place. What a gold mine of human diversity. The clothing alone would fill the alien's notebook, not to mention the way people walked, talked, or wore their hair. But the alien couldn't see these people's emotions. No one could see the fact that she was not yet a widow of a month, and inside, pain was tearing her apart.

"Cynthia!"

She looked up, and there was Purvell, calling her name and coming straight for her, arms open. Cynthia cried like a baby with relief as she surrendered into the arms her oldest and dearest friend.

Purvell insisted on driving the car back to St. Simons for the hour-and-a-half trip so Cynthia could tell her everything. They stopped for lunch, so by the time they reached exit 29, it was clear that Purvell's work was cut out for her.

❦

"I love this place," Purvell said as they walked into the beach house. "And you say there's a little apartment below. Oh my God, look at this view." She stood at the window overlooking the beach.

She turned to Cynthia. "This place is amazing. I see why you fell in love with it. You're going to stay, aren't you? Please don't tell me you're thinking about selling it and moving away. The whole island is an escape from the real world, and the history is so interesting. I did a little research of my own before I came. Maybe I need to relocate here and sell real estate," Purvell laughed, but Cynthia thought it would be great.

"I don't know, yet. For now I'm staying, but I don't know if I can afford it by myself. This week while you're here, I thought we could go to Atlanta and meet together with my lawyer and Philip's doctor. I don't want to go alone to see them and would feel good having you by my side. You don't mind, do you?"

"*Mind*. Cynthia, I would mind if you *didn't* want me. You pick the day, and let's stay the night, and maybe we can go shopping. Nothing like a little mall therapy, I always say."

Purvell was just what she needed.

❦

The next morning the two friends packed into Cynthia's car on their way to Atlanta.

Cynthia made an afternoon appointment with the doctor, Tom Kennedy, who was a friend and golfing buddy of Philip's, as well as a later appointment with the attorney. Their plan was to get business done first and then play it by ear since Cynthia didn't know what she could handle, minute to minute.

Driving into Atlanta was strange, to say the least, but

having Purvell sitting next to her and knowing she wouldn't be alone helped so much. Her emotions were so erratic, and she needed a second set of ears.

The women arrived in Atlanta around lunchtime and found a restaurant close to the doctor's office. Her appointment with Tom was at one fifteen, and the lawyer's was at three.

Tom would be going over Philip's autopsy results with her. She was looking forward to their visit, because she needed to find out exactly what had happened.

"I'm a little anxious wondering about what Tom is going to tell me today," Cynthia shared with Purvell as they ate their lunch. "It seemed clear that Philip had a heart attack like his father did."

"It does, but wasn't his father much younger?" Purvell asked.

"Yes, but it does seem a coincidence. I'll find out soon enough, I guess," and they continued their lunch, Purvell changing the subject to where they would go shopping.

Purvell wanted to go shopping at Phipps Plaza and Lenox Mall if Cynthia felt up to it. She had made reservations for them at the Ritz Carlton for the night.

They were in the waiting room only a few minutes when soon the nurse called her name and led them to Tom's office. Tom was sitting at his desk. He jumped up to hug and kiss Cynthia on the cheek.

"Tom, this is my best friend, Purvell. She flew down from New York City to be with me for a while. We have an appointment with the lawyer later, so I thought an extra set of ears would be good for both visits."

"Cynthia, have a seat. It's so good to see you and a pleasure to meet you, Purvell." He shook Purvell's hand and showed the ladies to a small sofa in his office.

After a few minutes more of chit-chat, Tom got to the point.

"It disturbs me that Philip never went to the cardiologist I referred him to. I explained to him that it was important for us to see what was going on."

Cynthia was shocked. "What are you talking about, Tom? Philip never mentioned anything to me about a cardiologist. I would've made sure he'd gone."

Tom looked puzzled and stared at Cynthia blankly. "You mean he never told you about my recommendation after his physical? He came in saying he'd been more tired than usual, and I recommended some extra tests and an EKG. The EKG showed a slight abnormality. Combined with the fact his dad and grandfather died young, I felt it necessary for him to have a full cardiac work-up. I suspected something called Brugada Syndrome. It runs in families and usually effects men who appear in perfect health. They drop dead of a heart attack for no apparent reason. I thought everything must be fine when I never received any report from the cardiologist, and Philip never said a word."

"Why wouldn't he have gone? I'm stunned by what you've told me." Cynthia felt ill and faint. Her stomach churned.

Purvell put her arm around Cynthia and took over the questions.

"You mean Philip had an idea something was wrong and ignored it?"

"No, I recommended more tests to confirm or discredit what I considered a possibility. I was very insistent with him about getting it checked out. Maybe with the wedding and move, he pushed it to the back burner. According to the autopsy, it appears he died from what I suspected. Your son should get checked out, since it runs in families. Philip definitely had a history."

"Could you have prevented what happened, Tom?" Cynthia feebly asked.

"If diagnosed, yes, we would have given him a pacemaker, and he could have lived a fairly normal life."

Cynthia was at a loss. Had Philip followed through, he would be alive right now. And why didn't he tell her? She was a nurse. It wasn't like she wouldn't understand. Her emotions went back and forth from devastation to anger. His physical had been months ago, with plenty of time to get what Tom was telling her checked out.

Tom continued to recite facts about Brugada syndrome, answering their questions for another twenty minutes, when he finally said, "Listen, you ladies can sit here in my office as long as you want. I'll have my nurse check to see if you have any more questions for me before you leave." He rose to his feet, leaned over, hugged and kissed Cynthia on her cheek, and looked intently in her eyes. "Call me anytime for anything. Phil was a great guy and a close friend. He will be sorely missed by all. Purvell, it was nice to meet you, and I'm so glad you could be here with Cynthia." He left the room.

They sat for a minute or two talking and decided they had no more questions, so they thanked the nurse and left.

Since they had an hour before the meeting with Cynthia's lawyer, they found a little coffee shop where they could kill some time.

"Purvell, why wouldn't Philip have told me about this? I don't understand."

"Well, you know how it can be when you're so busy. You lose track of time. He probably meant to do it and kept pushing it off until the next week. You told me how distracted and overworked he was. Did you ever resolve the thing about the other woman?" she asked hesitantly.

"I guess. I took his word for it. I mean, after all, why would he move if there was another woman? Other than his late hours, strange phone calls, being stressed out, and the woman who Christopher seemed to see when he was with his dad on occasion, Philip was fine with me."

She hesitated, realizing the words she'd just uttered didn't sound resolving, "I don't want to talk about it now. I have enough on my mind at the moment. We can talk about it later," Cynthia replied.

Cynthia could barely drink her coffee. She wasn't looking forward to telling the kids this latest piece of news. Philip's grandfather, father, and now him. And the effect it could have on Christopher since it appeared to be hereditary. She was so angry that Philip had neglected a simple visit to a doctor.

They left the coffee shop for the attorney's office.

Cynthia had always left the managing of their money in Philip's hands, since he was the investment banker and had all the knowledge. He never really encouraged her interest, and when she asked, he told her not to worry, because he had it under control. Now she wished maybe on occasion she would have taken a look to know what was going on. She considered herself a modern woman, but her lack of knowledge in their finances was embarrassing. When she'd made the appointment, their lawyer, George, had offered his condolences but had an edge in his voice that puzzled Cynthia. She would find out shortly.

George's office was on Peachtree St. in an office building on the third floor. The receptionist greeted her with condolences and said George would be out shortly. Why was Cynthia so uneasy about this meeting?

Not only was George their lawyer, but he'd done their taxes for years.

"Cynthia, it's always good to see you but not under these circumstances. I can't tell you how sorry I am, and I want to do whatever I can to help." George said. He next looked at Purvell. "And is this your sister?"

The women laughed. "No, George, it's my friend, Purvell. She's here for moral support." Purvell took Cynthia's hand.

"Well, come in, ladies, and have a seat."

George walked behind his desk and waited until both women had taken their seats. He then pulled out a thick folder and looked up at Purvell and then Cynthia.

"I'm guessing since you've brought Purvell, I'm free to give out any information concerning wills and financial figures?"

"Yes, George, anything at all," Cynthia replied.

"According to your wills, you and Philip were the survivors of each other's estates. I have filed all the papers with the county and requested copies of the death certificate and letters of testamentary for you. Nothing complicated there." He paused, paging through some of the papers but never looking up. He coughed a few times, as if he were delaying his next sentence.

Cynthia looked over casually at Purvell and caught her eye. Purvell gave her a look of apprehension. She looked back at George and waited.

"What is it, George? There's obviously something you don't want to tell me."

He looked up and spoke. "Your will gives me permission as the attorney handling Philip's estate to request bank and investment statements to help settle things. The stocks seem to be fine, but some of the investments are a little bit more risky then I would have expected from Philip. You'll probably want to get someone you feel comfortable with to go over and take care of that now. It's the personal bank accounts," he paused again. "You just sold a house and bought a new one, so I expected to see a clean wash between the two, but Philip had a separate account that some of the proceeds from your home went into after the sale. A loan was taken out for the new house in the amount of $800,000."

"We planned on using the proceeds of the old house to pay for most of the new house. We were still going to have a small mortgage," she quickly told George.

"That's not a small mortgage, and there is only $50,000 left in that account, with no trace of the rest."

For the second time that day, Cynthia felt sick. Where was their money from the house sale? What had Philip done? She thought about her fears of another woman.

She couldn't believe it was that. Surely George had missed something.

Somehow, she found her voice. "So how can we trace where the money went? I thought we were to clear about $500,000 or more when all was said and done," she said, as calmly as she could.

"You'll have to meet with the closing attorney on your house to find out where it went. They won't talk to me, only you."

Again, a long silence.

"Have you thought about whether you would stay on St. Simons or not? Maybe you'll come back to Atlanta."

"No. I'm staying on the island," she said with determination.

Purvell leaned over and squeezed her hand. "Sweetie, there has to be a reasonable explanation for this. I bet he put it into some stocks or other investments to make some money."

"I talked to some of his financial buddies, and they all said he hadn't mentioned anything. They also said he hadn't been himself," George volunteered very reluctantly. "Very on edge."

"The bank had him working a lot of late hours..." she trailed off.

She had to get out of there to think. George was sitting behind his desk looking at her with sad pathetic eyes. She wouldn't have it. She would take charge.

"George, I appreciate all you've done for us. I believe I have some work to do figuring out what's going on." She stood up, Purvell following her lead. She extended her hand, George taking it in his shaking hers and then Purvell's. "I'll let you know what I find out." And they were out the door.

"Purvell, you're going to have to drive. I want to go back to the island."

"I understand," was all Purvell said.

On the five-hour drive back to the island, they talked about her suspicion of another woman. She filled Purvell in on Christopher and Arthur's reports, what she'd seen at the mall, the phone calls, and Philip's late hours. "Purvell, I thought I knew him so well."

"You just need to call the closing attorney. There's no use in getting worked up over this until you have all the facts." Purvell's advised. "There's probably a simple explanation."

So the next day, Cynthia made the phone call to the closing attorney. He was out of town for a week and would have to call her back. She was so glad Purvell was there for her to lean on.

CHAPTER 19

*I*t's already Friday, Purvell is leaving on Monday evening, and then I will be alone again, Cynthia contemplated as she drove her car back home from the grocery store.

Purvell's visit had been quite eventful, she thought, as her mind drifted to the meeting with George. She would have to wait till the closing attorney arrived back in town to get some answers.

Was Philip living in a world she wasn't aware of? There were many signs indicating the possibility. Did she willingly look the other way so she wouldn't have to deal with it? Why wasn't she more persistent with her doubts? All this could possibly have turned out differently.

The next surprise of the week was the call she received from the Southeast Georgia Health System. She sent a resume to them before they moved. While she and Purvell were drinking wine on the deck her cell phone rang.

"Hello."

"Hi. Is this Cynthia Lewis?"

"Yes. What can I do for you?"

"I'm Alice Perkins from the Southeast Georgia Health System human resources department," the woman said in her deep southern drawl. "We understand you're looking for a position in ICU, is that still correct?"

"Why, yes," she said automatically. Was she really still looking with everything else going on?

"We'd love to schedule an interview with you next week, Tuesday at ten a.m. with the ICU nurse manager Jackson Irwin. There are some opportunities coming up, and after looking over your resume, we'd love to meet with you," the woman went on. "Will Tuesday work?"

She was dumbfounded, but she managed to say yes.

"Great. I'll email you directions and some other forms to the address in your resume. See you on Tuesday," she said, hanging up.

Cynthia held the silent phone to her ear, not saying a word until Purvell spoke.

"Is everything okay?"

Cynthia slowly turned to her. "It was the hospital I'd hoped to get a job at. They want me to come interview next week. Do I want to work?"

"Sweetheart, let's talk about this. From what the lawyer said, I think you'll need the money, and what are you going to do all day? Yes, you need to mourn, but what better way than to help others? I say, go for it. You'll start making friends, and I know this is the last thing you are thinking of, but I'm your best friend, and I can say it. You may even find love again."

Love again? It was the last thing on her mind.

Distracted by her thoughts, as she pulled into her driveway, Cynthia resigned herself to the fact that Purvell was right. She would take whatever job the hospital offered her.

She'd been so preoccupied going over the events of the week, she hadn't even noticed the car parked in her driveway. It was Christopher's Honda.

"What are you doing here?" she asked as he came to greet her.

"I didn't have any big plans for the weekend and wanted to see Purvell," Christopher said, looking down at his feet,

"I really wanted to see you, Mom, and make sure you were okay," Christopher told her.

She started to cry as Christopher put his strong arms around her.

On Saturday morning, the doorbell rang. Cynthia opened it to find the woman who had been so kind to her at the barbeque restaurant the night Philip died, holding what looked like homemade cinnamon buns.

The woman smiled and said, "Hey, remember me? Betty."

Remember her? Cynthia would never forget this woman who'd brought her back from the brink of anguish only a few weeks ago.

"Yes. How did you find me?"

"Well, you know, it's not that big of an island, and most folks come to our restaurant, well, they talk. I listen a lot. Just wanted to make sure you were okay. Felt I needed to come see you today," said Betty. She was all dressed in white like the night Cynthia had met her.

"Come in, won't you? I have a friend visiting me, and my son, Christopher, is here for the weekend. He goes to college in Charlotte. I'd love for them to meet you."

"How nice," Betty said. "I would love to meet them, too."

Betty followed her into the kitchen where the aforementioned duo was laughing hysterically, only snapping into control when they realized there was company.

"Oh, please, don't let me cause you to stop. Laughter is the best medicine," Betty told them. "I'm Betty Franklin, a friend of your mom's." She extended her hand to Christopher.

Purvell walked forward and took Betty's hand. "Hi, I'm Purvell Whitlock, Betty. I'm so glad Cynthia has a friend here. I'll be able to go back to New York feeling so much better."

Betty smiled. "We met the night her husband died."

There was silence for about five seconds until Christopher

piped in. "Hey, Betty, what's that in your hands?"

"Oh, I made some cinnamon rolls for y'all. Do you like them?"

"Like 'em… I love them," Christopher responded, taking the plate.

"Hey, Purvell and I want at least one," Cynthia told him with a laugh.

"I know how it is. I have two sons that eat us out of house and home. Good thing my husband and I have a restaurant," Betty said with a chuckle and toss of her head.

"How about a cup of coffee, Betty?" Purvell asked.

"Don't mind if I do. I have to be to the restaurant by noon but would enjoy a little relaxation and company before I go."

"Let's sit and have one of those rolls with our coffee," Cynthia said as she led them to the kitchen table.

"Have you and your husband always lived in this area, Betty?" Purvell asked.

"I have my whole life, but Jack hasn't. I met Jack when he was seventeen and I was fifteen at church youth group in Brunswick where we lived. I was born in Brunswick, but Jack and his family moved there a year before we met. His dad worked in one of the mills on the water. Jack told people that the first time he laid eyes on me, he was in love. My daddy didn't like the fact Jack was paying so much attention to me since Jack was new to the area, but Jack won him over, and when I graduated from high school, Jack asked for permission to propose. My daddy said if I wanted him, it was okay. The rest is history. We opened a barbeque restaurant and have two sons, John and Luke."

"I also have a daughter named Millie who's married," Cynthia told Betty, "She attends Berry College up in Rome and is graduating this May with a degree in business."

"My boys are both majoring in business at the College of Coastal Georgia. Jack wants them to run the restaurant but neither have an interest. They seem to have bigger fish to fry. Jack says he's ready to retire and have them take over. It's a constant argument between the three of them since neither boy wants the restaurant. John is twenty-two and is also graduating in May. He wants to work in a bank, and Luke is twenty-one and wants to be an accountant. Jack, bless his heart, won't hear of it. He's worked his whole life building the restaurant for them, but the boys want to sell it. I try to stay out of it," Betty said, obviously a little sad as she looked off. Cynthia rose to get another cup of coffee and heard the doorbell. She couldn't imagine who else it could be and was going to answer it when Christopher yelled he was getting it. She glanced over at Betty and noticed the way she looked toward the kitchen the door.

Christopher walked in the kitchen with an uncharacteristic look of concern.

"Mom, remember that woman I told you about I saw Dad talking to a couple of times?"

"Yes," she said, hardly understanding why he would bring it up at this moment.

"Well, she's standing at the front door and wants to talk to you."

"What!" Cynthia felt the blood drain from her. "What did she say?"

"Just, 'I would like to speak to Cynthia Lewis'," Christopher said.

Oh my God, she thought. It was true. Another woman.

"Cynthia, I'm here. You don't have to face any of this alone," Purvell told her as she held her arm.

"I'm here, too," Betty said. "I sensed this morning when I woke up that I needed to visit you. I'm like that sometimes."

Cynthia barely heard them. The two women followed behind her as she approached the door and opened it.

There stood a slender attractive woman about five-foot-eight with dirty blonde hair. She looked like she was in her mid-to-late thirties. She wore a hooded velour light pink track suit that pulled across her large, obviously store-bought breasts. Her hair was tied back in a ponytail held by a matching scrunchie. She had a pink Michael Kors handbag slung over her shoulder.

"So, you must be Cynthia," the woman said, looking Cynthia up and down. "I'm Connie Dickson."

"Yes. What can I do for you?"

"Well, first I want to say I'm so sorry about Phil's untimely death. He was a great customer of mine. I made *a lot* of money off him. In fact, he still owes me money. I figure you don't want any trouble, so you can just pay me," she said.

Cynthia was sick. There was another woman. She didn't want to believe it.

Just then Purvell pulled the door open wide and gave the women a threatening look.

"Look, Connie we don't care what 'Phil' was doing with you. How disgusting to approach the widow of someone you were involved with."

"What? Involved with? Seriously? He was a gambler, and I was his bookie. Played cards, the horses, sports games, you name it. You really didn't know? How naive can you get? He was addicted," she laughed more. "He paid me most of it after you sold your house, but he still owes me $100,000, and I'm here to collect, so cough it up. I'm sure he left you some crumbs," she said, her hands on her hips and a smile on her face. The woman was evil.

Now, it was Betty's turn. "Maybe we should call the police and settle this," she said, pulling out her cell phone.

Purvell added, "Philip is dead, and the way I look at it, so are your chances of getting any money. We have no idea if 'Phil' ever owed you anything, and any proof you give us will go straight to the police because we have nothing to lose here."

It was apparent the woman at the front door came to see if she could intimidate Cynthia but hadn't been expecting the army behind her.

"There's no need to call the police. But *you* need to know, your husband was a big-time gambler and had been in deep.

He would call me all times of the day to place bets and panic when he'd lose. Once, he cried like a little girl and asked me to give him some time to pay up, but he couldn't stop. Your loving husband," she laughed, "not the fella you thought he was at all," she said, obviously enjoying the hurt she could inflict.

"If you show your face around here again, the police will be called," Purvell said firmly.

Connie appeared concerned for the first time since the door had opened then looked Cynthia in the eyes and paused.

She gave a short laugh. "We'll see," she said and quickly turned, taking the steps down to her black BMW. The three women watched her leave in silence.

Cynthia walked over to a chair and dropped into it.

"That's where all the money went. The reason Philip wanted to move was to get the money out of the house to pay off his debts. It all makes sense now. He needed the money. If he would have just told me," she thought about him working longer hours and how tired and stressed he'd felt. Why hadn't he told her?

Having forgotten her son was there, she looked up and saw Christopher. He heard every word and had tears in his eyes. The image of his father had been tarnished. Cynthia rose from the chair and wrapped her arms around him as they cried together.

Betty left so she would make it to the restaurant on time but not before assuring Purvell that she'd keep a regular check on Cynthia as they exchanged phone numbers.

❦

Later that afternoon, Cynthia and Purvell sat out on the deck with a bottle of wine as they watched the tide.

"Purvell, I'm in total shock over this. I didn't know him at all," she started crying. She was relieved it wasn't another woman, but gambling? They had worked so hard to save their money.

Purvell moved her chair closer and topped off their glasses of wine, squeezing Cynthia's hand after putting the empty bottle down.

Cynthia angrily continued. "I don't know who I am anymore. I was living a lie. How could he have done this and kept it hidden from me? Is it my own fault? Am I a fool, or did I just look the other way, so my life would stay the same? What happened to the me you knew in college? What am I missing? Can you tell me?" she was drunk at this point and the doubts she'd so carefully denied and kept hidden were coming out all at once.

"Sweetie, I can only tell you this. I think we all ask those questions at some point in our lives. I did a few years ago, wondering why I never found someone to spend my life with. I decided it didn't make me any less a woman, and it was time to live my life to the fullest. When I did that... well, I'm not going to tell you what I discovered, because it might be different for you, and I don't want to interfere with what you need to find out on your own. Just know I'm always here for you."

After a pause, she continued, "I know you're worrying about money, but that will all work out after you see someone to help you make heads or tails of this mess. You'll make it through one day at a time."

Purvell was right.

"So what do you say we plan your visit to see me now? It'll be good for you to get away."

They got on the Internet and bought a ticket for her to come the Sunday after Thanksgiving and stay until Friday. Her mother and Granny would arrive the Sunday after she came back for their visit. Christmas was going to be hard, but with the help of her family, they would all make it through and create some new traditions in this house.

CHAPTER 20

On Tuesday, Cynthia took a deep breath and said a prayer before walking into the building where Jackson Irwin was waiting for her at the main desk.

"Cynthia? Hi, I'm Jackson, nurse manager for ICU here at Southeast Georgia Health Systems. Glad you could come in today. My office is down this hallway."

Cynthia followed him down the hall, taking a glance at the floor. It reminded her of the tiles in the ER and her dream. If she worked here she would see that floor every day. She pushed it out of her mind, looked forward and walked down the hall. She loved what she did too much to let something like this get in the way.

She took a seat in front of Jackson's desk.

"I must say, you have some good experience as a nurse and glowing references. What brings you to the area?"

She wasn't expecting to be asked that question, and she didn't want to go into the whole story. She wanted the job out of merit, not out of pity.

"I've always loved the area and wanted a fresh start," she said. It was close enough to the truth.

"I kind of did the same thing myself. You'll love it here, especially when spring rolls around," Jackson said with a smile.

The interview went for about a half hour before Jackson wrapped it up. "I think I've asked you all I need for now. You're certainly qualified for the job. I'm going to be interviewing a few more people over the next several weeks, so I'll be in touch. We'll be making a decision after that, and I'll let you know before the holidays. If this doesn't work out, would you be interested in other areas of the hospital?"

She hadn't thought about it, but she needed a job.

"Yes, I would, but ICU is my specialty. I'm really very good at it," she said, surprising herself at how confident she sounded.

Jackson smiled and extended his hand. "It was a pleasure meeting you, Cynthia."

That felt good, she thought, as she walked out the door.

She headed down the hallway without even glancing at the tiled floor beneath her feet.

✤

Later in the afternoon, she began to panic. What had she done? Was she moving too fast? Should she really stay here? Questions and doubt started filling her mind. She was pacing the house like an animal when she decided a change of scenery might be good and thought of Christ Church down the road.

The day she and Philip visited, she'd wanted to spend more time walking around the old graves but knew Philip wouldn't be interested so never said anything. She'd done that a lot, actually. Maybe she wouldn't be in this predicament if she hadn't been so accommodating.

Still new to the area and not sure where she was going, Cynthia drove past the church and immediately started looking for a place to turn around. She was pulling over when she saw it.

The two stone pillars were made out cement mixed with shells called tabby, common in the area. Matching metal plaques read, "Wesley Memorial." The pillars stood like sentinels on either side of a path leading to a Celtic-looking stone cross in the distance.

Something was calling her. She parked her car and walked through the pillars onto the path. The area was a series of trails with a huge cross in the center, surrounded by bushes and a circle of light-colored stone. The day was nice and warm, not a cloud in the sky, with only the sun radiating on her. She sat on the first bench to the right, feeling very spiritual, closing her eyes and lifting her face to the sun's warmth.

Her mind and her heart went right into a prayer.

God, was she doing the right thing taking the job and staying here? No answer. Why did she feel she didn't really know Philip like she thought she did? No answer. Why did she feel she didn't know herself at all? No answer. What should she do? Still no answer.

Her mind went over all she knew. Philip had been a gambler and hid it from her for years. Still, she couldn't help but wonder: If she had taken the time to get involved in their finances, could she have prevented all this? Had she been willfully living a lie?

One thing for certain, the knowledge of this secret part of Philip's life was helping her to move forward. It hadn't even been a month since he died, but it felt longer. She wondered how different it would be to go through all this in Atlanta.

She surprised herself by remembering a prayer from a book published long ago, *My Utmost for His Highest,* by Oswald Chambers:

"O Lord, You are the God of the early mornings, the God of the late nights, the God of the mountain peaks, and the God of the sea. But, my God, my soul has horizons further away than those of early mornings, deeper darkness than the nights of earth, higher peaks than any mountain peaks, greater depths than any sea in nature. You who are the God of all these, be my God. I cannot reach to the heights or to the depths; there are motives I cannot discover, dreams I cannot realize. My God, search me."

She rose from the stone bench and looked around the tranquil area. Whoever designed this memorial had certainly been inspired. The only sounds Cynthia could hear were birds chirping and the rustle of the trees. She followed the trail to the right, feeling one with nature and God.

Some of the trees were huge, towering over the smaller ones hung with the ghostly Spanish moss that waved lazily in the breeze, a calming motion. Some bushes and vines bordered the paths, but most grew freely in the small forest. The trail continued deeper into the woods. Cynthia didn't know or care where it led or how far it went, because she felt so at peace. It was as if the trees were singing a sweet song to her. It was like time stood still.

After a while, she heard voices in the distance and headed back to where she'd started. There were more visitors. It was someone else's turn. Looking at her watch, she saw she had been there over an hour-and-a-half. The best hour-and-a-half she had in weeks.

The new people greeted her; she smiled, returning the greeting and got into her car to drive away. Christ Church would have to wait for another day. She was hungry for something to eat and thought she'd try to find a place to stop at on the way home when she saw it, Jack's Barbeque. She pulled in the gravel parking lot filled with cars. It looked different by day.

She stepped in line to place her order when Betty came up behind her and touched her arm.

"You know your money's no good here. Come sit down with me, but first tell me what you want, and I'll have Jack bring it over."

"Oh, Betty, that's not necessary. Let me order like everyone else."

"No, ma'am, you will not." Betty led her to a table. Jack came over, and they both ordered something.

"You saved me a trip. I was coming over to invite your

family to our house for Thanksgiving."

Cynthia hadn't even thought about it. It would be nice to be around other people.

"Yes. I think it would be great to spend it with your family. How thoughtful and nice of you. It'll be my son, who you've already have met, my daughter Millie, and her husband, Jimmy. I insist on bringing dessert, though."

"I can agree to that," Betty said with a smile.

Cynthia liked this woman and was glad they were becoming friends. Her first friend in this new place.

"So, what's new?" Betty asked.

Cynthia told her about her job interview and her upcoming trip to New York to visit Purvell.

"Your trip sounds like it'll be good for you. Purvell is a good friend, I can tell. And a job will make you a part of our community. You'll be loving it here by this summer and wonder why you ever lived anywhere else. So much history and a nice way of life."

"Today, I discovered a little area by Christ Church. A memorial to John and Charles Wesley."

Betty looked peaceful and said, "I go there all the time. Such a beautiful place. It's as if time stands still when you're in there."

"I felt the same way. I'm almost embarrassed to say it, but I think I heard the trees sing to me."

"Don't be embarrassed. I hear them sing every time I'm there." Both women laughed.

Jack came with their food and visited while they ate. Cynthia went back to her house with a good feeling, so much better than when she'd left.

❦

Later that evening, she called Millie to tell her about Thanksgiving plans.

"I really don't think we should be going anywhere but

the beach house. How do you know this woman and her family?" Millie quizzed her.

"I met her the night Dad died, she was a friend to me, and I've started to get to know her. She's very nice, and it's good I'm making friends, since I plan on staying here," Cynthia said. She felt as if she was being treated like a child, and she didn't like it.

"I'm really worried about you, Mom."

"I can understand you feeling that way, but I have to face a new life without your dad. While Purvell was here, she convinced me I needed to get away for a little while, so the Sunday after Thanksgiving, I'm going to New York to visit her for a few days before the grandmothers come. It'll be good for me to spend time with her and have a chance to think."

"I guess that sounds good. I just miss Dad so much and can't believe he's not here. So much change, Mom. The baby, dad, and you moving."

Cynthia's heart ached thinking about what Millie was dealing with at such young age. She was happy Millie didn't know about her father's gambling and wanted to keep it that way. It was bad enough that Christopher knew. Millie was fragile right now, maybe even more than she was herself.

"I can't talk about this anymore," Millie said.

"How about if you and I spend some time talking next week when you're here, okay?"

"Okay. Sorry mom."

"Sweetheart, I love you so much. Say 'hi' to Jimmy for me." They said goodbye.

※

For the next two days, Cynthia felt so sad and lonely. The mornings and afternoons were more bearable, but in the evenings all the heartache would hit her. She missed Philip and her family.

It had been a month since Philip's death, and she was still standing. Cynthia was never one to feel sorry for herself, but this had thrown her for a loop. She was depressed and didn't want to admit it to anyone. She felt weak, and it made her feel like a failure.

She thought about going for a run, but something happened to her desire and motivation. She wasn't familiar with the area and didn't know where to go. It was just an excuse. She walked on the beach, instead, thinking it would make a difference, but when she walked back into the house, she felt no better seeing some of the still-packed boxes and the familiar furniture.

Jekyll Island was where this all had started, but could she bring herself to venture across the bridge and go there? Since it was such a beautiful day, she decided she was going to pack a lunch and visit the fishing pier to think.

As her car started up the bridge, she stole a glance over the side, taking in its beauty. At one time, she'd wanted to run the bridge, but now it looked overwhelming. She drove over the peak of the bridge and got a better view of Jekyll Island. She turned the car left onto the causeway leading to the island, paid the toll, and was on her way.

Since it was a weekday, there weren't many cars on the road or people at the pier. She parked and threw her lunch box over her shoulder, slowly heading down the long walkway to the end of the pier. To the right was a man and a woman, obviously a couple, reminding her of the day she and Philip had come here. To the left was a lone man with six fishing poles going at once.

She decided to sit on a bench not far from the man fishing and watch the boats coming in and out. She pulled out a bottle of water and took a long drink, wishing she would have brought her camera.

The man with the six fishing poles looked to be in his late thirties or early forties. With her sunglasses on, she was able watch him out of the corner of her eye without him knowing.

This kind of fishing was nothing like what she was used to on White Lake. The man had some kind of contraption designed to hold all his fishing gear, so all he had to do was wheel the whole thing out on the pier. The poles were attached to the railing, lined up like soldiers ready for battle. She'd love to get a closer look but didn't dare.

Her hand went into the lunch box, and she took out some fruit.

The man reeled something in, hooting and hollering to himself. "Jesus, Mary, and Joseph," he said, in either an English or Scottish accent, she couldn't be sure. "Look at this bloody thing." He turned to her, holding the fish up for her to see.

She looked around to make sure he wasn't talking to someone else. Then she threw her fruit back in the lunch box and walked down to the area he'd taken over with his gear.

"Have you ever seen anything so bloody beautiful?" He had a yellow and orange blowfish on the line.

"Do you eat those?" she asked.

"No, darling, I would never eat something this beautiful. I'm going to have you take a picture, if you don't mind, so I won't be accused of telling fish tales, and then I'll throw her back in." He smiled a big friendly smile.

"I've been curious about what kind of fish you catch on this pier?" she asked.

"A lot of shark, believe it or not. Not real big ones, but the wee type. They taste pretty good. And then there's flounder, croakers, black sea bass, sea trout… you said 'down here' … where you from?"

" I just moved here from Atlanta, but I'm originally from Wisconsin. I've done a lot of fishing in my life but nothing like this."

"You live on this island?" he asked.

"No, over on St. Simons. I decided to come over here today since it was so beautiful outside. I thought the pier might be interesting."

He reached out his hand. "My name is Ian Roberts. I live here on Jekyll and manage the campground. How about you?"

"I'm Cynthia Lewis. Like I said, I just moved here from Atlanta, but I was born and raised in Wisconsin. I'm a nurse, hoping to get a job at the hospital in Brunswick. You're not originally from here, yourself, are you?"

"No, I'm from a place called Berwick on Tweed in England, right on the Scottish border. Came here fifteen years ago to visit a friend and stayed. Discovered I liked the warmth here better than the cold in England," he laughed. "Been running the campground for the past six years. Before that, I worked for different manufacturing companies but find this fits my free-spirit lifestyle," he chuckled and straightened up, showing a slight belly he rubbed with his hands.

This guy didn't realize it, but his conversation was helping her forget her problems for the moment.

"Ian," she said. "I wonder if you would like to share my lunch with me?"

"I never turn down a meal from a pretty lass," he said with a big smile.

She pulled out her sandwich and gave him half, plus the fruit and some cheese.

Coming to the fishing pier had been a good idea. She asked Ian if she could ever fish with him sometime. "It would be grand," he said.

❧

The kids showed up the Tuesday before Thanksgiving, Christopher first and Millie and Jimmy soon after, since Millie's classes had run late. What a relief to have the house filled with people. Cooking and laughing with the kids was the best medicine for her.

Jimmy changed since the loss of the baby. The event transformed him into a responsible adult. Before it seemed Millie was always taking care of him, whereas now Jimmy was taking care of her. Millie needed him since Cynthia could only handle herself at the time.

Millie and Cynthia spent Wednesday making three pies — pumpkin, apple, and pecan — to take to Betty and Jack's. Cynthia remembered last year when Jimmy asked for pecan pie and felt it was important to make a dessert that Jimmy would enjoy, a kind of peace offering.

The two guys dedicated themselves to going through the bulk of Philip's things, so she wouldn't have to, placing several boxes aside that they thought she needed to look at when she felt like she could.

They all went for a long walk on the beach in the afternoon together.

"Mom, have you run the beach yet," Millie asked.

"No sweetheart. I just haven't felt like running. I've been walking though," Cynthia said. She wasn't sure why, but didn't feel she could run.

The next day, they went over to Betty and Jacks at about one o'clock.

The kids each took a pie to hold on their laps for the ride over. Jimmy immediately noticed the pecan pie.

"Millie, you made me a pecan pie."

"Actually my mom did just for you."

Jimmy turned to Cynthia, who was getting into the driver's seat.

"Cynthia, I can't tell you how much this means to me," he said, giving her an awkward hug.

She was emotionally walking on very thin ice that day. The hug was all she needed to break down and cry.

Christopher gave Cynthia his pie to hold onto and said he'd do the driving. She was learning to let them take care of her on occasion, as hard as it might be for her to accept.

When they pulled up to Betty and Jack's house, the guys

noticed a motorcycle parked in the driveway and figured one of Betty and Jack's sons must be the owner.

The house was located around the corner from their restaurant off of Frederica Rd. It was a white two-story with black shutters and a burgundy front door. The bushes and landscape looked well-established and taken care of. It was a cute, inviting home.

They walked up the steps to the front door, but before they could ring the bell, the door flew open, and there stood a young man who could only be one of the sons.

"Hi, I'm Luke. Saw you coming. Come on in … hey, Mom, they're here," he hollered.

Betty entered the foyer and gave Luke a look.

"I'm so glad to see you," she said, hugging Cynthia.

"You already met Christopher but not my daughter, Millie, and her husband, Jimmy."

"Millie, I've heard all about you. It's good to finally meet."

"You too, Betty," Millie said politely.

"And this is your husband, Jimmy?"

"Ma'am, it's a pleasure to meet you. Cynthia has told us all about you and your husband. What fine folks you are to have us over."

Jimmy and his Southern charm.

They followed Betty into the family room and there sat Ian Roberts, the fisherman she'd met the week before, alongside an attractive woman.

"Ian, hi. What a surprise."

All eyes went to Cynthia.

"You know each other?" Millie questioned.

"We met on the pier last week," Ian said, standing up. "Your mother's a good fisher woman."

Millie looked surprised.

"So how do you know Betty and Jack, Ian?" Cynthia asked quickly.

"I patronize their restaurant so much they had to invite

me for Thanksgiving," he teased. "Actually, Betty here has a thing for me, and it gives us a chance to see one another."

Betty gave Ian a playful slap on the arm and said, "Jack also likes to fish and invites this poor soul over for dinner on occasion." She turned to Ian, "You're a mess!"

"You're only noticing that now?" Ian responded, turning back to Cynthia. "And this is the lovely Collette, my girlfriend."

Collette stood up. Wow, what a woman. Tall with long, flowing dark hair, a beautiful tan, a curvy body, and shapely legs that seemed to go on forever. Ian was grinning from ear to ear. Collette drew the attention of Christopher and Jimmy, as well.

"Ian mentioned meeting you on the pier," Collette said in a low breathy voice.

"Collette here works at one of the local spas as a massage therapist," Ian told them, still grinning.

The young men in the room stared in an almost embarrassing sort of way. Just then, Jack walked in with what Cynthia guessed was their other son, John. Introductions went around again, Jack asking if anyone wanted something to drink. The festivities were on their way.

Cynthia, Betty, and Millie retreated to the kitchen with the pies. Cynthia insisted Betty allow them to help out, Betty reluctantly giving in.

"It was only a matter of time before you crossed paths with Ian. He's like a mascot for Jekyll Island and adds a lot of color to life," she said, taking the pies and placing them on the counter.

"Mom, I'm a little concerned to think you just take up with anyone. Obviously this man is a nice person, but you need to be more careful, in my opinion."

This was embarrassing, and she didn't know what to do but thank God, Betty did.

"Millie, would you go get Jack for me, and then I need someone to set the silverware around the table, if you wouldn't mind. Tell Jack to show you where everything is before he comes and finds me."

Millie headed out to find Jack.

"Sorry, Cynthia. I didn't know she was having such a hard time."

"I don't think I told you this, but she lost a baby a little over a month before her dad's death. And now my emotions are like a roller coaster, so I'm not the rock she's used to having. She's a little overprotective of me because of it all," Cynthia said, starting to tear up. "Sorry, I can't help it."

"Well, of course you can't. Millie will get better with time, as will you," Betty said with authority.

Just then Christopher came in all excited.

"Ian's going to show us his motorcycle. Do we have time before we eat?" he asked.

Betty looked up and said slowly, "I think so. Just tell Ian to not get carried away like the last time. He'll know what I mean."

"Awesome." Christopher was gone almost instantly.

"What will Collette do?" Cynthia asked. "Should I invite her to come in by us?"

"No. She doesn't seem to have any interest in the kitchen. I'll send Millie in to keep her company when she finishes."

Dinner was delicious. Jack deep fried a turkey, and Betty made the rest. The pies were devoured, Jimmy taking two slices of pecan.

Betty told Cynthia that she and Millie would take care of cleaning up, so she could go sit down and relax. She began to protest, but Betty gave her the same look she'd given Luke earlier. Cynthia obeyed.

When they were done, Cynthia saw Millie give Betty a hug before she joined them in the family room. Millie's whole demeanor seemed different. It was the old Millie Cynthia knew and missed. How had Betty done it? She told Cynthia that God had blessed her with the ability to see the hurt inside people, and Cynthia believed it. She'd been on the receiving end of Betty's touch.

Ian made quite the impression on the four young men. In fact, they were all going over to Jekyll Island the next day to fish with him. He was like a Pied Piper when it came to the "lads," as he called them.

On the ride home, Cynthia looked out the car window and thought about how different holidays would be from now on. There was nothing to do but accept it. Today, at least, had been another good step towards healing.

CHAPTER 21

Grand Central Station was the busy bustling place Cynthia remembered.

She pulled her suitcase across the large open area to the clock in the middle where Purvell had said to wait for her. Purvell was meeting a client in the area so Cynthia took a cab from the airport to meet her here. It had been some years since Cynthia visited Purvell in New York. Purvell preferred to come to Atlanta to get away from her busy life and kick back in the slower-paced South.

It was Sunday, and she wasn't going home until Friday, giving her four full days with Purvell. They were going to shop, go out to eat, ice skate, and take in the Christmas spirit, New York style.

Cynthia had hesitated the day before she left, but Betty and Purvell both convinced her a change of scenery would be good. They were right. She didn't want to face the empty house, the remaining boxes, the impending Christmas, her finances, and, worst of all, thinking about her husband who hadn't been who she thought he was. She was furious with him for dying, for not going to the doctor, for gambling, for lying. The hundreds of thousands of missing dollars made her feel sick. She'd worked hard for that money, too. He may not have been cheating with another woman, but this was cheating just the same.

As she continued to walk through the station, her stomach churned. She felt all alone in this city full of more people than she could imagine. Where was Purvell? Just then, her phone rang, and she saw Purvell's name on the screen.

"Hi, where are you Purvell?"

"Are you at Grand Central?" Purvell asked.

"Yes. I'm a little overwhelmed, I have to tell you. It's been several years since I've been here. I can't believe it's so busy on a Sunday. Will you be coming soon?" Cynthia asked, trying not to sound concerned.

"I was tied up with a client down the block, but I'm on my way. Might be about forty-five minutes to an hour, so why don't you get a cup of coffee. There's a Starbucks, just ask someone and they'll point you in the right direction. I'll meet you there, okay?"

"Okay. Bye," she said, and Purvell hung up.

Her eyes filled with tears, but she willed them not to spill over. In her preoccupation, she dropped the jacket she'd had over her arm.

"Excuse me, but you dropped something."

She turned to see a man holding out her jacket, gazing at him through a puddle of tears.

"Are you okay?" he asked, as he handed her the jacket.

Not knowing what to say, she said, "Thank you. I'm looking for Starbucks."

"That's nothing to cry about," he said, laughing to ease the mood. "It's at the end of the Lexington Passage." He pointed in the direction behind her.

"Thank you," she said again, quickly heading in the direction the man had pointed. She was a little embarrassed, but told herself that she would never see him again.

At Starbucks, she ordered an Earl Grey Latte and took a seat at a small table, checking her phone frequently between watching people flit about the hectic train station.

Soon Purvell showed up, looking fabulous in her wool coat, cloche-style felt hat, leather gloves, and boots. She was dressed all in black except for the pink plaid scarf wrapped around her neck. Purvell had always been a well-put-together woman.

"It's so good to have you here," she said, kissing Cynthia on the cheek. "If you're done, let's grab a cab to my place, and we can rest for a bit. I've taken the week off so I can be with you. Tonight I thought we could meet some friends of mine for dinner, and tomorrow night I have a little holiday party, which I'd love for you to attend with me. Just a bunch of realtors and property developers. It's more of a way to rub elbows and let everyone know who you are," Purvell told her as they walked to the front of the station to catch a cab.

The cabs were lined up, just like in the movies. All the activity helped calm Cynthia's mood, and soon she forgot about her earlier tears.

Purvell's apartment was small and looked like a physical version of Purvell's personality. It consisted of an open kitchen, dining, and living area, a bedroom, and a smaller study/bedroom with a bathroom in-between, all decorated colorfully in warm jewel tones.

"Why don't you unpack and get settled in while I fix us a snack?" Purvell suggested. "There should be enough space and hangers in the closet, but let me know if you need more. We're going to meet my friends around eight at the Union Square café." She left the room, closing the door behind her.

Cynthia dropped down to sit on the daybed and sighed. The day had been long and challenging but she would put a smile on her face and have dinner with Purvell's friends. She did the right thing by coming to visit didn't she? She needed to stop doubting herself and take advantage of this time away from her situation.

❦

Purvell's friends consisted of a married couple, Sidney and Jane, a fellow realtor, Randy, and his partner, Allen, and a woman named Bella. Purvell had obviously told them about Cynthia, because they were all very careful about the questions they asked. In one respect, Cynthia appreciated it, but she hated the fact people had to accommodate her. She needed a minute alone, so she excused herself and went to the ladies room. No one was in there, so she relaxed and pulled her comb and lipstick from her purse. She fixed her hair, getting ready to put on the lipstick and paused, staring at her reflection, again feeling alone.

As she left the ladies room, she was so distracted by her thoughts that she walked into a man on his cell phone with enough force to spill his drink.

"Please excuse me," she said, never looking him in the eyes as she made her way back to her seat at the table.

❦

The dinner was excellent. Since the restaurant was not far from where Purvell lived, they walked back to her apartment.

"Purvell, I'm tired. Today has been a long day. Do you mind if I go right to bed when we get back to your place? I want to be my best for Macy's tomorrow."

"Of course, dear. I understand. I have a little work I can do, so don't worry."

Cynthia said good night, got ready for bed, and crawled under the covers. The day had been exhausting. Two minutes after she laid her head on the pillow, she fell into a deep sleep.

❦

Cynthia was up before Purvell the next morning. She made herself a cup of tea and got comfortable in a chair with a blanket while she watched out the window as the world woke up in New York City.

It's amazing what a good night's sleep away from your problems could do for you, she thought. Somehow she'd worked through her feelings overnight while she slept and had a different resolve upon waking.

"Hey. You're a little early bird, aren't you? I see you found the tea. Did you sleep okay?" Purvell asked.

"Yes, I did. The day bed is very comfortable. I was asleep as soon as my head hit the pillow. I guess the traveling wore me out," she responded.

"Life in general can wear you out," Purvell added and went to the kitchen to start the coffee maker before coming back to sit down on the sofa.

"So shopping today at Macy's and 5th Avenue?" Cynthia begged.

"You sound like a child. Anywhere you want, my dear. Do you want to sit on Santa's lap, too?" Purvell laughed.

"Only if you will, too," Cynthia said. "We could each sit on one knee." To her surprise, she started crying. "What am I going to do, Purvell? Philip lied to me and left me in a situation I'm not sure I can fix."

"Come, sit here next to me."

Cynthia came over to the sofa and sat down.

Purvell put her arms around her and held her while she sobbed. "The past can't be changed. Over the next months, you'll feel the anger come out, but don't let it consume you, or you'll never be able to move on. Work on letting go of the anger, and your life will come together again."

The two women continued to talk for thirty minutes or so, deciding some shopping therapy was needed. They dressed, and after stopping at a small restaurant for one of the best bagels Cynthia ever had, they were on their way.

Macy's was decked out for the holidays. How could you not get into the spirit shopping there? They had lunch in the basement of Macy's and talked about the evening.

"This party we're going to is being given by a developer I work with quite a bit named Daniel Benton. He's about our age, very handsome, and as nice as can be. His wife died about five years ago, I think of cancer. The women are after him, but he manages to keep away and doesn't play the field. Has no kids, just himself, and lots of money."

"I can't imagine losing your spouse and having no kids," Cynthia said. "Poor guy."

"Yeah, but he keeps busy with his work. Hey, wait until you meet some of the women at the party. I play the game, though, it's part of the fun," Purvell smiled a devilish smile and took a bite of her sandwich and a drink of water.

"I don't know how you do it," Cynthia told her.

They had to take their packages back to Purvell's apartment before going to 5th Avenue. Once on the Avenue the pair had a lot of fun. Cynthia mostly looked, but did manage to buy a few presents for Christmas.

New York was like another world. With people everywhere and all the decorations, Cynthia was able to put her sadness aside for a short time and get into a festive mood, looking forward to the party that evening.

They arrived back at Purvell's around five with plenty of time to get ready for the party at eight. Purvell said they'd take a cab to the hotel where it was being held. Time did seem to go faster in this city, because before Cynthia knew it, the cab was there and it was time to go.

Daniel Benton walked around the atrium at the hotel. He'd been throwing this party for about ten years. It used to be more fun for him when his wife was alive. She always found a way to make it special. Now he left the party up to someone on his staff, only looking over the final plans and giving his okay.

The guests wouldn't arrive for an hour, but he liked to

go early to look at everything and make sure he got what he paid for. He didn't become a successful business man by sheer luck.

"Hi, Uncle Daniel." He turned around to see his sister's son, Stephen. Stephen was a graduate of the University at Albany's business school. Since Daniel had no children, he was grooming the boy to take over his company someday. Stephen had worked several years as an intern for him during the summers and holidays, but after graduation, he'd became his right-hand man.

"Oh, hi, you startled me a little," he said as he put his hand on the boy's shoulder.

"Everything looks great," the young man said as he looked around. "You know how to throw a party, Uncle Daniel!"

The space was decorated exquisitely for the holiday season, with a large Christmas tree in the middle and slightly smaller trees in each corner. All the trees were decorated with white lights and red, silver, and gold ornaments.

The tables were draped with gold, floor-length tablecloths and topped with silver square overlays. Floral centerpieces in the middle echoed the colors of the trees. Daniel already arranged for the centerpieces to be delivered to an area hospital after the party for others to enjoy. The food was being served buffet-style since people would be drifting in and out during the evening.

"Would you mind going in the kitchen and seeing how things are coming along?" Daniel asked Stephen.

"Sure, I'd be glad to." He left Daniel alone.

Daniel watched the boy walk away, pleased that there was someone he could trust to someday take over the business he'd built. He walked off to the right, where a man was warming up with a few holiday numbers on a baby grand piano. The man tipped his head at Daniel as Daniel walked to where the bar was set up. The bar looked well-stocked, just the way he wanted it to be. The whole set-up looked good.

As he walked around, he felt a pang of empty loneliness.

He missed his wife especially during this time of year. He was alone except for his sister, brother, and their families, both of whom lived in the Saratoga Springs area, where he'd been born and raised. He would drive up there on Christmas Eve, go to church in the evening, and then spend Christmas Day with them, coming back to New York the day after, alone. Now was not the time for sentimentality, so before he could travel too far down that path he put it out of his mind.

The party was a thank-you to the realtors and developers he worked with. Without them, his success would not be what it was. They sold, rented, and helped develop the properties he owned. When he was a young man starting out, he came to New York to make his mark as a realtor like most of them. Now he was a very wealthy man because of it, but also a lonely man.

The staff was busy getting everything ready for the guests. He made a quick stop in the men's room to center himself before everyone arrived. The evening was going to be a success, as it always was. He reminded himself to make sure he asked Purvell about the woman she was having dinner with last night who bumped into him at the Union Square Cafe. It was the same woman he'd seen at Grand Central Station looking for Starbucks earlier in the day. A strange coincidence. There was something about the woman that made him curious. How could he come up with a smooth way to ask Purvell without showing too much of his hand?

He walked back to the atrium just in time to meet the first guests. He greeted each guest by name and pointed them to the bar area, repeating the gesture with each new arrival. Eventually, he saw Purvell walk in and slowly made his way over to make small-talk with her.

"Purvell. I'm so glad you made it. One of my star realtors," he said as he put his arms around her and pecked her on the cheek.

"I wouldn't miss your party for anything, Daniel," she replied. "I hope you don't mind, but I have my best friend from college visiting, so I brought her along. I want you to meet her. She stopped in the ladies room. Oh, here she is."

Daniel couldn't believe his eyes. It was her.

"Daniel Benton, I'd like you to meet my best friend in the world, Cynthia Lewis. She's visiting from St. Simons Island in Georgia."

Daniel eagerly extended his hand, and Cynthia returned the gesture.

"It's a pleasure, Daniel. Purvell has nothing but good things to say about you. I hope you don't mind her bringing me along," she said, looking him straight in the eyes.

"I'm pleased to have you here. St. Simons Island, you say? I've never been there. Have you lived there long?"

"No, just a few months actually, but I feel I will love it," she replied.

"We better let you get to your other guests," Purvell said. "We're going to head to the bar for some wine." They left.

Daniel watched them walk away, not believing what happened, but was even more intrigued. The woman didn't recognize him, and he was disappointed.

❦

"So how did you like the party?" Purvell asked Cynthia in the cab on the way back to her place.

"It was all I thought it would be and more. What interesting people," she said.

"Oh, I know. I'm so used to it by now that normal people are unusual to me. What did you think of Daniel?" Purvell asked.

"When you went to the ladies room and stopped by some friends, he sat down and talked to me for quite some time. Asked a lot of questions."

"Really? What kind of questions?" Purvell was curious.

"About the island, why I moved there, what I did for a

living, my family, that kind of stuff. He even suggested we stop by his office before I leave. I told him we had a very tight schedule and wouldn't have time to stop by. It was very curious. I'm afraid I was a little evasive with him and came off as rude."

"Don't worry about it. I make him lots of money," Purvell laughed.

Cynthia didn't want to say it, but she'd felt as if he was watching her all night. The rest of the evening she avoided looking his way. When he shook her hand as they left, it seemed like he didn't want to let go. She had to be imagining it, she thought. He was very attractive. Oh, what was the matter with her? He was just a very polite guy.

They rode back the rest of the way to the apartment in silence, and both women went right to bed because tomorrow promised to be a busy day — they were going ice skating at Rockefeller Center. Cynthia had always wanted to skate there since she was a little girl. She hoped that ice skating was like riding a bike, and you never forgot how to do it.

As she laid in the daybed, her thoughts went to Philip and his gambling. Right now, everyone was keeping her busy, but at some point that would all stop. The mundane daily existence would set in, and her new world would become her reality. She soon dozed off.

She was skating on White Lake with fluffy snow falling all around. The lake was frozen, and bare white birch trees stood like soldiers in the darkness. Everyone she loved was there, even her mother and Granny.

The kids, Philip, her brother, Ron and Sandra, some coworkers from Atlanta, and even Betty, Jack, and Ian were there skating like Olympic champions. Off in the distance, she saw blurred people also skating. One blurred figure seemed separate and started to follow her. Who could it be and, why didn't the figure show them self?

❦

Only two days remained before she left on Friday. They spent the morning in Chinatown, where Cynthia bought handbags and jewelry for Millie, her mother, and Granny. She even managed to find herself a few things, too.

Rockefeller Center was fun for both them. They felt like girls again gliding around the ice rink. After about fifteen minutes of testing their skills, they were skating backwards and swooshing in and out like the old days back in Wisconsin. It appeared skating *was* like riding a bike.

Purvell took Cynthia to one of her favorite restaurants after they had their fill of skating, an Olde English pub called the Churchill Tavern. Cynthia couldn't resist the fish and chips, while Purvell elected to have her favorite, bangers and mash. She said it was her occasional splurge, and she ate every bit of it.

When they arrived back at Purvell's, they put their pajamas on and crawled into Purvell's bed to talk.

"Cynthia, you know if I can ever be of help to you, I'm just a phone call away. There's nothing I wouldn't do for you."

Cynthia was touched by Purvell's kindness and wanted to cry. Her emotions were a roller coaster ride that seemed would never stop.

"Time will heal you, you'll see, and you can always rely on your faith in God." Purvell took her hand and smiled. "And you can always escape up here to this crazy place to forget." They both laughed, Cynthia through her tears.

After about an hour of talking, Cynthia crawled into the daybed in the other room but lay there for an hour thinking about how she would cope when she got back to the island. She would have company until the New Year, and then everyone would be gone, and she would be alone. One day at a time, one foot in front of the other, she reminded herself.

She knew she needed to get to sleep, because tomorrow was her last full day in New York. They were going to the Met and getting Chinese takeout for supper. Friday, her plane left at noon. For the first time since Philip had died, she didn't think of him and her unknown future as she slowly drifted off to sleep.

CHAPTER 22

C ynthia was back at the Jacksonville airport two days after she returned from New York to pick up her mother and Granny for their Christmas visit.

She sat in the same area as she had when she waited for Purvell to arrive the previous month. Soon she saw them heading her way. She stood up, and they rushed over with warm loving faces as she started to cry.

"Oh, Cynthia," her mother said, wrapping her arms around her as if she were a child. "Sweetie, we are here to take care of you. Now just let us be in charge."

Granny piped in: "Darling, don't you worry, we'll be here for several weeks. Trust me, it will be okay."

After she gained control of herself again, she looked at them and smiled.

"What would I do without you two? You're both right. Let's get your luggage and head to the island."

And off they went.

On the ride home, Cynthia told them about her New York trip. Both women loved Purvell like a daughter and were interested in all aspects of her life. They were most distressed that she'd never had a husband or children and, as always when they talked about Purvell, spent a good bit of time on the subject of her lack of them. Cynthia honestly couldn't see Purvell with children, but she didn't tell them so.

As they approached the island, the silhouette of the bridge into Brunswick came into view, the mid-afternoon sun shining behind it. She thought about how much she'd wanted to run it. She hadn't run in months. The only other time she'd not run for a long time was when she was pregnant.

"I'd like to take you both over here to Jekyll Island one day," Cynthia said, pointing to the right as they passed the turn-off to the island and started to approach the bridge. "I've made a friend over there by the name of Ian who fishes on the pier. You'll love him, and also I want you to meet Betty and Jack Franklin, the owners of a barbeque restaurant on St. Simons. They had us all over for Thanksgiving." As Cynthia spoke, her spirits picked up realizing she had started to make a life here.

Since there were four bedrooms in the beach house and the apartment below it, was easy to make everyone comfortable. Cynthia had her room, Christopher and the grandmothers would each have their own rooms, and Millie and Jimmy would stay in the apartment below. Christopher was coming Friday after he finished his last final in the morning, Millie would come by herself on Sunday, and Jimmy would come on the following Saturday. Cynthia was looking forward to it with bittersweet feelings. This was supposed to have been her first Christmas here with Philip and as a new grandmother.

While they were carrying in suitcases, Cynthia's phone rang and saw it was Betty.

"Hi Betty, we just walked in from the airport."

"Oh, good. Guess everyone's safe and sound then. Listen,

Jack and I want you three to be our guests tonight at the restaurant if you're up to it. I can't wait to meet your mother and grandmother. I hope they like barbeque," Betty rattled on.

"They like pretty much everything, so let me get them settled in and ask, then call you back, okay?"

"Sounds good. Talk to you later." She hung up.

"Betty invited us as guests to her restaurant tonight, and she can't wait to meet you both," Cynthia told them.

"Oh, goody," Granny replied with a grin on her face. "I love meeting new people." She took off upstairs to find her room.

"Well, Mom, hope you don't mind, but I think it's decided."

"Cynthia, you know I love meeting new people, too." She followed Granny to find her room.

Cynthia called Betty back and they decided on six o'clock.

The rest of the afternoon the women visited and walked on the beach to satisfy Granny. The now 95-year-old woman never stopped.

When they came in, Cynthia poured them all a little glass of wine, and they sat in the living area.

"Cynthia," her mother said, sitting in a leather chair next to the fireplace. "Please don't tell me you're going to keep that urn of Philip's ashes on the mantel."

"Why not, Mom?" she replied, a little startled at her mother's reaction.

"Grace, hush about that. Philip's not been gone that long now. If it makes Cynthia feel better, who are you to criticize?" Granny said from the sofa.

"Well it's just this cremation stuff is new to me. I mean, what are you going to do, keep the ashes with you forever?"

"I'm not sure what I'm going to do with them yet, and I felt the mantel was a safe place for them." In actuality, she didn't know where to put them.

Granny piped in: "I had a friend die who was a huge animal lover. Every pet she ever had was cremated. Dogs, cats, fish, hamsters, birds, ferrets, and even an iguana she had for a month. Had a shelf in her laundry room with all the little urns lined up and labeled. In her will, she stated that their ashes were to be mixed with hers after she died. Her kids thought she was crazy. It also said that the ashes were to be spread over Lambeau Field, because she was also a huge Packer fan. Lambeau Field said, "no way," which upset the kids, because they wanted to get rid of the ashes. They did mix them with the animals, and now the kids have to take turns keeping the urn each year." Granny shook her head at the thought and quickly changed the subject. "Come on, Grace, we need to start getting ready for supper with Cynthia's new friends. I'm getting hungry." She stood up, waiting for Cynthia's mother to follow suit. As she walked over to the stairs, she turned and gave Cynthia a wink.

That Granny, Cynthia thought. *She is something else.*

⚜

The restaurant wasn't too busy, so the three women, Betty, and Jack sat in a corner where they weren't seating customers for some privacy.

Betty made fast friends with the two older women.

"Now, how did you meet?" Granny asked.

Cynthia jumped in. "I wandered in here, and we hit it off. Betty is my first island friend," she said with a big smile, not wanting to recall that dreadful night.

"I knew a guy up by us that was in the barbeque business for a short time," Granny said, turning to Jack. "The guy's name was Don Stankowski. He had a cottage on White Potato Lake close by us. Ordered a big metal barbeque oven custom made that he could pull around with his truck to parties and public events. While he was in the testing stage, he burned down his home and partially damaged the place next to him when the fire got out of control. Rebuilt his house but died before they finished it."

"How did he die?" Jack asked.

Granny was in thought and all of a sudden came back. "Have you ever heard of pasties?"

"No," Jack said with hesitation.

"They're a meat pie we make up north. Has your meat, vegetable, and potatoes all in a pie crust. Don thought he would start a pastie business instead, so he was experimenting with different meats and vegetables. Accidentally made some with poisonous mushrooms," she dropped her head, shaking it. "We think he must have gotten the mushrooms in the woods. They found him on the floor with the half-eaten pastie in his hand. A real shame," she said, with great remorse.

Cynthia had to turn away to stifle a laugh from the look on Betty and Jack's face. They'd just had their first dose of Granny.

On the way back to the house, Cynthia asked, "How do you like my new friends?"

"Oh, I think they're just splendid," Granny said from the front passenger seat. "In fact, Betty's coming over to make cookies with us next week Monday."

"But Granny, I don't have any friends to give the cookies to here, and we can't eat all of the ones you make," Cynthia said.

"Betty has that all worked out dear, don't worry."

Cynthia wished the only thing she had to worry about was an overabundance of cookies.

The next morning, she told them about Philip's bookie visiting and the gambling. Both of their faces revealed the shock Cynthia still felt.

"Honestly, I don't know what I think and feel about Philip right now. I'm angry, but then I feel sorry for him, because when you lose that kind of money and just keep going, you're sick. And then he never went to the cardiologist when his doctor suggested he go for a work-up. It could have saved his life," Cynthia said.

"Cynthia, stop it. Leave it in the past; it's done. You have to look to your future," Granny told her with concern in her eyes.

"I know, but I'm not sure what to do. I'm not sure who Philip was or who I am right now, and I'm almost fifty-six years old." Tears streamed down her cheeks as she spoke.

Granny took her hand. "You will, sweetheart, you will, but it's not going to be easy."

"Do the children know?" her mother asked.

"Just Christopher, because he was here at the time."

"You need to tell Millie, so she won't feel as if she were left out in case Christopher lets it slip, and you know he could by accident."

Her mother was right. She would tell Millie the first opportunity.

❦

"Why don't we spend this week exploring the island? It might make you feel more grounded. What do you think?" Granny suggested the next morning.

So the rest of the week was spent with the three of them discovering the area. It was good for Cynthia since it helped her become familiar with her new home.

They went to Barbara Jean's for crab cakes twice and visited the Maritime Museum, the lighthouse, and Christ Church. Cynthia took great pleasure in showing them the Wesley Memorial. She knew the place would be a refuge for her as long as she lived on the island.

Before she knew it, the weekend was there, the kids arriving. There was so much activity that Cynthia had no time to think about anything else.

Millie arrived mid-afternoon. Cynthia decided to get her alone for a walk on the beach before it got dark to tell her about Philip's gambling. *This is going to be hard*, she thought, but Millie listened, cried, and said, "Mom, are you going to be okay? How bad is this going to be financially?"

"I'm not sure yet, but that's why I've applied for a full-time job at the hospital," she admitted. "I'm committed to staying here. I like it." She smiled at Millie.

"Okay, Mom, if it's what you want. I'm in full support."

Cynthia hugged her daughter, never wanting to let her go. Millie seemed better and more herself since Thanksgiving when she and Betty had cleaned up after dinner. Cynthia was grateful.

❧

Betty rang Cynthia's doorbell Monday morning at nine a.m. "I'm here to bake the cookies," she announced.

Just then Granny headed down the stairs with her flowered apron on. She greeted Betty as if they'd been friends their whole life and ushered her into the kitchen.

Soon Granny, her mother, Millie, Betty, and Cynthia were at the kitchen table sipping on tea and coffee and discussing cookieology — which cookies to make, and all the ingredients they needed. Betty suggested they consider donating some of the cookies to a shelter in Brunswick. Betty and Jack donated food items often from the restaurant to help out. Granny loved the idea.

That afternoon and for the next two days, the five women made cookies. They packaged some to keep and the rest were for the shelter.

They delivered the cookies on Thursday to a very happy group of people, but no one was happier than the five women who'd baked them.

Jimmy arrived on Saturday night. Cynthia was starting to like him. He was one of those people who didn't make a good first impression because he tried too hard, which resulted in him appearing a little shallow and self-centered. After the loss of the baby, Jimmy had proved himself to be a man who truly loved her daughter. What more could a mother want?

Christopher and Jimmy went fishing with Ian all day Sunday while the women found the artificial Christmas tree and did some decorating to help things feel somewhat festive.

The guys came home with Ian in tow and plenty of fish for their supper.

"I was just wondering, Cynthia, if you'd thought about where we'd go for Christmas Eve service? How about the Methodist Church next to the memorial garden by Christ Church?" her mother suggested.

"What a great idea, Mom."

"I'll look online to see when the services are," said Millie.

Cynthia was ashamed she hadn't even thought about Christmas Eve, but the church was a great suggestion. Ian asked if he and Collette could come along, too, so it was settled.

※

Christmas Eve was on Tuesday night. They decided to attend the seven thirty service at Wesley United Methodist Church.

Because her mother was uncomfortable seeing Philip's ashes on the mantel, Cynthia moved the urn to the top of a dresser in her bedroom closet. As she was getting ready for church, her eyes drifted to the urn. She walked over to it and then slowly reached out to touch it. The marble was cold and smooth under her hand. She had a hard time thinking that Philip was in there, but he was.

"Oh, Philip, what am I going to do?" she said aloud, closing her eyes. "I loved you so, but it seems I didn't really know you. I still miss you so much."

After a few minutes, she went into the bathroom to take a shower and have a good cry. All her life she'd found a shower comforting when she needed to let go of some anger or hurt. As soon as the water hit her body, she felt the release. Naked and pure, crying it all out, and washing it away down the drain was like a kind of renewal for her.

230 Susan Amond Todd

This was the one place she was safe from anyone knowing how she really felt.

Her mind went to the past, going over each month, week, day, and hour since they'd decided to move here. The time had gone fast. Would the rest of her life be like this? The day after New Year's, her mother and Granny would go home. The kids would go back to their lives at school shortly after. She still hadn't heard from the hospital about a job and was becoming concerned about what she would do with her time and how she would support herself.

Suddenly, her crying stopped, and she felt a ray of hope spread over her heart. Was this God's Christmas gift to her? It was the same feeling she'd had at the Wesley Memorial, a wave of wellbeing telling her to stay strong and have trust in a higher power, have faith and believe that all would be okay.

❧

It was late morning on Christmas Eve. Daniel Benton had a few loose ends to tie up at his office before he headed up to Saratoga Springs to be with his family for the holiday and was walking out the front door of his office building when he bumped into Purvell Whitlock. He'd thought about her friend, Cynthia, several times since the party. This could be his chance to find out more about her.

"Purvell, Merry Christmas."

"Daniel. Merry Christmas to you, too. I thought you went out of town for the holiday?"

"I'm leaving soon. Just had to take care of a few things before I head out of the city. I was thinking of grabbing a bagel and coffee at the place across the street before I hit the road. Want to join me?"

"You read my mind, I was just thinking how I would love a bagel myself and was going to cross over there."

This was going to be easier than he thought. They ordered their bagels and coffee, Daniel's treat, and sat down to eat, making business small talk when there was a break in conversation.

Finally, Daniel got up the nerve to ask: "So did your friend have a good time visiting you? I hope she enjoyed the party."

"She had a great time. It's like being girls again when we're together. We even went ice skating at Rockefeller Center," Purvell laughed.

"She's a very attractive woman. Does she visit you often?" he looked down into his coffee and then back up to a smiling Purvell.

"Daniel, you're interested in her."

"Don't be silly. I just met her. She seemed very nice, different then what I'm used to around here, that's all," he responded, trying to get back into control.

"I know what you mean, but I have to tell you, Cynthia lost her husband two months ago. I knew them both from college; in fact, I was there the night they met. Her husband died unexpectedly. Cynthia is doing well but is very fragile and vulnerable, though she hides it well."

Daniel thought about Cynthia's tears when he saw her at Grand Central Station and her distraught look when she walked into him at the restaurant and understood now why she didn't recognize him at the party. She was also a little standoffish when he sat down and visited with her. It suddenly made more sense.

"Okay, so I admit I did find her attractive and was interested, but under the circumstances... well ... " he let the sentence hang in the air.

Purvell took a bite of her bagel and studied Daniel for a moment. "Tell you what, Daniel. When the time is right, I'll let you know, and if you're still interested, I'll put in a good word for you."

CHAPTER 23

October, Ten Months Later

Although the past year on the island was not the way Cynthia had expected it to be, she'd made a life for herself. It consisted of work, walks on the beach, spending time with her few friends, and being alone. After the first of the year, the Southeast Georgia Health System had finally called, offering her a full-time position in their ICU. Betty invited her regularly to her house or the restaurant, and Ian took her fishing or out to eat with he and Collette on occasion. Life was boring, mundane, and relatively predictable.

The kids would come visit when they could, but she never heard from any of her old Atlanta friends. She'd been told that sometimes when you had friends as a couple, you could lose the connection when one spouse died, and it seemed to have been true in her case.

There was no trip to White Lake, either, since she had no vacation time built up yet or any extra money. Her mother and Granny preferred to stay up there in the summer, since it was hot on the island, so it would be the holidays before she saw them.

She also heard from Purvell, who she suspected was in regular contact with Betty, her mother, and Granny. She was fortunate to have such good friends, because she truly needed them.

In the spring, Cynthia, Ian, and Collette joined the Wesley United Methodist Church and would meet and sit together on Sundays. Cynthia went frequently to the memorial garden next to the church just to sit and think.

The evenings were the worst, because Cynthia was in the house alone. Days she worked were better, since she didn't get out until eight, sometimes later, but she was often so tired, she simply dropped into bed when she got home. Other nights were rough.

She still wasn't running; she just didn't have the heart for it.

Millie and Jimmy moved to Charlotte after graduation from Berry College in the spring. Millie took a job with a big Charlotte accounting firm, and Jimmy started working at a bank. This was very convenient for Cynthia since Christopher was going to school at UNC-Charlotte.

Since the first anniversary of Philip's death was coming up, Cynthia decided it would be better for her to go to Charlotte so they could all be together. Plus, it might be easier to be there than on the island.

The week before her trip to North Carolina, she got a call from her attorney. He was getting close to settling Philip's estate. Philip had investments all over the place, George had discovered. She worried about how much all this searching was going to cost her.

The attorney asked if she had thought about putting the beach house on the market and finding something smaller or moving back to Atlanta. She hadn't in either case and didn't know what to do, therefore she called to talk to Purvell. Purvell didn't answer, so she left a message.

Cynthia had grown to love St. Simons and didn't want to leave. Going back to Atlanta was not an option. She had started to feel like she belonged on the island.

Later in the evening, Purvell called back, and Cynthia

told her what the lawyer said.

"I have a great idea. Why don't you move into the apartment down below and rent the upper part of the house out to my clients here in New York? They're dying to go somewhere warm in the winter. They'll pay anything. We could start after the New Year," Purvell suggested.

Cynthia liked the idea. The apartment was a comfortable size for her, and she could stay right where she was and make money to pay the mortgage.

"I knew I could count on you, Purvell."

❦

Friday morning, the day before the anniversary of Philip's death, Cynthia headed to Charlotte. She was staying with Millie and Jimmy in the townhouse they were renting. Millie had taken the afternoon off, so she could be there when Cynthia arrived.

Christopher would meet them after his last class and spend the night. They were going to dinner at All American Pub, a favorite place of Millie and Jimmy's.

Christopher came up with the idea to drive to Crowder's Mountain on Saturday morning to go hiking, something Philip would have loved doing with them, and so the day was planned.

❦

Betty Franklin pushed open the swinging door to the large restaurant kitchen in search of her husband, Jack. *Where is that man?* she thought. It was nine thirty, and the restaurant had begun to slow down. She was thinking of going home.

"Jack," she hollered.

"Back here."

She found him working hard over the smoking ovens. In the past, their sons Luke and John had helped out, but the boys went to visit some friends in Atlanta. She hated how Jack had to do so much alone without the boys there.

"Hey, I'm thinking of calling it a night. Do you need me anymore?" she said.

"I always need you, darling," Jack responded with a big grin. She loved him as much as the day they were married, and she was sure he would say the same. They were soul mates. She gave him a playful pat on the arm.

They started this restaurant together the first year they were married. It was Jack's dream, so it was also her dream. Jack wanted the boys to take over one day, but neither had a desire to do so. He was so determined to pass it on to them, but their interests were elsewhere. Betty understood, but Jack didn't. She suggested they consider selling the place but couldn't convince her husband, at least not yet.

"Well if you don't need me for work then I'm heading home. How late do you think you'll be?"

"Well, I got a little cleaning to do and some things to get ready for tomorrow. Maybe midnight. Don't wait up for me."

"Okay." She gave her husband a kiss on the lips.

As soon as she was in her bed at home, she fell asleep. Several hours later, she woke as if she'd heard something. She knew she needed to get up. These kinds of things happened to her all the time. She knew when she was needed.

The first time it had happened was when she was a little girl. A grown man wearing work clothes was sitting on a park bench close to where she and her brothers and sisters were playing. Even at an early age, Betty knew when someone looked troubled, and this man did.

He sat with his legs apart, elbows on his knees and his head in his hands. Betty walked over and stared at him until he looked at her. She said, "Mister, is something' wrong?" He looked into her eyes and proceeded to tell her about how he'd just been paid, gone to a bar, and spent it all on drink. He was afraid to go home to his wife and kids.

Betty had been raised in a good Christian home, but she heard the adults talk about drinking, and she knew it was no good. The compassion Betty felt for other people overwhelmed her. She went over to this man, putting her small dark brown hand on his shoulder and closed her eyes. She told him she would pray for him. She said to go home and tell his wife he was sorry and to never drink again. His wife would surely forgive him.

Betty saw the man several years later in a grocery store. He recognized Betty and told her that since the day they spoke, he'd changed his life. He gave her a five-dollar bill. Betty took the bill and put it in the collection plate on Sunday. She knew who'd really helped this man.

Why had she thought of that tonight? She realized that she was alone in bed, and it was one. Maybe Jack had fallen asleep watching TV, but it appeared he wasn't home yet. Could he still be at the restaurant? She called his cell phone, and there was no answer.

She dressed, grabbed her keys, and went outside to drive to the restaurant.

That's when she smelled the smoke.

❦

Crowder's Mountain was only forty-five minutes from Charlotte. The park offered several trails at different levels, challenging everyone from the new hiker to the serious rock climber. They spent most of the day exploring several of the trails and then some time leisurely sitting by the lake, reminiscing about Philip. Cynthia felt it was very cathartic for them to be together in such a peaceful place.

When they were getting ready to leave, Cynthia pulled her phone out of her backpack.

"Huh, Ian called and left a message earlier today. I guess being on the mountain, the phone call didn't go through.

Must want to see if we're having fun." She pressed the screen and listened.

"Cynthia, Ian here, ah… I need you to call me when you have a moment, lass. It's important." He hung up. That was odd.

"Listen, I want to call Ian, so why don't you drive, Christopher?" Cynthia said.

"Sure, Mom. Everything okay?"

"I'm not sure," she replied, worried by the tone of Ian's voice.

She dialed Ian, and he answered on the second ring.

"Cynthia, I was getting worried about you."

"The kids and I were hiking. I guess being on the mountain affected my phone service. Is something wrong?"

"Last night after Jack's Barbeque closed, the ovens caught fire," Ian said.

"Oh no. Was the fire bad?" Cynthia asked.

"Looks like the place will have to be leveled, but listen, Jack was in the place when it happened and tried to fight the fire by himself. He was hurt bad, Cynthia. He's at the hospital …" Ian's voice dropped off.

"What about Betty?" Cynthia asked

"She's her strong self as usual. When will you be back?" Ian asked.

"Tomorrow," she said with resolve. Betty was there for Cynthia at the worst time of her life. Cynthia needed to be there for Betty now.

"That sounds good, Cynthia. I'll tell Betty. A safe trip to you, and if there's more to tell, I'll call, okay?"

"Thanks, Ian, you are such a dear friend." She hung up.

"I'm sorry, but first thing in the morning, I'll be going back to the island. Seems there was a fire at the barbeque restaurant, and Jack was injured. I need to be there for Betty and the boys."

"We understand, Mom," Millie said with concern in her voice.

Cynthia went right to the hospital in Brunswick when she arrived back in the area the next day and found Betty sitting next to Jack in the intensive care unit where Cynthia worked.

She stood outside the room for a few minutes before going in so she could observe Jack. The barely recognizable man in front of her had scorched patches on his face, an eye swollen shut, and the hair on his head had been signed off. His arms and hands were bandaged, but the rest of his body looked untouched.

"Betty." Cynthia said as she walked in the room. Betty's eyes glanced up in her direction, calm and collected as usual, but Cynthia spotted a touch of relief. Cynthia went to her, and the two women hugged. It was only a year ago the two became friends after Philip died.

"Oh, Cynthia. I'm so glad you're here. Jack told them he wanted no one but you taking care of him," Betty said, never taking her eyes from Cynthia.

Along with the burns on his hands and arms, Jack suffered smoke damage in his lungs, but that wasn't the real problem. When the firemen found him, he was unconscious on the floor of the restaurant. The ER doctor said the stress of the event, along with his injuries, had caused a heart attack. Unknown to Cynthia, Jack was already under care for a heart attack from eight years earlier.

Cynthia pulled up a chair next to her friend and took Betty's limp hand into hers. "Can you tell me what happened?"

"This is all I have been able to piece together," Betty started. "I went home at nine thirty. Jack closed up at ten thirty, all the employees were done and out by eleven thirty, and Jack stayed by himself to do a few things in the office. I expected him home around midnight so I wasn't concerned and went to sleep. At one, I woke up with a start and knew I had to go to the restaurant when I saw that Jack wasn't in bed. First thing I noticed when I stepped outside was the smell of smoke and I just knew it was our place. My car pulled into the parking lot just as they were bringing Jack out of the building and wheeling him over to the ambulance. He wasn't conscious, but I knew he wasn't dead. I followed the ambulance to the hospital and have been here since."

"Where are Luke and John? Haven't they been here with you?" Cynthia asked.

"I don't know. I've been trying to call them and can't get an answer. They're living in an apartment over by the school. This weekend they were going to Atlanta, but I think should be back by now," she said, taking a paper from on top of the nightstand and writing something down. "Here's their address. Maybe you could call Ian and see if he could go over and find them."

Ian was the perfect person to find them, so she stepped out of the room, called him, and put him on the task. She went to the cafeteria and got them each a sandwich before she came back.

Cynthia stayed with Betty the rest of the afternoon. Ian didn't find Luke and John until later in the day when they arrived back from Atlanta. They were on the way to the hospital, so Cynthia told Betty she was going back to her house but would be seeing her the next day when she came in for work at seven in the morning. Betty was planning on spending the night, but Cynthia suggested she go home the next day for a rest when Cynthia came in to work, promising to give Jack extra special care.

The women parted with a hug. Cynthia held it together until she was alone in her car. She prayed Betty wouldn't have to go through what she herself had.

❦

The next three days Cynthia worked her usual twelve-hour shifts, glad she could be of help to Betty. Jack stayed the same, opening his eyes and nodding yes or no, occasionally speaking a word or two. The poor guy was not sure what had happened even though they'd explained it several times. It wasn't unusual for patients who'd faced a trauma to not remember the details right away. Most remembered more in time.

She was off for the next three days and decided that since Betty's sister was up from Florida, she'd let the two women have their time together. Jack seemed to be doing a little better. Cynthia would be there for Betty when her sister went back home.

Cynthia rose early Thursday morning and decided to take a walk on the beach and enjoy the sun rise — she needed some time to herself to think. Out on the deck, a whip of salt-filled air assaulted her face, blowing her hair around her head. The beach was desolate as usual this time of the morning.

What would my life be like now if Philip were still here, she wondered as she took a drink of her coffee. Cynthia couldn't even imagine.

She started thinking about how quickly life can change. When she'd gotten married, she'd had a dream of how she thought her life would materialize. It was something she thought most all women did.

As she walked along with her eyes fixed on the sand below her feet, she saw pieces of polished sea glass, empty beer bottles and soda cans, a deflated beach ball left behind, an empty food wrapper, and some tangled fishing line. The man made obstacles interfered with the beach's tranquility, but there were natural objects, too — a dead jellyfish, clumps of seaweed, smooth polished stones, and shells of varying sizes and colors.

Occasionally there would be a dip in the sand where water collected and a few lone fish were trapped until the tide came in, allowing them to escape. She felt like she was a fish trapped in one of those dips, waiting for her own tide to come in.

Purvell's idea about renting out her house was going to buy her some time, she hoped. There was no doubt in her mind that Purvell would get top-dollar for it.

Then she thought of Jack and Betty. What would they do? Betty had a faith stronger than anyone she'd ever known. Cynthia had been leaning on it for the past year. *A whole year ago,* she thought. It seemed like a lifetime. You never knew what was coming in with the tide, she thought to herself.

❦

Sunday morning Cynthia was back at the hospital. Jack seemed to be about the same, so Betty had gone home the night before with her sister to sleep in her own bed. After going to church in the morning, they were coming back to the hospital.

Cynthia went into Jack's room to find him wide awake.

"Hey, Jack. It's so good to see you. Doing okay?" she asked, knowing he would just nod his head, but he didn't.

"Talk to you," he said so soft and raspy that Cynthia barely heard him.

"Talk to me? You need to save your strength for later when Betty is here. She would love to hear you talk," Cynthia told him.

"No," Jack responded "You."

"Me? Okay." She pulled a chair over, getting as close as she could, and put her hand on the side of the bed. "What's up?"

Jack stared into her eyes with such intensity that Cynthia became afraid. His breath was labored, but he began to speak. "I was wrong... too stubborn... Luke and John... college... should have sold... too much alone... boys feel guilty ..." he trailed off, laying his head back in exhaustion for a moment. "Tell them... I'm sorry." His head went back down.

"Well, they'll probably be coming by later. You can tell them yourself," Cynthia replied.

"No. Tell Betty... I love her." Again his head went back, and he was asleep.

Poor Jack, Cynthia thought. All a parent wants is what they think is the best for their children, but sometimes their children have other ideas, and you learn the hard way. Hopefully he'd feel better after his rest and he could tell Betty himself.

But Jack never woke up from his nap. An hour after Betty and her sister came back to the hospital, he had another heart attack and died. He was on her watch and died. She felt like she'd let Betty down and was beside herself. Betty was as calm as always and insisted that she would be fine with her sister and that Cynthia should go home and take care of herself.

When Cynthia's shift was done, she drove from the hospital in a daze until she glanced to the right and saw the bridge. She made the decision then: she was going to run it today before the sun set.

When she got home, she pulled her scrubs off, tossing them on the bedroom floor. She found her running clothes pushed into the back of the closet. In a matter of minutes, she was ready to go. After grabbing two bottles of water and her purse, she was on her way.

She decided to park on the Jekyll Island side of the bridge behind the sign and the palm trees. Off-shore, the sky was looking a little dark and ominous, but it didn't mean anything. Storms would often disperse before ever reaching the shore.

After locking her purse in the trunk, doing some stretching, and taking a long drink of water, she headed over to the road. She wanted to make sure she was running against traffic, so she needed to go on the other side of the bridge. Several cars from both directions flew by her. Don't think about it, she told herself, just do it. She ran over to the other side, stopping to look up at the looming bridge in front of her. *Sure looks different standing here than it does being in the car,* she thought.

Making sure her hat was secure and tying the string in her shorts tighter, she started up the incline to the bridge. Even though it didn't look all that steep, she felt it running. Now was not the time for her to wonder if she was in good enough shape to run the three miles from one side to the other. It was too late for that. She was committed, and even if she had to walk part of it, she would not stop until she was finished.

The trek to the top was slow-going, but she did it without hesitation. What a view. To the left was the Port Authority, businesses, and manufacturing plants. To the right was the open ocean and marshes. The view was awesome. She would do this again.

As she started down to the other side of the bridge, she noticed the dark clouds were rolling in to shore. She could see several clouds in the distance, a solid stream of showers pouring out of them. Maybe if she turned around quickly enough, she could beat the rain to the other side. She had no choice but to try.

As soon as the coast was clear, she ran to the other side of the bridge so she would be against traffic and took off. No such luck. As soon as she reached the peak, the rain caught up to her and quickly escalated to a down pour. She continued, determined that not even Mother Nature was going to get the best of her. Once she reached the other side, she kept running toward her car, immediately jumping in soaking wet. She grabbed a beach towel that she kept on the back seat and started drying herself off.

Soon tears started. Tears for Jack, Philip and her lost grandchild, tears for her loneliness, her financial concerns, and her sad, mundane life. She was so confused and lost. Who was she? Where was she going? Why did this happen? And then she asked… Is this it, all there will ever be for me? She'd been searching for answers for a whole year and still had none.

Where would she find them?

The rain clouds rolled out as quickly as they'd rolled in, the sun now shining strong. She opened the door of her car and got out to look at the bridge she only minutes ago conquered. It glistened as if covered with diamonds.

She'd been sleep-walking through life this past year, not participating but only going through the motions. Today, with this rain, she'd been baptized back into the living world. Running the bridge had shown her to keep going. Her life wasn't over but beginning a new chapter.

A new determination came to her. She had already decided to stay here, but now she decided she would become a part of this place and let *it* become a part of her.

CHAPTER 24

Sliding the turkey into the oven, Cynthia felt a cloud hanging over the preparations. This Thanksgiving was small with only her mother, Granny, Christopher, and herself. Millie and Jimmy were spending it with his family. Originally, Betty and Jack's family were coming, but since Jack's death, Betty decided to go to her family in Spartanburg. She was staying there until after the New Year. Since Cynthia hadn't talked to her since the day of the funeral she wasn't able to tell Betty yet what Jack said the day he died.

Today was not the day to be thinking about it, so she decided to divert herself by focusing her attention on improving the mood in the kitchen.

"Where's Christopher?" she asked her mother.

"I think watching TV, dear," her mother responded, looking up from the green bean casserole she was quietly preparing.

Cynthia walked into the living area and stood in front of the TV. "How about you find a radio or something with some Christmas music we can listen to in the kitchen?"

Fifteen minutes later, Christopher showed up with a boom box blaring "White Christmas" in Bing Crosby's crooning voice. That was more like it. They all started singing to the music and, much to Cynthia's surprise, she felt better. Much better.

Cynthia's mother and Granny thought the idea of renting out the beach house was a great idea.

"That Purvell is one smart cookie," her Granny said. "And she has the connections to help you. Sure would like to see that girl, it's been years."

"It has," her mother, said, "Maybe the two of you could take a trip together to visit us at White Lake. Talk about it next time she calls you, dear, and see what Purvell says. Tell her there are two old ladies in need of her spunk." Her mother looked at Granny, and both of them laughed.

"You know, that could be fun. I'll definitely ask her," Cynthia responded.

"So, dear, what can we do to get this house ready?" her mother asked.

"I'm waiting to hear back from Purvell when I might have my first renter, but in the meantime, anything I don't want to leave up here I'll need to pack up and move to the garage, unless I want to use it in the apartment. I'm thinking this year of only putting a tree up for Christmas, not all the rest of the decorations. We can start boxing things up and when Christopher is home I'll get him to help move the heavier stuff. How does that sound?"

"Like a plan," her mother said. "What are you going to do with that thing holding Philip's ashes?"

Her mother didn't like the urn, and Cynthia had forgotten to move it to her room before she arrived.

"I'll have to move it to the apartment with me, I guess," Cynthia said with a smile.

The women started the next day boxing pictures and other personal items that there wouldn't be room for.

Since the apartment already had furniture in it, all Cynthia needed to do was stock the kitchen and move her clothes and things down. She'd do most of that when she knew she had a renter.

One day while they were baking cookies, the phone rang. It was Purvell.

"Guess what?" she said, "We have our first renter. They want the whole month of January!"

Although she was happy, Cynthia was sad at the same time. She needed to get over it and be grateful for the renter and the incoming revenue. The apartment was nice and would suit her fine.

"Cynthia… are you there?" Purvell asked.

"Yes, I'm here. Thank you, Purvell. What would I do without a friend like you?"

"I feel the same way, Cynthia. These people up here are loving the thought of going to St. Simons Island. I just tell them about the history and Jekyll Island, and they want to come down and visit 'y'all.' I'm having fun renting it out," she laughed.

Cynthia's mother motioned to her and mouthed "White Lake."

"Oh, yes, Mom wanted me to put an idea in your head. She wants you and me to come visit White Lake, so keep it in mind for a vacation."

"Tell her I will. It's been ages since I've been there. What a nice escape it would be from this place," she laughed.

The women talked for another thirty minutes, Cynthia telling Purvell about work, hiking with the kids, Jack's death, and running the bridge. Purvell told her about the latest restaurant she'd been to, her great sales month, a weekend trip to Boston, and a new guy she'd met. They hung up, and Cynthia went back to cookie-baking, reminiscing about her trip the year before.

The trip felt almost a million years away.

✤

It was the night of Daniel Benton's annual holiday party, his staff outdoing themselves again on the preparations. As he walked the room, he couldn't help but wonder if Purvell Whitlock's friend was visiting again. He thought occasionally of her. It had been a year since the woman's husband died, so he decided if she was in attendance with Purvell tonight, he was going to ask her to lunch before she returned home.

Purvell arrived just before they started serving dinner. She was alone.

"Good evening. I was afraid you weren't coming, Purvell."

"Got tied up with a client," she said smiling and giving Daniel a hug.

Should he say something? What the hell, he was dying to find out.

"Thought your friend might be visiting again. You know the one you brought with you last year …" his voice trailed off.

"No, Cynthia couldn't come this year. Last year I kind of insisted she visit so she could get away after her husband died. She has family visiting her now. I just talked to her the other night."

"Is she doing well, I mean it's been a year since her husband died, is she having a hard time, or is she, you know, doing well?" Oh my God, he thought. I sound like an idiot. He hoped Purvell didn't notice.

"As well as can be expected, I guess," Purvell said. "She's actually having to rent out the upper part of her beach house while living in an apartment built below it. I'm helping her out by mentioning it to people here in New York that like to get away to somewhere warm in the winter. Have you ever been down there? It's beautiful and full of history."

"No I haven't but it sounds as if I've been missing something," as a thought occurred to him.

"You really should check it out sometime," Purvell looked him straight in the eyes and smiled.

"Well, please tell Cynthia I wish her the best and maybe next time she visits I could take you both out for lunch or dinner," he said rather awkwardly and went to visit with his other guests.

CHAPTER 25

Cynthia's house was ready for renters by January 1, thanks to her mom, Granny, and the kids. The grandmothers had already gone back to White Lake, and the kids back to Charlotte, so she spent New Year's Eve alone in the apartment under the house. It would be her home for the next several months.

It turned out that the apartment below her house was rather nice and cozy. Because of her aversion to the urn containing Philip's ashes, Cynthia waited until her mother left to place it on an end table in the corner. She wasn't sure what else to do with him.

Her first renters from New York flew their private plane into the little St. Simons airport on January 1. The party consisted of three couples, the women staying the whole month and the men flying in and out from New York on the weekends. Watching and listening to their comings and goings provided Cynthia with entertainment when she was home.

By the look of all the bags the women carried into the house from the shared rental car, they did a lot of shopping. She guessed they must be checking out the expensive boutiques on the island and maybe even driving up to Atlanta.

Since it had been unseasonably warm, the women often started their happy hour on the deck at about four. Cynthia would occasionally sit silently on the patio below with her own glass of wine and listen to them. She gathered from the conversation she overheard that they did sightseeing not only on St. Simons, but on Jekyll and in Savannah. The women also enjoyed walking the beach for a couple hours every morning and went out to lunch daily.

The men would fly in arriving Friday morning, hit the golf course for a few rounds, take the women to dinner, and repeat the same on Saturday and Sunday. Monday morning, bright and early, the men would jump in their plane and fly back to New York to do the whole thing again the next weekend.

Cynthia kept to herself while these people lived in her house by going to work, running, and visiting Betty or Ian when she was lonely.

When Betty got back after the New Year, Cynthia invited her over for lunch one day so she could finally tell her what Jack said the day he died.

"This will be good for the boys to hear," Betty told her. "They don't talk about it much, because they know how much I miss their dad, but I know they're feeling guilty for not being there, thinking maybe if they helped more with the restaurant, their dad wouldn't have had so much to do, and the fire wouldn't have happened. They're both having a very hard time. Thank you," she said. She hugged Cynthia, and for the first time, Cynthia saw Betty cry.

One night during a storm, the electricity went out as it did on occasion, Cynthia's phone ringing shortly after. One of the women upstairs was wanting to know what Cynthia was going to do about it. Cynthia told her where to find candles and said she would call the electric company. After she hung up, she went back to her glass of wine and the book she'd been reading by candlelight. The storm passed, and the lights went back on as usual.

The January people left and soon, the February people came. They were an older couple and barely left the house, providing Cynthia with no entertainment at all. The March people were a childless couple in their late thirties. Different friends showed up, visiting for a few days here and there and partying every night. They would be leaving soon, and the people renting for all of April and May would arrive.

❦

Betty came to visit often. The two women walked the beach, sometimes not uttering a word between them, finding strength in being together.

One day, Betty showed up with some good news about the restaurant.

"A man called me yesterday wanting to know if I was going to rebuild the restaurant. I told him I didn't know what I was going to do. I own the land it was built on. Says he's interested in buying the property to build a little shopping center. What do you think I should do?"

"I think you should call Brad Davies, the realtor we used when we bought our house here. He'll know if these people are trying to scam you or are legitimate," Cynthia told her and went to find Brad's number.

Brad told Betty that the piece of property the restaurant occupied was quite valuable, and she shouldn't rush into anything. Maybe she would want to develop it herself, since it could bring her in a steady income. Betty told him she thought about opening a deli in the future since she only knew the restaurant business and would give what he suggested some thought.

Ian dropped by one day to see how Cynthia was doing and bring her some fish.

"So when might you be throwing a line in with me, lass? It's been a long time."

"It has been a long time. Let me check my work schedule."

She went to her desk and pulled it out from under some papers. "I can do next week Thursday. How about if I bring Betty along, too?"

"That's a great idea," Ian said. "It's a date."

⚜

Early in the morning on the day she was meeting Ian, her phone rang. It was her attorney, George. *Now what*, she thought.

"Hi George."

"Cynthia, so glad I was able to get you. Have some news that might be good. Philip sure did believe in diversity when it came to his investments. I found an insurance policy at the Savings and Loan he worked for right out of college in Wisconsin that I guess you didn't know about. He's been paying into it all these years. Not sure how much money it is, but it could be good," George told her. "I also found some more stock investments."

"That's great news," she said, stunned.

"I'm going to make some phone calls and find out how to get you the money from the insurance policy. Knew you would love to hear about it. I'll be in touch. Call me anytime if you have any more questions."

"Thank you so much, George."

⚜

Cynthia drove over to Betty's to pick her up so they could visit Ian for the afternoon. Except for trips to the beach with Cynthia, Betty hardly left home much since Jack had died.

Cynthia rang the bell and was startled when Luke answered the door. It was the first time since the funeral that she'd seen him or his brother.

"Luke, it's so good to see you. I told your mom I was stopping by. Going to take her for a surprise. Is she ready?"

"Um. Yeah, I guess so."

"How's school going? You and your brother doing okay? Maybe next time Christopher is home, the three of you can go fishing with Ian," Cynthia babbled.

"We're okay. Have Christopher call me or John. I'll tell my mom you're here." He left Cynthia in the family room alone.

She walked over to some family pictures on a corner table with an old fashioned tatted doily on top. Her Granny tried to teach her how to tat once but she'd never caught on. Maybe Betty or one of her sisters did it. She would ask.

Covering the table were some pictures of the boys when they were younger, a couple of them in football gear, Jack and Betty as a young couple, some family pictures obviously taken for a church directory, and some people she didn't know. Cynthia leaned down closer to the table to get a better look at a more recent family picture with all of them smiling. It was from a happier time, something Cynthia understood all too well.

Betty walked in, purse and jacket in hand, breaking the moment. "So where are you taking me?"

"We're going fishing with Ian," Cynthia said with a laugh. Betty was dressed for something much finer.

"Tell you what, I'm going to grab myself something to change into at Ian's, and we can be on our way."

"Sorry, I wanted to surprise you," Cynthia said with a shrug of her shoulders.

"Oh this is a surprise all right." She went to grab the clothes.

❦

Betty was in the best spirits Cynthia had seen since Jack's death. The two women talked and laughed like old times as Cynthia drove to Ian's.

The "Blue Beast," one of Ian's motorcycles, sat in his driveway. She understood why Christopher couldn't wait to visit Ian when he came home for a weekend. He was a big brother to him and the male role model Christopher needed in his life.

She was sure Ian let Christopher drink when he was with him, even though Christopher was underage, because Christopher would often call to say he was spending the night and would see her in the morning. She didn't care as long as he didn't drive. A little male bonding with Ian was good for him.

As she and Betty walked to the front door, she noticed the big grin on Betty's face. She was happy to see it. Ian opened the door before they could knock.

"Hello, lasses. How are you this lovely day and welcome to my chateau." Ian stepped back and bowed with great flair, sweeping his right hand through the entrance to his home.

Cynthia walked in and spotted Collette and Cynthia's two closest friends from work, Teresa and Mindy. "Surprise," they all yelled.

"We know your birthday isn't for awhile, but we could all get together today to celebrate. Happy birthday, lass," Ian said, planting a kiss on Cynthia's cheek and putting a bouquet of pink roses in her arms.

She'd forgotten her birthday was even coming up. How strange but how wonderful all at the same time.

Ian cranked up his gas grill and flipped hamburgers for the ladies. Collette had made a chocolate cake with raspberry filling and chocolate ganache frosting. The top was covered in little dollops of the ganache frosting crowned by raspberries.

"This is a work of art," Cynthia told her. "Where did you ever learn to do this?"

"I worked for a bakery before I became a massage therapist," she said.

"We need to talk," Betty said. "I'm thinking of opening a little deli, and I could use a girl with your talent."

It was late afternoon when the friends went home.

Cynthia thanked them over and over. She didn't normally like surprises, but this one had been wonderful.

She gave Ian a big hug. "Thank you so much. I would say you shouldn't have, but I'm really glad you did this. I forgot my birthday was even coming up. I still want to go fishing with you, so you owe me a date."

"How about this weekend? It's supposed to be beautiful."

"Just let me know what time," she said, hugging him again and holding on for a few extra seconds so she could get a grip on the tears threatening to come, but mostly because she missed the feel of having someone's arms around her.

CHAPTER 26

*C*ynthia walked the beach, wondering why the April renter hadn't shown up yet.

She would try to call Purvell again to find out when and if they were coming. Purvell had been incommunicado lately, and she wasn't sure why. Spring was a busy time of the year for realtors, so she would give her the benefit of the doubt. Maybe the new renter would come on the weekend.

She decided to continue renting out the house for at least part of the year, since it was bringing in good money for her. After George had finally closed Philip's estate, she'd met with a financial advisor. The advisor suggested that Cynthia refinance her mortgage to make it more manageable and enable her to keep the house. Between renting the house out for six months a year or more and working full time, she should be able to keep her head above water without dipping into retirement funds.

She was even taking two weeks off in July to finally visit her brother Arthur in England.

Pursuing her master's was also on her mind — nothing and no one could get in her way this time.

The sun was going down behind the trees, and the air was becoming a little cooler. Time to head back and make herself some supper. She needed to go to bed early since she was working twelve-hour shifts the next three days. Though her life may look boring, she was happy with her job at the hospital and enjoyed living on the beach, knowing that every morning, she could hear the water coming in and out.

❦

On the way home after her fourth twelve-hour shift of the week, Cynthia was looking forward to four glorious days to herself. The renter still hadn't shown up, and she and Purvell had still been playing phone tag. Cynthia wondered if maybe the person had backed out. Purvell told her it was someone who needed time to work on a project away from everyday life.

That night as she pulled in the driveway of her house, her question about the renter was answered. There was a car parked off to the side, and the lights were on inside the house. Part of her was hoping the person had changed their mind so she could move back in, but then again, the money was helping out her situation.

Exhausted from the three long days of work, she pulled around to park next to the apartment and quietly went in. Christopher called earlier in the week and said he was coming to visit on the weekend. She hadn't seen him or Millie in a while and couldn't wait. Since she was off the next several days, she would get a look at the renter tomorrow, but tonight all she wanted to do was eat something and fall into bed.

❦

The person renting her house must have gotten up early and left because the car was gone and everything was quiet when Cynthia started her day the next morning. Before heading to the beach for a morning run, she sat on the patio below the upper deck, drank a cup of tea, and ate a scone.

Christopher would be in late on Friday. No doubt he already had a fishing day planned with Ian on Saturday. Since Ian had become a substitute father for Christopher, she encouraged the time they hung out together. Christopher and Philip had been close, so she was grateful for someone who wanted to fill the void. She couldn't think of a better person.

Having finished her breakfast and a few stretches, she headed to the beach and started with a slow relaxed jog, immediately thinking and sorting her mind.

Her life with Philip was beginning to become a memory, and at times when she closed her eyes to recall a moment, she found the event playing out like a movie, she on the outside watching a scene from her life.

Is this how it happened when you started to move on? She wondered. Her breath caught as she stifled what was trying to be a sob, but she told herself to stop. She was ready for a change.

Walking back to her house after her run, she saw a figure on the deck. The renter must be back. She'd sneak into the apartment unnoticed if she could and stay as quiet as possible. That might be hard this weekend with Christopher around, but for now she didn't want to be seen.

Daniel Benton was as nervous as a schoolboy wanting to ask a girl to prom while he stood on the deck and watched the woman walk towards him.

He'd flown his plane into the St. Simons Airport the day before, rented a car, and settled into the beach house before the sun could set. The house was very nice and large enough for him to have invited several people to come along, but he preferred to be alone.

He needed a place to get his thoughts together, where he wouldn't be disturbed. A group of developers from overseas had asked him to speak at an upcoming convention. They wanted to hear about how he'd climbed to the top of the New York City real estate market. After he talked with Purvell Whitlock at his holiday party the idea came to him about renting Cynthia's beach house. Staying here would give him an opportunity to get a good start on his presentation. It also was a good opportunity for his nephew, Stephen, to take charge of his company without Daniel around. He could always fly back if Stephen needed him. If all worked as planned, Stephen would someday run the company, and he could stay in the wings and semi-retire.

He also had an ulterior motive. Cynthia Lewis. Was he crazy coming here? Some would say yes. He became intrigued after talking to her over a year ago at his holiday party. Even though he only knew what Purvell told him, there was something about her that he found appealing. He often felt women were only attracted to him because of his success and money. He could tell Cynthia didn't seem to care, and he liked that. He hoped after a year and a half as a widow, she would be open to getting to know someone else.

As she came closer, he raised his hand and waved. She waved back. He watched her disappear under the deck and climb the stairs to where he was. She looked the same as he remembered her.

"Cynthia." He extended his right hand, and she extended hers, grasping his. "Daniel Benton, Purvell's friend. She told me about renting your place, and I thought since I've never been down here, what a great opportunity."

"Yes, of course, I remember you. I had such a lovely time at your party and talking to you when I was visiting her. Purvell told you about it, you say. How nice of her. I've been having trouble getting a hold of her lately, but I think I'll try again tonight," Cynthia responded with a smile.

"I'm working on a presentation, so I'll be here alone but would like to check out the sights on the island," he told her. "Maybe you could show me some of them if you have time?"

"Ah… I work full time as a nurse, so I have a pretty tight schedule. I'll let you know if I have some time available. I've got to go get cleaned up, so see you later." With that, she was gone.

He was annoyed with himself — he'd been too pushy.

❦

"Purvell, what the heck kind of game are you playing with me?" Cynthia said when she finally got a hold of her friend.

"I have no idea what you're talking about," Purvell replied coyly.

"Daniel Benton is living above me in *my* house. You had nothing to do with that?"

"One day in passing, he told me about a presentation he was working on and how he found it hard to get anything done here, after I mentioned my friend was renting out her beach house. He needed a place to get away. I'm looking out for you, Cynthia. You know, renting the place out, nothing else," Purvell said

"My gut tells me you're stretching the truth on this one, but I'll give you the benefit of the doubt until I find out otherwise," she said reluctantly.

"You will hardly know he's there. He's got to get going on his presentation, that's all. Trust me on this."

❦

The first thing Cynthia saw when she opened her eyes was the clock on the bedside side table. It was 9:12. How had she slept so late?

Christopher had gotten in at about eight thirty the night before, bringing all his stuff into the small apartment.

She didn't hear the TV or any movement, so she thought he was still asleep.

Grabbing a robe, she walked out to the empty living area, checked his room, which was empty, and then went to the patio, which was also vacant. She saw a note on the kitchen table when she came back in.

Hey, Mom, went to breakfast with Daniel.

How interesting. It seemed every time she emerged from the apartment, Daniel was there.

Tuesday she was going to the grocery store, and he asked if he could tag along. What could she say? Then one night, when she was going for a walk on the beach, he'd conveniently showed up wanting to walk with her and asked her to visit Christ Church and Fort Frederica with him the next day. She said yes.

She did have a good time with him. He'd taken her to lunch at Southern Soul Barbeque as a thank-you, a place she went to now that Jack's had burned down. It was a beautiful day, and they sat at one of the picnic tables outside to wait for their food.

"So how long have you been on the Island?" he asked.

"Oh, a little over a year and a half. Hard to believe it's been that long, really. I feel a like I've been here forever. I love it."

"I know what you mean. The place is magical. I haven't been here long, and I've already forgotten the hubbub of New York," he chuckled, looking her directly in the eyes.

"Yes we… I felt the magic the first time I visited. I'm fortunate to be able to live here."

He went on to tell her about growing up in Saratoga Springs. His father worked in a brewery, just like Philip's did. How strange. He wanted more, so he put himself through college in Albany. Both of his parents passed away several years ago, his dad never understanding why Daniel couldn't be content staying in Saratoga Springs. Daniel had gone to New York after college, got into real estate, and worked hard. The rest was history, as he put it. He met his wife, Julie, in college. She worked in banking, but once Daniel became successful, she left the industry and worked with him. Six years ago, she was diagnosed with an advanced stage of breast cancer and lost her battle two years later. He missed her terribly. They never had children.

Hearing about him had made her comfortable, and she shared more than she usually did with someone new. He'd been very easy to talk to. She told him about her upbringing in Wisconsin, her family, going to school at Madison, working as a nurse, and being a widow.

"I think you mentioned you've only lived here a year and a half," he said. "Did you move here after your husband died?"

"No, we lived here when he died," she said, suddenly feeling uncomfortable and exposed like you do when you've said more than you intended.

He seemed to sense this and changed the subject.

"I would love to hear about your children," he said, and she gladly expounded on them.

It was the first time she'd been out with another man since Philip died. It felt good, but Daniel would be going back to New York when his two months were up. She was sure by the end of May, he'd be tired of her island and ready for the "hubbub" again.

When he'd asked what she was doing on Thursday, she told him she was busy getting ready for company, without telling who it was. She felt she needed some space, especially after telling him so much.

She spent Thursday morning cooking and baking, then went to see Betty for lunch, and later dinner with Ian. When she'd arrived home, Daniel's car had been gone, and she wondered where he was, surprising herself when she felt a little disappointed.

About eight thirty, there was a knock on her door. It was him asking if she would come up to the deck and share a glass of wine. She told him another night since she had company coming. He was gone all day Friday.

What was going on? She enjoyed his company, but he would leave her world in several weeks, and she would never see him again. He lived in a place so different from hers.

She snapped back to the present and read Christopher's note again, when she caught a glance of herself in the mirror. Not knowing when they would be back from breakfast, she better get dressed and cleaned up in case Christopher invited him in. Why did she care? It didn't matter. But she *did* care.

A half-hour later, she heard the laughing and thumping of feet on the deck above her. She slowly went up, playing it cool as she climbed the sheltered steps to the top, surprising them.

"I see you've met Christopher. How was breakfast?" Cynthia said as smoothly as she could.

"Yes," Daniel said, laughing. "He was roaming around on the beach and when I found out who he belonged to, I invited him to breakfast."

"Hey, Mom. Daniel has his own plane and said he would take me for a ride before I go back on Sunday. Isn't that awesome?" Christopher was as excited as a small child. "I asked Ian, and he said to bring him with me when we go fishing today. This is going to be a fun day. We're going out to dinner with Ian after fishing at Barbara Jean's, Mom's favorite place, so you'll have to come along." Christopher said.

"Well, I don't want to intrude..." Daniel said, not sounding like he really meant it.

"Don't put Daniel on the spot, Christopher. He's here to work on a presentation, and we might be taking him away from his work," Cynthia offered.

"I'm actually doing really well with it and could use a break, in fact I'll treat for dinner," Daniel said with a big grin.

"Well, okay, I guess it's settled then," Cynthia said. And she was surprised by how much she was actually looking forward to it.

❧

Christopher rode home from Barbara Jean's with Cynthia, going on about Daniel this and Daniel that. It made Cynthia realize how much Christopher really missed the things he did with his dad.

"We're getting up at six tomorrow morning to fly in Daniel's plane," Christopher told her.

"Great," she responded.

"Hey, we should invite Daniel to lunch for taking me in his plane, Mom." Christopher said in an overly excited voice.

"You need to calm down. Tomorrow I want to spend lunch alone with you before you leave. Daniel is just renting the beach house. He'll be gone by the end of May, and we'll never see him again."

"He told me he loves it here and is thinking of buying a place right on this section of beach or maybe Jekyll. I think he's loaded, Mom. Ian likes him, too. They made plans to go out in one of those big fishing boats while he's here. I really think we're going to be seeing more of him," said a convinced Christopher.

❧

"Mom, Daniel's plane is awesome. I think I want to learn how to fly," Christopher said as he walked through the door into the apartment the next morning.

"When you've graduated from college and get a job, you can do and buy whatever you want. The key words here are graduated and job," Cynthia informed Christopher. "Now go get your stuff together so you can leave after lunch."

Christopher stuck his head out of the doorway. "Oh yeah, I asked Daniel to lunch anyway. Daniel says thanks but he won't be able to because he has some phone calls to make, but he would love it if you would have a glass of wine out on the deck later. What's up with that, Mom?"

Cynthia felt herself blush. "I have no idea."

"Do you like him, Mom?"

"No more than you. He's a nice guy," she said as she turned away.

It was the only response she could give.

❦

She did join him for a drink that night and every night for the next week. On the nights she worked, she found herself quickly getting her charting done so she could be on her way home.

They talked about their childhoods, finding many similarities, but their lives after college were very different. Daniel had been all over the world, and she had stayed where she was, focusing on being a nurse, wife, and mother.

"It was sad when we found out Julie couldn't have children," he told her. "Instead, we concentrated on our careers. When she died, I was devastated. A child would have been nice, but it wasn't meant to be for us. How did your husband die?"

"My husband died of a heart attack the day we moved in here," she said abruptly. It felt good to finally get the words out.

Daniel looked at her in shock.

"This was supposed to be the next chapter in our lives. Instead of *our lives* it was just *my life*," she said. "Then I found out he had a gambling problem and, long story short, this is why I'm renting out the house you're in," she said. It felt good to share with him.

"I see," he said. "Well, it appears you're doing well for yourself."

"I'm doing okay," she said with pride.

Then one morning as she was leaving for work, she found an envelope with her name on it taped to her door.

Dear Cynthia,

I have unexpected business in New York and not sure if and

when I'll be back. Have enjoyed getting to know you better.
   Daniel.

She read the note again and felt the same disappointment she felt the night she didn't see his car in the driveway. In her vulnerability, she'd let him into her heart so carelessly. How foolish of her. She should have known better. They were from such different worlds.

The next several weeks were lonely. She'd enjoyed his company and missed it, even though the time she spent with him was short. It was her first connection with another man since Philip's death, and it had felt good.

❧

Two weeks passed when she heard a car pull in the driveway. It was Daniel and with him was another man and two women. One of the women must have been his girlfriend. She decided to keep a low profile and visit Betty's more while he was here. Opening up to him had been a mistake, it appeared.

She managed to avoid him for several days when, one night, he knocked on the door.

"Hi. Everything okay upstairs?" she asked him.

"I've been missing you. Where have you been?" he asked genuinely.

"Oh, just around." It was a lame answer. She knew it.

"I brought my sister, brother, and his wife with me this time. After telling them about how nice this place is, they wanted to come see for themselves. I want them to meet you," he said. He looked down at his feet then back up at her.

She felt like a fool. Still, she would be cautious.

"How about joining us for dinner out tonight. We're going to Barbara Jean's, and since it's your favorite place, I hoped you would come along," he said.

She smiled at him. He was very charming, and she'd

missed his company. "Yes, I would love to. What time?"

"Wait for me. I'll be down to get you about six thirty."

He knocked on her door at 6:31 p.m..

She opened the door to a smiling Daniel. He was freshly shaven, his sandy blonde hair neatly arranged, wearing black slacks and a wrinkle-free white shirt with his monogram on the pocket. "I'm so happy you can come with us tonight," he said. He stepped forward, taking her hand and then putting his arms around her. She hugged him back, taking in the smell of starch and aftershave, bringing back memories. She placed her head on his chest, closed her, eyes and inhaled.

The evening was one of the nicest she had since moving to the island. They came back to the house, opened a bottle of wine, and visited for a while. He had a nice family. When she went to leave, Daniel insisted on walking her down to her apartment.

As she turned to thank him for the evening, he took his right hand and tenderly touched the side of her face, looking deep into her eyes then kissing her full on the lips. When he pulled away, he looked into her eyes again. Neither of them said a word. She smiled as she watched him walk to the stairs and disappear into the night.

CHAPTER 27

*C*ynthia was scheduled to work the next three days and wasn't able to see Daniel and his family. On the third night, when she came home late, the house was dark, and the rental car was gone.

Her heart sank. Why had she expected more? He came here for a working vacation to get his presentation done. She quickly willed herself to shake off her mood. No more feeling sorry for herself.

She ate some leftover chicken and quickly went to sleep.

Over the next week and a half, Cynthia kept busy, deciding that it was the best line of defense.

When time permitted, she visited Betty and Ian and took walks on the beach when she could. Then on Wednesday, there it was in the driveway when she arrived home from work.

The rental car.

Cynthia's heart did a little flip-flop, and her face felt flushed. How embarrassing. She was too old to be acting like this. He left without a word or even a note. He must have seen her pull in, because he came out before she could open the door of her car.

"Hi. I've been waiting for you," he said happily.

"Hi," she said. "I wasn't sure you were coming back"

He looked down at her in the car. "Yeah, my life is like that. I sometimes don't know what I'm doing tomorrow, but I am back."

There was a long pause.

"I would love to have you share a bottle of wine with me on the deck tonight."

"I'm exhausted tonight from work and have twelve-hour shifts the next two days," she said. "But maybe later this week if you're still here."

"Oh, I'll be here," he said.

❦

Two nights later when she came home from work, a bouquet of roses was at her door with a note.

Going fishing with Ian tomorrow morning. How about you come to dinner, and I cook what I catch in the evening? If you could go for a glass of wine, I'm on the deck above you.
Daniel.

She changed and climbed the stairs hidden under the deck, and there he was. She found him so appealing. He was about six feet tall, his body somewhat fit for a man in his late fifties, lightly tanned, with warm and gentle brown eyes and sandy blonde hair with a peppering of gray at the temples. He wasn't just handsome or cute but *attractive*.

"Thank you for the flowers. I would love some wine, and, yes, dinner sounds wonderful."

She had two glasses of wine while they sat in lounge chairs. They talked until she had to go to bed. As she floated off to sleep, she reminded herself about how he would be leaving soon. She didn't need to get involved any more than she was already.

❧

The day had been warm, so she decided on a casual royal-blue sundress and a black cardigan in case she got chilly. The night before, Daniel asked for her phone number so he could text her what time to come up. He texted about four to say dinner would be at seven thirty, and he hoped she liked flounder. She did.

It felt strange knocking on her own door, but she did, and Daniel welcomed her into her house. She looked around with a feeling of missing her house and smelled the nice aroma coming from her kitchen.

"Do you cook for yourself often?" Cynthia asked.

"Yes I do, as a matter of fact. I have to go out to eat so much for business that cooking for myself is a treat. Do you like to cook?"

"Yes, and I like to bake, too."

Just then they heard the wind pick up and heavy rain pelt the windows. She was glad she made it up there before it started.

Cynthia sat in her kitchen and watched Daniel put together a delicious-looking meal of pan-fried flounder, salad, and vegetable pasta as the rain storm picked up outside. Just as he placed the plates on the table, the lights went out.

"Oh no. This happens frequently when a storm comes through. I have some candles in a drawer over here and a lighter." She walked over to the drawer, got them out, and lit them, illuminating the room.

"I have a great idea," Daniel said. He stood up, leaving the kitchen, and flipped the gas logs on in the living room. "Let's eat in front of the fire place."

She found a blanket and placed it in front of the hearth while Daniel brought their dinner in on a tray. He handed it to her.

"I'll go grab the glasses and wine bottle," he said.

When he came back, he kicked his shoes off and plopped himself down next to her, laughing. "This is kind of fun."

She agreed.

The meal was delicious. Daniel cleared the plates away while she poured more wine into their glasses and remembered the night she polished off a whole bottle in this very room not long after Philip's death. Stop it, she told herself. It was not the night to be thinking about the past.

Daniel propped up some overstuffed pillows from the sofa so they could stay by the fire. The warmth was so relaxing. They didn't speak a word for the longest time; just looked at the fire. Daniel touched her cheek, and she turned her head to him. He cupped his hand around her jaw. "I think you're a beautiful woman, not just outside but inside."

Before she knew what she was doing, she closed her eyes and leaned forward, kissing him lingering in the moment. When she opened her eyes, he was looking at her.

Soon their arms moved slowly and gently around each other, kissing and touching, the light of the fire adding to the romance. He ran his fingers through her hair then slowly down her back.

She felt something familiar coursing through her veins that hadn't been there for a long time. It was like an old friend, but was she ready for it? A peacefulness came over her, and Daniel spoke as if he could read her mind.

"I understand if you're not ready for this… we can wait."

His words surprised yet comforted her. She didn't think she wanted to wait, but was it the right thing for her to do? She more than liked the man; she had begun to fall for him. But what if she got hurt? What about Philip? She was so tired of being alone.

Daniel continued to look her in the eyes and ran his fingers through her hair.

She was over thinking the situation. She needed to go

with what was in her heart and take a chance. That's what life was all about.

With a calmness she hadn't felt in a long time, she closed her eyes and let go.

Before long, they were naked in front of the fire. She felt comfortable and trusted this man.

Making love with him was like nothing she ever felt or done before, a reckless abandon that felt so good. He was strong yet gentle, allowing her to see a different side of him.

It was so unlike her to do this, but at the moment, it was exactly what she needed.

❧

First one eye, then the other opened, and Cynthia found herself under a blanket on the floor in front of the fireplace. Daniel was still sound asleep, even though the sun had started beating in through one of the large windows facing the beach.

Lifting the blanket, she saw they were both naked. What had she done?

Her few items of clothing were scattered on the floor close by. If she maneuvered herself quietly from the blanket, maybe she could retrieve them, put the dress on, and silently go to her apartment. He never stirred as she slowly slipped her dress over her body and headed out the door and downstairs.

Once safely in her apartment, she removed her dress and turned the shower on, getting in once it was warm. The water felt good. She heard her phone ring but could do nothing about it for the moment. The events of last night whirled in her head. She couldn't deny enjoying herself. Daniel embodied an air of strength about him that rendered her weak. Again, her phone rang.

When she was done with her shower, she wrapped herself in a towel and checked her phone. She thought it might be one of the kids. It was Daniel, so she called him back.

"I was worried," he said. "I woke up, and you were gone. Everything okay?" he asked.

"Yes, I thought it best I come down here to get a shower," she assured him.

"I'm making us breakfast, so how long before you can come back up?"

"Give me forty-five minutes," she replied.

"Okay," he said and hung up.

This time, when she came to the door, she didn't knock but opened it and said, "Hello, it's me," as she walked in.

He was wearing one of her aprons, causing a flashback of Philip on the morning of his fifty-fifth birthday when he'd made them breakfast. Was she ready for this? She believed she was. She was distracted by the smell of breakfast and realized she was starving. It looked great.

"When did the lights come back on last night?" she asked. "They're usually out only about an hour."

"I have no idea," Daniel replied. "I went around and turned them all off so when they did come back on, we wouldn't be disturbed."

Cynthia gave him a look of surprise, and then they both laughed. He pulled her to him and kissed her like he had last night. He wrapped his arms around her. "I love you," he said ever so softly, like a whisper into her hair.

Even though she had made love to this man, she was not prepared say those three words. Not yet. She liked him but *love*? It would take more time before she could say it. She quickly pulled away. "So what's for breakfast?" she asked, acting as if she hadn't heard him and walked over to the stove.

They spent the rest of the day together talking and walking the beach, but they didn't make love again. After sharing a pizza delivered for dinner, she announced reluctantly that she needed to go to her place so she could get ready for work the following morning.

It had been a beautiful day.

❧

Since she was working, they only saw each other briefly over the next several days. On her first day off, he told her he had to go back to New York for business but would return in eight days. Before he left, he wanted to talk with her about something important — would she meet him later on the deck for some wine? She said sure.

She climbed the steps, and there he was, waiting for her, wine chilling.

After talking for a few minutes, he said, "Come sit here." He patted the cushion next to him on the love seat.

She sat down, and they talked about New York and what it was like living there.

"I told you I wanted to talk to you about something," he said, visibly nervous. "The past several weeks I've enjoyed my time here. You more than anything else have been the reason why. I don't want it to end."

"I've enjoyed it, too," Cynthia said.

"I know this is sudden, but why don't you quit your job and come to New York? You could easily get a job as a nurse, and Purvell is there."

She was shocked and didn't know what to say.

"I love it here, and I don't think I could afford New York on a nurse's salary."

"You could live with me, but if you don't feel you're ready for that, you could stay in one of the apartments I own and really see what New York is like. See if you like it. I'll take care of you."

She was speechless. She had no idea this was coming.

"Daniel, I don't know."

"Why not?"

"You've taken me by surprise. I hardly know you."

"I understand. I've fallen in love with you, Cynthia Lewis, and I don't know anyone like you. I want you in my life. I told you I have to leave, but I'll be back to finish my month here. I hope you'll give me the answer I want if I give you some space to think about it. Will you think about it?"

She never dreamed this was what he wanted to talk to her about. What could she say?

"I'll think about it, but don't push me. I've begun to care about you, too. But this has all happened so fast for me. I'll give you an answer when you come back." She got to her feet and walked down the stairs to her apartment.

The first thing her eyes went to when she got inside the door was the urn containing Philip's ashes.

⁂

Over the next week, Cynthia thought about what Daniel proposed. She had no answer. There was no denying she cared for him and desired to get to know him better, but to leave here and move to New York? She had gone through so much to get to where she was.

She shared none of this with anyone, because she wanted to make this decision on her own with no advice. It had to be all her choice.

As the day approached when Daniel would return, she could no more make a decision then the day he asked her. What was she going to do?

And then, suddenly, she knew.

⁂

The next day at work, she met with her supervisor, Jackson, and explained she was having some personal problems and needed to take a short leave of absence. Jackson was not happy about her request, but she had been a good employee. He agreed to let her have it, but depending on how long she was gone, he couldn't guarantee her same job when she came back. She may have to take another position. She told him she understood, gave him a hug, and said thank you.

❦

Ian agreed to drive her to the airport for her nine o'clock flight. She swore him to secrecy as to where she was going. He'd been given the keys to her place so he could look after it while she was away. Cynthia told him he and Collette could stay there whenever they wanted while she was gone and enjoy the beach. Christopher and Millie might show up for a weekend here and there, but when Christopher came, he should keep a close eye on him. He said he understood.

"You can tell them you know where I am, and I'm safe. I need some space to think and clear my mind. Will you promise me?"

"I would do anything for you, Cynthia, but are you sure this is the answer to your problems? Sometimes it's best to face things head-on and get them over with. I don't know what it is you're running from, but I'm assuming it has to do with Daniel."

She looked at him, surprised. "Why do you say that Ian?"

"The day we went fishing, he spoke of nothing but you. Asked me all sorts of questions, like did I think you were ready to move on? I told him only you could answer his questions."

"Yes, it's him, but I don't want to talk about it, and I'm not running."

"If you say so," he said. They were at the drop off entrance to the airport. He gave her a peck on the cheek. "Lass, I hope you find your answers. Be off with you, and keep in touch. My lips are sealed."

She hopped out of the car and closed the door. A momentary hesitation rose up in her chest, and she wanted to tell Ian to come back, but he pulled away, disappearing into the mass of vehicles leaving the airport.

It was better this way. She knew what she must do, and she was determined to work this out on her own. There was a part of her that had gone missing over the years, one she desperately needed to find again no matter what her decision would be about Daniel.

CHAPTER 28

O'Hare Airport in Chicago holds the title of being one of the world's busiest airports. The number of people traveling in and out of this Midwest airport was truly mind-boggling. Watching all this activity made Cynthia's two-and-a-half-hour layover go by quickly

When her flight number was called, she walked down the stairs to the tarmac outside and then up the portable stairs to the small plane she'd be traveling in. The airport she was flying into wasn't able to accommodate large planes.

Her plane wasn't full, so she sat alone in row 5, seats D and E, and belted herself into E, the window seat, so she could see the view. Once in the air, the plane followed the shore line of Lake Michigan. When she saw a familiar landscape out her window, she knew she was almost there.

She stared at the farmland and fields below — a geometric grid in shades of brown and green, soon to be emerging crops. When more homes and neighborhoods became visible, she knew the plane would be descending shortly to the airport in Green Bay. From there, she would set out for her final destination.

After retrieving her luggage, she rented a car. Before getting on her way, she sat for a moment thinking about what she'd just done, feeling pleased with herself. This was the first step toward moving her life out of the limbo it had been in, whether it involved Daniel or not. Her idea was to go to the only place where she knew the outside world couldn't touch her. White Lake.

The trip would take about an hour, giving her enough time to unwind, get her mind in the right place, and fine-tune the story she would tell her mother.

Before starting out, she made a call on her cell phone.

"Hi, Mom, it's Cynthia. Guess what? I just landed in Green Bay, and I'm on my way… Just wanted to give you a heads up … We'll talk when I get there… Should be there about two thirty… I will… Bye."

That wasn't so bad.

She headed north. The roads weren't busy, except for the occasional semi and slow-moving car. Out her car window, she saw the familiar farmland and Guernsey cows blissfully wandering the fields.

The whole time she drove, Daniel's words echoed over and over in her head. She had just started feeling good about the way she'd taken over her finances and was supporting herself. She liked knowing what was going on instead of being told not to worry about it. She liked visiting New York, but living there was another story. Seeing Purvell more often would be nice, and she was looking for adventure, but she loved her life on St. Simons.

"This is all your fault, Philip," she said aloud.

When she passed the sign for Lena, she knew her exit was coming up. So many life events had happened since the last time she visited. As she approached the lake, she first passed the boat landing. Not far after to the right was where Uncle Freddie had once lived. It looked out on Granny's little white cottage across the road. Her mother's place was down the hill from there and so was the house where Aunt Bea had once lived. Aunt Bea and Uncle Freddie were siblings of her mother's father, Granny's husband. Cynthia wasn't sure how they acquired the land they'd built their homes on, but she knew it went way back.

While she enjoyed the drive, she used the time to rehearse her story. Granny and her mother didn't need to know that after Daniel left, no one would be renting. Her mother would go for it, never asking a question, but Granny was another story and could not be put off so easily. She would have to make it work, since it was all she could come up with.

After parking the rental car behind her mother's car, she took a deep breath. Before she could even open the door, her mother was there with open arms.

"Oh my God, Cynthia. I just don't know what in heaven's name you will do next. How you can just leave and show up here is beyond me. What about your job and the kids? Do they think you're crazy? I mean, for Pete's sake, why would you want to be here when you have that island to live on?" In between her string of questions, her mom gave her a hug and a kiss.

Cynthia hardly wanted to let go. She wanted to keep her head on her mom's familiar chest as if she were a child, smell her familiar perfume and just listen to her mother's voice. If it were only that easy.

Cynthia must have lingered a little too long, because her mom seemed to know immediately that Cynthia needed her support.

"Let's bring in your luggage, and get you settled. You've picked a good time to come; they're predicting the weather to be warmer than usual," her mother said, pretending she didn't see the tears that Cynthia wiped from her cheeks as she turned to hide her face.

When she turned back, Cynthia said with a smile. "Great, Mom. I hope I can get in a lot of walking, running, and boating."

Cynthia stood still for a few seconds and looked at the

cottage. The sight of the sturdy granite steps and wraparound porch lifted her spirits ever so slightly. Coming here had been the right thing to do.

The porch had been great during the summers when they were kids — they could all play outside even on rainy days. The cottage, which had once been painted a dreary shade of green, had changed about fifteen years ago when her mother decided that sunshine yellow with black shutters and white trim was much better. Cynthia agreed. She took a deep breath, letting the fresh Wisconsin air clear her lungs and head.

She was home.

Once everything was inside, Cynthia surveyed the familiar rooms. Nothing had changed in them since last time she visited. Same furniture, pictures, rugs on the floor — everything.

"I'm putting you in the bedroom upstairs facing the lake. Let's get you settled in before you head up to see Granny or she comes down here, okay?" her mother suggested.

"Good idea, Mom," she said, glad Granny wasn't there at the moment.

Cynthia loved the set of log stairs leading to the second floor. Her grandfather built this cottage with his brothers so many years ago.

She looked around the second-story bedroom, remembering all the summers she'd slept in this room. Although the room was small, it contained a double bed, dresser, night stand, and chair — it was tight, but cozy. The walls were painted a soft green, and the bed was covered in a pastel quilt made by Granny. The exposed beams on the ceiling had been insulated in recent years so her mother could live there comfortably year-round.

On the dresser, her mother placed a little bouquet of wild flowers. "Mom, thanks for the flowers," she said, hugging and kissing her.

"Did you see the box next to it?" her mother asked.

She hadn't until her mother mentioned it. She picked up

the small square box wrapped in pink tissue paper and tore it off. Inside was her charm bracelet from high school.

"I forgot about this," she said. "You've been saving it all this time?"

"I was saving it to give to Millie one day, but I think it needs to be with its original owner, don't you?"

She looked up at her mother and then back down at the bracelet. "Yes, I do." She hooked it around her wrist.

"Well, darling, you get settled in here, and then come down so we can talk." Her mother left the room, closing the door and leaving Cynthia alone.

Cynthia sat down on the bed, and for the first time since she'd left the island, a wave of anxiety ran through her.

She picked up her cell phone, turned it off, and put it in a drawer. The kids would get a call later from Ian, but otherwise this time alone would be unplugged. Daniel would try to call her, but he wouldn't get an answer until she was ready.

❧

Granny made the hike several times a day down the small hill to Cynthia's mother's cottage, saying it was what kept her young. They did put some restrictions on the 95-year-old woman when there was snow on the ground, but otherwise, she was free to move about as she pleased.

She arrived for supper and accepted Cynthia's story without questions — at least for now.

For supper, they had her mom's tater tot casserole, a once-a-week meal when she was growing up, like many of her friends. It tasted just as good, if not better, than she had remembered.

The dishes had hardly been cleared when the two older women started the interrogation.

"So what made you decide to abruptly catch a plane up here?" her mother asked. "If I were you, I would have waited a little longer. I mean, it's nice in the day but chilly at night. What about your job?"

"I love this time of year, Mom. I wanted to come visit, because of the renters, that's all. I found it hard having them living above me in my house." Was she convincing? "The people at work understand that I needed some space and a change of scenery."

"Okay, okay, just wondering. You know, I think the last time I had you all to myself up here was before you were married," her mother said.

"I have something to say," Granny said. "Who do you think you're talking to here?"

Cynthia sat in silence. She knew better than to interrupt her Granny. It could only make any situation worse — Granny could smell emotion like a hunting dog.

"I think you're running away from something or maybe someone," Granny said.

How did Granny always know? Did she have the gift of sight like Betty? She avoided her eyes.

"Mother, don't be silly. What would Cynthia be running from?" Cynthia's mother said to Granny. "She has that beautiful island she lives on, a great job, and wonderful friends. I mean, under the circumstances, her life is very good."

Her mother seemed content with a life alone after Cynthia's father died. Cynthia wasn't sure she wanted to be alone.

Granny kept her steady gaze on Cynthia, ninety-five years of instinct honed to perfection. Could Granny see she was running away from a man? A man she'd made love to? Who had helped her forget Philip and his gambling? It would be liberating to share this with them, but she just couldn't. "I decided to come here for several weeks before I visit Arthur in England; that's all there is to it."

Granny surveyed her carefully. "Okay Cynthia. We're glad to have you visit."

And not another question or word was spoken about it that evening or in the weeks to come by her mother or Granny.

True to her mother's word, the weather was unseasonably warm for the last week of May. Cynthia spent her first week home visiting relatives and friends with her mother and Granny, glad to get it out of the way. Once the word was out about her visit to White Lake, invitations for lunch and supper started pouring in.

Most of her relatives wanted to know how she was doing as such a young widow. What they really wanted to know is, was there someone else in her life? Her answer was the same with everyone. She was doing fine and enjoyed her life on the island. Relatives can be so nosey, she thought.

After getting through all the visits, it was time to get down to business. What the heck was she going to do? Maybe going back in time doing the things she did as a young person on the lake could help her reconnect with … with what? Truthfully, she wasn't sure.

It was now June, and the days were getting longer and warmer.

Early Monday morning during the second week of her visit, she made a cup of tea and wandered out to the porch to find the perfect spot to watch the sun rise. The air was chilly still in the mornings, so she wore a light jacket.

With both hands around the cup of tea, she wondered for the first time about what might have happened when Daniel came back, having intentionally avoided any thought of it out of guilt until that moment. She turned her phone on twice since she put it in the dresser drawer having seen missed calls and messages from her kids, Purvell, and

Daniel. As irresponsible as it was, she turned the phone off again without responding or checking the messages. Ian knew how to get a hold of her if he needed to. Never before had she run away from anything in her life, but something about it felt good — the right thing to do.

She still wasn't sure what to do. She loved her island life, her friends, and her job. She had begun to love Daniel, but she felt he was asking her to give up so much of what she worked hard to achieve since Philip's death. What was *he* willing to give up? She spent the past fifty-plus years accommodating others, and she wanted it to stop. What he was suggesting felt like going back in time.

After thirty minutes or so, her mother joined her with a cup of coffee.

"A penny for your thoughts," she said with a smile.

"Mom, I'm not sure what I'm thinking. That's the problem." She took her mother's hand.

"Funny how we think that at some point in our life we'll have all the answers to all our questions. Even Granny would agree with me on this one. What you do have with age is experience. Experience to know everything always works out the way it should if you have faith. Now it might not be as you have it planned in your mind, but sit back and enjoy the ride, and prepare to be amazed at your life as it unfolds. Life is your own unique adventure," she said, looking out over the lake with a smile.

Cynthia reflected on what her mother had said, still clasping the familiar hand in hers, both women in their own worlds for a moment. After several minutes Cynthia broke the silence.

"When will I ever be as smart as you?" she asked.

"Oh, sweetheart, I don't know about that. I've just lived longer," her mom responded. "Learned most of it the hard way," she said, and they both laughed.

❦

"Mom, does that old trail still go around the lake?" Cynthia asked one day after lunch.

"Well, I'm not sure. I don't venture out that way. Are you wanting to walk around the lake, dear?"

"Yeah, Arthur and I spent a lot of time on that trail. I thought I might see how far I can go this afternoon."

"Have at it," her mother said. "I'm going to run into Walden Falls to get a few groceries with Granny."

Cynthia found the slight remnants of the trail were still there. It sent her back in time to when she and her brother would spend their days visiting all of their friends and relatives around the lake. Although the indentation of a path was still evident, vegetation had taken over, obscuring the trail but not hiding what was once there. She couldn't wait to see how far it went.

The first cottage on the path, right next to her mother's place, years ago belonged to one of her favorite people on the lake, Aunt Bea, who was now long since gone. The cottage was two stories and built into the hill that led down to the lake. The main living area was upstairs, and downstairs was a place to hang out after you went swimming, playing games and shooting pool on a table off to the side. There was also a little bar and a refrigerator always filled with soft drinks in glass bottles. She wasn't sure who owned the place now.

Next was Mean Old Mrs. Deen, the lady Granny told them the story about. Cynthia had a new appreciation for the woman, since now her own husband was gone.

Several of the cottages looked neglected, but most appeared to have a fresh coat of paint, with additions on the back, and large screened-in porches.

Although she had to maneuver the occasional overgrowth and break in the trail, it continued to the place she was hoping to find. An area that all the kids on the lake went to, so they could get away from the adults and hang out.

She wasn't sure who owned the property they'd adopted as their own, but there it was, untouched and ready for another summer. In the middle was the hollow area ringed by big rocks for the fire pit, where they used sticks to roast hot dogs and marshmallows over a small bonfire.

In those days, you could truly be a kid, without always having to report your whereabouts like kids did today. They would be gone from sunup until sundown, covering every inch of the lake unsupervised.

She looked across the lake to her mom's cottage. At one time, she thought that this might be the place that she and Philip would retire, but now she found her island and never wanted to retire but to go on bouncing from one adventure to the next. She laughed, because she never thought of herself that way before. It had always been about what she would do with Philip, and now he was gone.

Life with Daniel would be an adventure, but was it the adventure she wanted? She'd been playing it safe her whole life, and here was an opportunity to fly. She could see a world she only ever dreamed of, but would she have to make compromises? Her life on the island was so different, but she liked it and didn't know if she wanted to leave.

The tears started, but it was good for her to get it all out before going back to her mother's. This is why she had come to White Lake. By the time she left here in a few weeks, she prayed she would have answers.

❦

Two weeks had already passed, and Cynthia seemed no closer to what she was looking for then when she first arrived.

One day, she decided to run to Kelly Lake, the next lake over.

When she and Arthur were kids, they'd frequently walk over to Kelly Lake for ice cream. The only problem was that by the time they walked back to White Lake, they needed another ice cream to cool down. She hoped the ice cream store was still there, along with the Round Roof Club, which made the best hamburgers ever. A thick beef burger on a generously buttered semmel bun with everything on it. The butter and juices would practically run down your arms. She hadn't worried about eating healthy then.

After telling her mother she was going out to run, she headed down the road leading to Kelly Lake.

The last time she walked this road had been with Philip three years ago. The kids were playing in the water, and the two of them decided some alone time would be nice, so they took off hand-in-hand, feeling young again.

The road to Kelly Lake curved after a long straightaway. She saw a slight movement approaching the curve ahead and wondered if it was fluttering leaves, but no — it moved again.

She slowed to a walk, thinking maybe she needed to turn around and run back, when she suddenly saw it. About ten deer in a pack. She stopped and froze. They looked at her and she at them. After what seemed like five minutes, two of the deer approached her until only a couple of feet away.

Several more deer came around her, looking, she not daring to move. The nose of one of the does came within an inch of her face, sniffed, and then tipped down, looking her straight in the eyes with soft compassion.

Cynthia began to cry. The doe bowed her head, and Cynthia did the same to the doe. The other deer walked around her and sniffed, Cynthia not afraid in the least.

Suddenly, the big buck with horns started to do what she could only describe as a scream, startling her. Then, as if someone had shot a gun, they all took off into the woods, their little white tails bobbing along out of sight. These beautiful creatures seemed to understand her feelings better than she did, leaving her with a sense of peace.

She was in awe at what happened. No one would ever believe her story.

Determined to get to Kelly Lake, she continued on. To her disappointment, the Round Roof Club had burned down, but the ice cream place was still open, and she took full advantage.

When she arrived back, her mother said Purvell had called looking for Cynthia.

"Darling, I don't like to do it, but I lied to her until I could talk to you. I said I had no idea where that crazy daughter of mine was, sorry about the *crazy*, and that if she found you to have you call your mother. I'm so glad Granny was at her place taking a nap, because I could never have pulled it off if she were here."

"You did good, Mom. Thanks. I'm going to get a shower." She went upstairs.

Her time was coming to a close. Soon she would need to go back to St. Simons. Daniel would have to be given an answer before she left for England.

❦

There were row boats all over the shore of White Lake. She saw friends and family around her, all still alive except one. Philip. He was smiling as everyone climbed in the boats and set off rowing to the center of the lake.

She motioned to him to get in with her, but he shook his head, blew her a kiss, threw the rope in, and shoved her off alone, waving. As she floated toward the other's she saw the boats around her were filled with mumbling, blurred people. In the middle of the floating boats was one lone person who she couldn't make out treading water.

She couldn't remember the last time she had one of her dreams. The next morning, she remembered the whole thing, feeling Philip was somehow telling her it was time to move on and she knew what to do.

❦

As soon as he looked down at his phone and saw who was calling, Ian answered it.

"Cynthia. It's about bloody time you gave me a call. I've been so worried about you. No word from you at all. Are you fine?"

"Yes, and I'm sorry. I'll be back soon," Cynthia replied.

"The kids are fine, but that Purvell is about to drive me insane. She is one tough cookie. I had to tell Betty what was going on, lass, to take some pressure off me. I'm just a simple man and not used to these female goings-on. I don't even have sisters, mind you. I think Betty already knew, but you said you only told me. You women."

"I'm so sorry. I'll somehow make it up to you," Cynthia said, "I've one more favor I think you might not like, but since Betty knows, she'll probably be willing to help you."

She proceeded to tell him what she needed and why.

"You have got to be kidding? This is a joke, right?"

"No, I'm serious. Like I said, get Betty to help. You are the best and dearest friend I have, Ian. I could ask no one else."

And with that, the two friends said goodbye.

Ian wasn't going to do what Cynthia asked alone, so he called Betty.

"Betty, my dear. Just heard from Cynthia, and she's fine but has a little job for us to do. Could you meet me at her house in about an hour? I'll explain when you get there."

CHAPTER 29

*T*he next morning Cynthia started to put her plan into action.

"I'm thinking about going fishing, Mom, but first I want to see if I can get myself to the inlet. It's been such a long time since I've rowed around the lake alone. No use in getting all the gear together if I can't make it over there."

"Well, dear, you're in great shape, so I think that rowing over there should be no problem," her mom said.

"I have good lower-body strength from running but not much upper, so I want to try it out first. See you in an hour or so," she said, and she took off down to the dock.

The row boat was ancient but sound. Obviously no one had used it in a while, but she found the oars and some flotation cushions in the small boathouse several feet up from the shore line. In five minutes, the boat was ready to sail.

She packed a lunch, several bottles of water, and brought the latest book she was reading.

The inlet had always been a hot spot for fish and ambiance. She hoped it was still so. The small area branched off from the lake through a narrow passage into a small pond not conducive to building cottages because of the marshy ground around it. Since nothing could be built, the area was quiet, giving fish a false sense of security.

It had been one of her dad's favorite places to fish on the lake.

She learned everything she needed to know about fishing from her dad. He and his cousin, Willie, upheld a reputation in these parts. Some said that the two needed no worm, just a line and hook on a string.

Willie would frequently show up at six in the morning or earlier, and the two would head out with a trailer and a boat full of gear. They'd come home hours later with buckets of fish they proceeded to gut and filet on a table outside under the trees. Her mother fried the fish as fast as her dad and Willie could gut them. It was the best fish she'd ever tasted.

Her arms were starting to hurt as she entered the shaded passageway to the inlet. The passage was lined with white birches on either side. The inlet was still with pink and white blooming water lily pads in one corner.

She decided to drop anchor by the water lilies and stretch out in the sun with the lunch she packed. Using the floatation cushions in the boat, she made a comfortable little seat for herself. No one seemed to come in here anymore, or maybe it was because not many people were vacationing yet. In Wisconsin, June could still be chilly, so most people visited in July when they could count on warmer weather.

As she relaxed, her mind began to wander, remembering a picture she'd seen of her dad when he was about twelve years old, looking like Huckleberry Fin with the lake as his backdrop. He was barefoot wearing cut-off denim shorts and an old T-shirt, holding his fishing pole in one hand and a line of fish in the other, sporting the biggest grin on his face. The look was that of innocence and daredevil combined.

Starting to feel sleepy from the lunch and sun, she sat up straighter to concentrate on why she was here. Truth be told, she had no intention to fish.

After deciding everything would be ideal for her plan, she spent another half-hour reading before rowing back, reminding herself to take some ibuprofen later.

❦

"Cynthia, there's a package here for you from Ian," her Granny yelled upstairs to her. "What in the world is he sending you?"

She needed to play this cool so no more questions would be asked. Too bad Granny was the one collecting the package.

"I'll be down in a minute." Here goes nothing, she thought.

The too sharp for her own good little woman stood in front of her, holding the box and shaking it a slightly. "It's kind of heavy."

"Thanks, Granny."

"What's in here?" she shook it again before surrendering it to Cynthia.

"Oh, just some things I needed."

"But aren't you leaving soon?" Granny asked with a sly look on her face.

"Yes, but I needed this," she said and quickly took the package upstairs to her room before any more questions could be asked. She would open it later when Granny was gone. She couldn't take any chances.

As she headed up the stairs, Granny called out. "Oh yeah, Purvell called again looking for you. That girl is persistent. Your mother stuck to her story in case you're wondering."

❦

Later when Granny was safely tucked into bed back in her little white cottage and her mother sound asleep, Cynthia opened the box. Ian and Betty were true friends for what they'd done for her. She hoped someday she could return the favor.

Carefully she put the item they'd sent in a canvas bag with a sweater and jacket on top of it. She pushed the bag as far back in the closest as she could. It would be safe there.

❦

The next day it rained, never letting up. Cynthia was leaving in four days to go back to St. Simons. She felt like a caged animal inside, frequently walking around the porch to see if there was any break in the conditions, but no luck. She would have to wait until the next day.

The next morning, she woke to the sun pouring in her bedroom window. She rushed downstairs and announced that she wanted to go fishing before leaving. So far, so good.

"Mom, do you still have some fishing poles, and where can I get some bait?"

"The fishing poles I think you'll find in the shed on top of the hill," her mom said. She handed her an old Tupperware bowl. "Just dig in my flower garden on the side of the cottage for some worms and put them in this plastic container. So are you going to catch us supper?" Her mother chuckled.

"You never know," she responded and turned, heading up the hill to the shed.

The shed was an old outhouse that had been repurposed. She opened the door to the dark, musty-smelling structure.

There were the same old poles she swore they'd used as kids. Finding the best-looking one, she started surveying the shelves for the old tackle box. It was sitting on the top shelf, looking as old as it had when she was a child. She found a rickety stool to stand on and just barely reached the box.

Inside was an unopened package of hooks. Just what she wanted. Even though fishing was not her main purpose in going, she thought she might as well try to catch something to avoid any suspicion. She grabbed the pole and tackle box and headed to the flower garden.

There was a bucket and small shovel sitting to the side of the garden. After digging up a clump of dirt, she threw it in the bucket and poked around for worms. They squiggled around, no idea what was in store for them. She put the worms and some dirt in the Tupperware container. She was finally ready.

"Cynthia." She heard her mother's voice.

"Yes, Mom?" She went back around to the kitchen door.

"I packed you a little something to eat, dear, and some bottles of water. You know, in case the fish are really biting and you don't want to come in," her mother said with a slight smile.

"Thanks, Mom. I just need to run upstairs and grab a jacket and sunscreen before I head out." She slid past her mother up the stairs and grabbed the canvas bag from the back of the closet.

"Bye. See you later." She headed down to the dock.

The boat was where she'd left it. After loading her gear and slipping the oars into the slots, she shoved off.

It couldn't have been a more beautiful day. The water was so calm, not a breeze in sight, and the air was warm enough to be comfortable. She would be able to take her time.

As soon as she entered the inlet, it felt as if she'd left the world she knew behind her. It was so calm and tranquil. More water lilies bloomed, reminding her of the Monet print hanging on her bedroom wall at her *home* on St. Simons Island.

Her *home*. It was the first time she'd thought of it as a home and not a house. Soon she would be back in her *home*, not the apartment below it. The thought put a smile on her face.

She anchored in the same vicinity as the other day and pulled the container hidden under the sweater and jacket out of the canvas bag, holding it close.

Inside were the ashes of her husband, Philip.

White Lake didn't have the significance for Philip it did

for her, but she was the one still living and could visit the inlet with the kids and know he was resting in this magical peaceful place. Maybe someday her ashes could join his.

After her dream with the boats on the lake, she knew Philip was telling her to let go of him. Seeing the urn of ashes would always prevent her from doing this. Spreading them here was the perfect way to help her move on but never forget.

She held the container with her husband inside for the last time in this world, bowed her head in silent prayer, and asked God to help her find a way in this new chapter. Carefully standing in the boat, she opened the top of the plastic container. Leaves and bark from the white birches fluttered along the shore line, coming her way. Just as she tipped the container over, the approaching wind swirled around her, drawing the remains up, out, and around the inlet, over the lilies, the water, and into the trees.

Cynthia sat down and could only watch in awe, amazed at what she was seeing. It was as if a small tornado had entered the inlet for a brief moment, dispersing Philip's ashes, dying away as silently as it had come in.

She sat for how long she wasn't sure in what she could only describe as a meditative state. When she found herself tying the boat to her mother's dock, she wasn't even quite sure how she'd arrived there.

Looking up to the cottage, she saw her mother and Granny sitting with someone. She was not in the mood for company. Which one of her mother's friends could it be?

As she climbed the steps to the porch, she recognized who it was.

Daniel.

Not now, not today. Who had told him?

"What are you doing here?" she asked.

Both her mother and Granny were in high gear, antennae up. What had he been telling them?

"Cynthia. Is there somewhere we can talk alone?" Daniel asked nervously.

"You young people go down to the dock for some privacy," Granny piped in, knowing full and well she had a bird's-eye-view right there on the porch.

Cynthia reluctantly went back down the steps to the dock, Daniel following.

"How did you find me?" she asked.

"After looking everywhere else, this was all that was left. I can see why you came here."

"I'm guessing Purvell must have suggested here because otherwise how would you know?"

"I'm not saying anything. I found you, and that's what my goal was. Now why did you take off on me? I came back, and you were gone, none of your friends or children divulging anything. What did you pay these people for their silence?"

"I needed space. You took me by surprise; we were just getting to know each other."

He hesitated before he spoke. "Do you remember the day you arrived in New York to visit Purvell at Grand Central Station?" he asked.

"Yes," she said, puzzled.

"You dropped your jacket and you were crying, needing directions to Starbucks."

"Yes, but how do you know that?"

"I guess you couldn't see through your tears, but it was me who handed you your jacket and gave you directions. Later the same day, you came out of the ladies room at the Union Square Cafe distracted, not watching where you were going and walked right into me. I was on the phone but recognized you and watched you sit down with Purvell. And then you show up with Purvell at my holiday party looking beautiful, me thinking you'll recognize me, and you act like it's the first time you've ever seen me. Talk about hurting a guy's ego."

Cynthia remembered all of it. It must be true, because how else would he know?

"I was going to ask you to lunch at the time until I found out you were recently widowed. I thought maybe the next year you might visit Purvell again and I could ask, but when you didn't, I found out about renting your house and thought, why not?"

She was shocked and overwhelmed.

"Cynthia, you are a breath of fresh air to me. I want you in my life."

This was more than Cynthia could take. Spreading her husband's ashes and not even thirty minutes later another man interested in her affections.

"I have to go," she said.

"Where?" he asked.

Cynthia raced back up the stairs past her mother and Granny, who both wore excited looks, to her room. She put on her running clothes and ran back outside past the two women and Daniel, straight to the road leading to Kelly Lake.

Usually her pace and breathing started out uneven, but today, with all the adrenaline in her body, she was running like a star athlete.

Who does he think he is showing up here? she thought. She'd only just said a final goodbye to her husband today. His timing was so bad. He was probably back there sweet-talking the old ladies and she would never hear the end of it. Wait until she spoke to Purvell.

With every thought, she went faster and faster, causing her to be worn out by the time she reached Kelly Lake. She was walking toward the ice cream place when who should pull up in a car but Daniel.

"Can I buy you an ice cream?" he asked with a pathetic smile.

She couldn't help but laugh and then she remembered she had no money with her.

The run had helped her clear her mind. "Yes, I think it would be okay."

He parked and met her at the storefront, ordering two custard ice cream cones. They sat under a tree away from any people.

"I stayed at the Kelly Lake Motel last night," he told her. "It's rather nice."

She laughed again, thinking of this high-power New York business man at the Kelly Lake Motel.

"Your mother and Granny invited me for 'supper' tonight, but I said only if it was all right with you. Is it?"

"Sure, why not?" she replied, realizing this man really must like her to go through all this.

"Will you drive me back? I've worn myself out."

"Be glad to."

They rode back in a companionable silence.

When they reached the cottage, she said, "I'll give you an answer tonight," and went in, avoiding her mother and Granny, and took a long shower.

❧

Supper was nice. Her mother made a roasted chicken, green beans, mashed potatoes, and gravy. Daniel was gracious as always.

"Why don't you two go for a little after-supper walk," Granny suggested. "Grace and I will clean up and have desert ready when you come back. My special lemon meringue pie."

The two went walking side by side into the night. Cynthia jumped right in.

"I said I would give you an answer, so here it is. You may find this hard to believe, but for the first time in my life, I'm on my own, and I like it. I'm making my own decisions and doing what I want, not what everyone else wants, and I'm not willing to give it up. And most importantly," she hesitated for a few seconds. "I don't love you."

She thought about how in the past she'd gone along with what everyone else wanted her to do, but not anymore. When she let go of Philip's ashes earlier in the day, she stepped through a new door that had been thrown wide open to her. One full of endless possibilities.

His face dropped.

"Just wait," she said. "I like you, but I don't love you, because I don't know you, and I'm not sure I'm ready for a committed relationship just yet."

He stopped and faced her, taking her arm and turning her towards him, studying her face for a few moments. "You know you will love me," he said with certainty and kissed her long and hard.

"Maybe," she said with a smile.

When they arrived back at the cottage, he said "thank you" to her mother and Granny and told them he had an early flight back to New York. In minutes, he was gone.

Her mother was first. "What a nice young man. Such good manners. You don't see that often around here."

"I want to know, are you going to marry him?" Granny never wasted any time.

"Granny!" Cynthia said, and the three women laughed.

❧

Three days later, she was back on St. Simons Island, having missed it more than she'd ever imagined.

The Sunday before leaving for England, she took Betty, Ian, and Collette to Barbara Jean's for dinner to thank them. She'd asked a lot from them while she was gone.

"The three of you can use my home anytime you want while I'm gone. I've decided to stay three weeks in England, and when I come back, the new and improved Cynthia is going to start the next chapter of her life."

"I kind of liked the old one; don't change too much," Betty said.

"I won't. It's more about me realizing I'm a woman with so much yet to give. I don't want to miss an opportunity."

And until she said it, she hadn't known she felt that way.

❦

Millie came down from Charlotte to be with Cynthia a few days before she left and take her to the airport for her flight.

"Mom, one reason why I wanted to come down here before you go is to tell you that Jimmy and I want to try having another baby. We're both so excited."

Both women cried.

❦

The much-awaited day came. Cynthia boarded the plane for her eleven-hour trip to London.

She hadn't heard a word from Daniel since he'd left White Lake. She got out her phone and was getting ready to press his number when she hesitated and put her hand in her lap. This was all too fast for her. She *was* running and didn't know how to stop. Until she got herself together, she couldn't be with anyone. Daniel would have to wait, and if she took too long, so be it.

Soon the plane took off, and she was on her way.

When the flight attendant came around, she asked for a pillow and blanket and found a comfortable spot to settle into.

The motion of the plane started making her sleepy. As she dozed, she began to dream.

Everyone was dancing the waltz, the men in white tuxes and the women in fancy flowing gowns. There were family members and friends dead and alive dancing together, all smiling and happy. She saw herself dancing with Philip in the center. Blurred people were dancing, too, but they started to disappear one by one. Then the people in tuxes and gowns started disappearing, and even Philip until it was just her and one blurred person. She felt a little anxious.

The blurred figure danced closer with his back to her. Cynthia saw that he also wore a white tux. As the music progressed, the person turned around and came toward her. She was uncomfortable and anxious, but when he was just a few feet from her, she recognized him. He kissed her and held her close before he also disappeared.

It was Daniel.

ACKNOWLEDGEMENTS

*U*nfortunately, there isn't enough room to express my appreciation to all the individuals who have helped me over the past several years as I wrote this book. The list is endless, including family, friends, coworkers, my customers, other writers, and sometimes even strangers.

Although I'm thankful for all these individuals I'm most grateful for my loving parents, Ralph and Joan Amond, to whose memory I have dedicated this book. I was blessed to be given to these two people as their child. My thoughts were of them when I pushed the period key at the end of the last sentence I typed. I closed my eyes and said "I did it mom and dad," and then I cried.

When I first told my family I was writing a book I don't think they had any idea how serious I was but they soon found out. My husband, Bill, and daughters, Elizabeth and Julianne, gave me the space I needed to spread my wings and do something I have wanted to do since I was a kid. I'm so grateful for the support and patience they have given me and love them for it. I want to also recognize my son-in-law, Robert, and my grandson, William, who is the light of my life and keeper of my heart.

Other family I would like to thank are my brothers, Drew and David Amond, for always being there for me. Love you guys. My sisters-in-law, LeAnn Amond, Kathy Amond, Cathy Wilber, and Patty McGee, for their support and interest in my book, but especially Patti for being the first person to read and give me feedback on my final manuscript. You are the sisters I always wanted. Special thanks also to my Aunt Lois Bednarowski for saying how much my mom would have been proud of me, and my cousin, Sara Sullivan, for all the Atlanta help she gave me.

I owe a debt of gratitude to Barbara Lawing and her Wednesday night writing group for giving me the confidence to write and jumpstarting me on my way.

My friend, Dr. Mark Carroll, was invaluable providing me with information pertaining to my medical questions as well as my daughter, Julianne Todd, who is a nurse.

I'm grateful to La McLeod for allowing me to use her mountain home anytime I wanted to get away and write. The majority of this book was written there.

I appreciate the courtesy The Jekyll Island Inn extended me when I visited by giving me a tour, answering my questions, and allowing me to wander around.

I want to thank Ana Sanchez-Moreland, Teresa Westbrook, Mindy Kelner, Susan Mills Wilson, Dianne Mason, Sue Marshall, Paul Mckellips, Ian Scobie, Anabel Mastandrea, and all my customers who asked "How's the book going Sue? You know I want a signed copy." You are just a few who have helped me with information, encouragement, ideas, advice, inspiration, friendship, and support. Thank you so much.

I thought this would be one book but the people I've created have more to do and I've enjoyed writing about them so be on the lookout for the next installment in the life of Cynthia Lewis called Return Home.

CPSIA information can be obtained
at www.ICGtesting.com
Printed in the USA
LVOW12s1739210917
549565LV00004B/749/P